SHEOL

THE SCOTT PFEIFFER STORY PART 2
BY SHANE WOODS

SEVERED PRESS
HOBART TASMANIA

SHEOL

WWW.SEVEREDPRESS.COM

ISBN: 978-1-922323-54-5

In loving memory of
LCpl Jake Pettit,
the 22,
and all those we've lost along the way.

PROLOGUE

I pressed my foot down firmly and felt the warm sand beneath give way. The further in it went the more granules rushed to fill in the void, more than happy to race to the front of the line to begin wrapping my foot in a cocoon of sun baked warmth.

I leaned back in my chair taking it all in as I closed my eyes. The steady light breeze blowing mixing with the scents of barbecue and an aroma of the breaking saltwater. The sun blanketing my body, keeping me separated from all I touch with a thin film of sweat and sunscreen.

'*This is it,*' I thought. '*All the loss, the drama, the tears and smiles, the smooth sailing and the struggle. This is it. This is what we worked for.*'

I felt a light tickle on the side of my thigh as the ash dropped off of my cigar, tracing the tips of my nerves as it fell. Bringing the stick of blended tobacco to my lips, I took it all in, visually this time.

The beach was sparsely populated at best. I was lounged upright in a folding chair, the majority of my view being the stark white of the sand split cleanly by the gently rolling cerulean waves. The scene was interspersed by the occasional human sloth, laid out and doing much the same as I. Nothing. Some read books, I myself had my buddy's latest zombie novel on the table next to me, my most recent stopping point marked by a little collapsed paper umbrella.

Opening the cover just a bit revealed the scribbles on the title page: "*Hey Scott, thanks for the laughs. We still owe each other that beer! -R*"

I smiled as I considered this. Maybe, just maybe, we still would. But it was going to take more than beer to peel my ass from this collapsible beach chair.

May take something closer to a pina colada, I realized as I looked at the empty bar glass next to the paperback on my table.

Turning to my other side, I eyed the most perfect rear end I'd ever seen. A little bubble, not too small, not too big, and startlingly pale despite the coating of sunshine. The paleness was contrasted in stark relief by a black bikini bottom wrapped tightly around the curve of each cheek and disappearing into a wonderful ending.

As I eased myself up to move from my seat, I grabbed my drink glass with one hand, and brought the other back, palm-forward, to give a firm, playful slap to announce my departure.

My hand glided forth through the air anticipating touchdown. It landed spot-on, creating a gentle ripple in the soft flesh that met with the solid *CLICK-KLANK* of my hand, marking the point of impact.

Wait.

CLICK-KLANK?

On this realization, the beach scene was torn clear of my grasp, as well as that round butt.

I let out a moan as my eyes opened, regaining sight as the comforting sunlight was stolen from me and replaced by the same harsh million-watt fluorescent glare that hadn't left since I got here. The ass under my hand quickly dematerialized, becoming the thin excuse of a mattress topping the metal wall-bunk.

Rolling away from the wall, the full recollection of where I was flooded into my mind. Grayson and Munoz and all the other faces until the Colonel last night flooded back into my thoughts. I sat up on my poor excuse of a bed, my shackles jingling in mockery at my every move.

They said it's just interviews, just getting a feel for what happened, and gathering information from someone who's been outside. If that's the case, why the hell am I shackled? Why are we kept separated? Where are my family and friends?

Then the icing on the cake was shown to me as the sleep finally left my eyes. I knew it. Asses don't click or clang. I've never in my life met one that did. It was my food slot on my door being thrown open. Just as I cleared my vision, a tray was pushed through to balance precariously on the ledge.

I groaned again, rubbing my eyes, then nursing my dead sore shoulder and hip. Apparently, I hadn't moved all night, and my body let me know as much. Twisting around, I located the Polaroid image I'd fallen asleep holding onto. I studied it once more before allowing it to fall to the bed as I encroached my way lazily to pick up my food tray and grab the accompanying drink off of the ledge.

2% milk and red fruit punch in their own tiny cartons. On the sectioned tray sat a pile of dry Frosted Flakes, cold watery scrambled eggs, an orange, and a single piece of toast. I'm really getting the star treatment here.

I plopped back down on my bed, the thick plastic tray resting on my legs, and began to tend to my breakfast. Just like my youth, when I spent more than a few short stays in county, the process was very similar. Cover the eggs with the supplied black pepper packet, milk on the cereal, choke it all down before you can taste it and follow with the full carton of juice.

As I did so, I found my mind wandering. Thoughts of my family and friends who were also present in this facility, those left behind, those unaccounted for, and sadly, those lost. Trying to divert my train of thought, and the inevitable emotional buildup to follow, I turned back to my now empty tray and wondered if this was standard fare for the facility, or just those of us here against our will.

Setting the tray aside and finishing my juice in one big gulp, I stood and stretched once again before making my way to the paired stainless-steel toilet and sink combo, dropped my trousers, and took a seat. There, I'd contemplated more of our situation, as well as what had passed and what was to come.

Though not just such mundane things as recollection of the recent past, but thoughts of the near future's possibilities, as well. What if this wasn't just interviews? What if, as my jail-food-filled gut told me, this *is* imprisonment? What if, at the end of all the story telling and explanation, they found it simply easier to just lock us away?

Surely that couldn't be the case though, right? It would be a smarter use of resources to just give us the boot, tell us thanks for sharing, then have us pack our things and leave.

Actually, I realized, that may be preferable on our end, as well. We'd been 'outside' since the beginning, more or less. It would probably be safer, even more comforting to go back to familiarity and live out our lives, short or long, waving our asses in the face of danger. Certainly, it would be preferable to having to escape from wherever we were at now, at least.

Before long I had finished and my right leg had begun to go numb, so I cleaned up, pulled up my bottoms and turned to the sink. No shower in this room, but the sink had running water, so I began brushing my teeth with the supplied tools then I grabbed the lone washcloth and got it nice and wet.

My intentions were a basic bird bath. Or, hobo bath, restroom clean-up, bird wash, whatever it is where you're from.

I was halfway through the "ass" portion of that when my door swung open to show Munoz and a half-dozen Privates standing there. Shit. Even my towel a few paces away seemed to be on the other side of the planet in that, pun partially intended, bare moment.

There I was, fully exposed and in all my glory, tainting a once-clean washcloth with my drawers around my ankles and my shirt off and pulled down to my wrist shackles. I think I handled it gracefully, but the others didn't seem impressed.

"Oh, hey! You're early!" I called to Munoz, who wore a single butterfly bandage and had a single crutch from the night before. "Just tidying up, y'all can come in and have a- "

"*Enough.*" He cut me off. Christ these guys love their interruptions. No wonder why everything military or government is an acronym.

"Oh, no, I insist!" I retorted, trying to keep my demeanor level, while reaching to turn the faucet back on. I then handed the soiled washcloth out to Munoz, my hand containing the offending rag just inches from his face. "Can you hold this for me? No? Okay, okay, my bad, dude."

"We are here to lead you to another interview," he instructed. "We are also under order that if you try anything at all, *anything,* puto, we are to fill you with bullets and let the janitor take care of the rest. Comprende?"

"Anything you say buddy!" I replied cheerily, watching his eyes grow as I flung the washcloth into my unflushed toilet. "Is that coffee?"

He retracted the coffee cup in his hand, so I reached for the little button to flush the toilet.

"What?" he started, then put his hand out. "Don't you flush that. Yeah, here, coffee."

"Oh, thank you so much!" I replied, still upbeat as I received the cup and took a sip before the taste found the proper receptors and I ended up spitting it right back out. "Is that fucking chicory? Really? Christ this *is* county jail, isn't it?"

"You ready?" he asked, returning my previous mischievous grin. "Get dressed. We got thirty seconds and we're walking."

As he spoke, I noticed a younger orderly walk by, then back up a step as she saw me in my full nude state. I took to ignoring Munoz and flashed a few poses, grinning ear-to-ear as I did, until two of the guards directed her away. At that point, I grudgingly complied and in moments I was making my way through the door and into the hallway. The orderly was nowhere in sight, but that was okay, I had a feeling Munoz wouldn't be allowing any more of my public displays today.

"Do you think housekeeping will go through my things?" I asked over my shoulder as we left. "I have souvenirs for family back home, and my unmentionables."

"Just shut up, and stop being difficult," Munoz instructed. "No more talking until it is time to talk."

"Well," I inquired, clearly testing my luck, "when will I know?"

"I'll tell you," he replied, cold as ice as he shoved my back to get me moving more quickly.

The others nearly naturally fell into step with each other until the hallway resounded with marching footsteps and my own rattling chains. The parade tones only broken occasionally as the guy in front would call to clear the hallway as we passed curious orderlies, a couple of doctor types, and several in either civilian attire or military uniform. This place seemed to be a child's set, Skittles bag mix of professions. We really just needed the police officer standing with the mayor and a construction worker to complete it.

From somewhere far off down a slightly darker hallway I could just barely hear the telltale shriek I'd grown to hate as it floated like a ghost train down the corridor.

"What the fuck was that?" I asked sharply, nearly freezing in place.

Munoz shoved me hard as he shot back, "The fuck I tell you about talking, asshole?"

"Ooo," I replied, "insults in English now, it must be serious!"

He shoved me again.

Okay. Point taken. I made sure for the remainder of the walk to pace myself to be almost in step with the others. Almost. This resulted in me inevitably falling behind, Munoz having to shove me forward again, which I'd counter with something along the lines of, "But mooooom, I'm just so tired. Billy kept me up all night with him playing video games!"

Eventually, and somehow without Munoz getting tired of my shit and ending me in the hallway, we made it to a door. This time, I was instructed to turn and face the opposite wall while I had three rifles trained on me. Apparently, our little ring of trust was broken. It's okay, Munoz and gang, the feeling is mutual.

A heavy, windowless steel door unlocked and was swung open, then I was turned back around and led through it. A room nearly identical to the one from yesterday was on the other side of the threshold. For a moment I thought it was the same, until I realized the mirror was on the opposite wall.

I was led to a seat on the far side, same as before. As I was sat down, I was instructed to turn in the chair and my shackles were removed. Where the restraints lay across my skin had turned an angry discoloration and still bore the marks of the cuffs. I rubbed my ankles and wrists, elated to be free of the bindings, and turned to Munoz as he took his seat.

I watched him casually as he began setting up the same equipment from the day before and doing so in the same ways.

"Can I talk now?" I asked him.

"I'd prefer you didn't." He glared for a moment before returning to the task at hand.

"Well, I'm a sucker for fine print, and preference doesn't mean set in stone," I informed him, then, trying to chill the temperature of the room, "What do you miss the most about the way things were before?"

"My wife and kids," he replied flatly, bringing his brown eyes up to meet mine. "My dog. My parents. My aunt. Everyone and everything I've lost. Now, about my preference…"

"Point taken," I deferred, sitting back in my seat heavily, now focusing my attention on the mirrored wall.

"So, what is it?" I began anew. "One room like this, a funhouse box like that, then another of these rooms? So, I bet, on the other side of that wall is another of these, then another mirrored wall?"

Munoz didn't reply as he made a sharp sucking sound before spitting something onto the floor, a toothpick working again furiously between his teeth.

A few quick beats later, and I could hear sharp footfalls, then a moment after, the door swung back open as Grayson entered followed by three more young military men, identical to those Privates from the day before, and then Nurse Hannigan. I stood to meet Grayson, my hand outstretched to shake his. He started to sit down! What nerve!

"You should shake a hand when it's offered," I commanded softly, the words dripping from my teeth, and, bringing my soft demeanor back as quickly as it had left. "It would be rude not to!"

"Ah, sorry, a bit more than usual going on this morning, I've been distracted," he replied kindly, but still keeping the strength to his voice. "Good morning, Scott, how are you?"

"Is that maple syrup?" I asked, motioning to the one amber drip still clinging to his white button-up shirt. "You bastard!"

"Hopefully we get things finished and cleared up today," he said, trying to placate. "I know, the meals in holding aren't exactly fulfilling. You remember Nurse Hannigan?"

He motioned to the blonde nurse with her little kit as she took her place next to me and went to grab for my sleeve.

"Yes, I do," pulling away, and to the nurse, "No headache today, I feel fine, thank you."

"Just a follow-up shot, Mr. Pfeiffer," she smiled. "We don't want the meds to leave your system too quickly, it's rough if they do."

"Right," I replied, and in a few moments, she had her injection finished up, applied the cotton ball and tape to my arm, cleaned up and left.

By the time she had done her job, Grayson nearly finished organizing his files and bringing his tablet to life. Munoz had gotten his recording equipment to come on as well. One of the Privates had also returned with a stainless coffee pot and another water jug. He arrayed cups on the table for each and retreated back to the other two men by the door.

It was difficult to tell the three young men apart, aside from skin tone. They were the same recruitment-poster perfect as yesterday. Maybe even two of the same. All cleanly shaven, identical uniforms except for patches. All three had their cover pulled low and tight over their heads. They all even carried identical M4 rifles.

"Let's see the tablet," I asked, remaining as informal as I could to see how far I could get.

"Way ahead of you, Scott," Grayson replied as he turned the tablet around to show me. All the same or similar images before, live shots of various parts of the facility, or maybe even right next to where we were. All of my friends and family I expected to see were still alive and accounted for.

"Can you tell me anything yet?" I inquired. "Where we are? How long will this take? What's going on? Why I heard one of those freaks shriek earlier?"

"Same as before, Mr., ah, Scott," Grayson replied. "Let's hear your story first. We need all the facts you can give. We're still in sort of a discovery process here. We need the main events that led to your tangles with Uncle Sam and Colonel Parker, but also any intel you can provide as to what life outside is like."

"You make it sound like you've never left this place," I observed, trying to feel out whatever info he would give me, even if not directly.

"We have limited resources topside while we try to get a handle on things," Grayson replied. It sounded programmed to me, but I went with it. But that word. *Topside*. Where the hell is this place?

"Well," I began. "Pour me a coffee? I believe we left off with Tony. After we saved those people."

"The coffee here is self-serve," he replied, turning the handle of the insulated carafe toward me, then, "but, yes. Your friend. Your second-in-command you've called him. He was…shot?"

"Yeah. Through and through. Back to front," I stated, pouring coffee into a paper cup and allowing the aroma to reach my nose as I anticipated something hopefully better than fucking chicory. Even in the end of the world you should always have a standard about coffee. Shitty brews make shitty mornings of course. Don't believe me? Try it.

"And the shot was long range, you said the sound came after the impact?" Grayson interrogated.

"Yeah," I replied, then pushed, "not a whole lot we could figure out beyond that. At least, not initially. Actually, the next few weeks went by with just the basics. Work, eat, scavenge, recover. The basics."

"Well, let's just start then," Grayson instructed. "Whenever you had new intel, or new happenings."

"Okay," I relented, smelling the aromatic steam from the top of my cup, relishing actual hot coffee. "It was maybe a few weeks after Tony got shot. After your infallible Uncle Sam left my best friend on that rooftop choking on his own bl-"

"Mr. Pfeiffer," Grayson broke in, "Let's continue. Calmly."

"Right." I stopped, then began anew. "A few weeks I said? Somewhere around there. Maybe two, three, so, anyway…"

ONE

Ohio weather is notorious. It's too damn hot and humid in the summer, with temps hanging in the 90s. The wintertime? Yeah, the exact opposite, with lake effect snow and temps hanging in the single digits and lower. It sucks, but it does afford us those perfect times of the year in between all of that.

This brings us to where I am now. The nights had been getting progressively cooler, yet not much real drop in the daytime temperature. This gave these perfectly cool mornings, crisp and clear, but not to the point of seeing your own breath just yet.

My target stood a good few blocks from me. I'd spotted the heathy looking doe moving with a few others at least an hour prior, judged their direction, took a chance, and set up my stakeout.

The new modifications Henry had done to some of our light pickup trucks were a Godsend. Scavenging several auto parts stores and garages yielded a ton of do-it-yourself window tint kits. This led to him retrofitting a couple of the Rangers and a Dodge Dakota with bed caps, tinting all the windows, opening the rear of the cab to the bed and finally he installed an internal tailgate release. We now had mobile hunting blinds for the upcoming hunting season. So long as you were cautious, and quiet, it did a very good job of keeping you hidden from prey, as well as those who would hunt you.

I'd waited a solid hour or more for at least one of the deer I'd witnessed to present itself to me. With the weather cooling down, we hunted for meat, not for buck or doe, not for trophy, and I was more than pleased to see a well-fed female break cover within range of my Mk. 18.

I pulled the short rifle nice and tight to myself, prone shooter position with a clear view from the back of the truck through the tailgate gap, a la The Beltway Sniper, but with a much wider area of attack.

The doe worked her way into the clear, then behind an abandoned car left forgotten in a driveway. I kept the rifle tight in place, my finger alongside the trigger guard. I could have taken the shot when she first appeared, but I lacked any and all interest in tracking a wounded animal through infected territory, and therefore waited for that perfect shot.

As I lay in place, my every breath coming shallow and slow, she began to slowly break cover. Head down and grazing, I got a front shoulder first. Then slowly, emphasizing that we had all the time in the world now, she began to move from the other side of the car.

I moved my finger to the trigger, ever so slightly applying pressure as the magnificent girl came into full view and I obtained the perfect shot I had been waiting for. Just another moment, and it was go time.

Her head came up quickly, but gracefully, as I slowly pushed the air from my lungs and began to leverage more pressure on the trigger. Just a moment before the crisp trigger gave way, she disappeared in a flash of movement and a loud bleating call.

I lifted my eyes from my optics and watched at range as a single runner hit the side of the deer full bore, spearing her against the car from out of the tall grass nearby. Before the doe could even react, two more joined the scene, both working feverishly at disabling her head and neck. The first runner let its head fall back as it let out one of those piercing shrieks to call others to the dinner table. Another runner joined, and moments later a few of the slower variety.

Blood erupted in fountains and flowed in rivulets as they dug in, rending flesh and bone from fur and skin. They ate ravenously, and I watched. Clearly, it was no longer a hunting trip, and I was back to intelligence gathering.

So, I watched, my rifle still at the ready and a sheet of window screen hanging over the gap, blowing lazily in the gentle breeze. I was in my binoculars now, trying to avoid the gore while I watched their actions, instead. At any given time, one or two of them would have their heads up, eyes and ears on a swivel watching for either more prey, or a threat. I wasn't sure. They did, however, make sure the shamblers had gotten their fill as much as they had gotten their own.

We had all been curious about this. They seemed to get slower, or 'become all slow and shambly', as Shannon had put it, whenever food was scarce or that particular freak hadn't eaten in a while. So why did the faster ones seem to help the slower? It was suggested we kept a few for studying, but no way in Hell was I going to have our enemy sleeping in our compound.

I watched the gruesome scene unfold for a few more minutes until my bladder couldn't take it any longer.

Reaching for the rope attached to the top of the tailgate, I drew it in, then grabbed the top of the gate and pulled it in tight until I heard the faint click of the mechanism on both sides. Then, I secured it further with bolt latches that Henry had installed and searched for a restroom.

I gave my contribution to the gallon jug next to me and reached through to place it on the front seat, then I followed it myself into the cab of the little Ranger.

Turning the key in the ignition, the truck started. Barely a hum now, instead of the old low rumble. Henry had also gone overkill on muffling the exhausts of our vehicles, as well as adding any sound deadening material he could find to the engine compartments.

It resulted in nearly dead quiet vehicles on the positive end. On the negative, it added several hundred pounds to some and occasionally resulted in cooling issues during the warm weather. We had one team stranded a week back with a hydro-locked engine.

Okay, some quick knowledge for those not 'in the know'. The vehicle overheated, and being in hostile territory, they kept driving it. Full of people and supplies, it didn't take it long before that overheating caused head gasket or block issues which, one or the other, froze the engine in place because it was getting coolant into the cylinders. Hydro-locked.

Back to reality. With the truck started, and my jug topped off, I did a very slow three-point turn and headed toward the hunting infected. I pressed the accelerator and rolled down the window as the little truck lurched forward.

The first infected took notice when I was about one block away from them. It raised its head from its meal and appeared to try to shriek or vocalize my presence, but the mouthful of venison…MY venison…seemed to keep it voiceless.

Now half a block away, I unscrewed the cap to the piss jug and propped it on my lap, holding it tight so not to spill a week's worth of myself, well, on myself.

As I glided almost silently past the feeding group, they finally took notice, just in time to receive a heavy dose of a week's urine. The jug hit the first one hard enough to knock it off its feet, and as it fell, the remainder of the truck-baked fluids showered the rest, and their meal.

Okay, yeah, it was in part a solid 'fuck you' from me to them that they may or may not understand. It was also because of how they use their scent.

We had a scouting team led by Dave recently get trapped out on the rooftop of a home. After 5 hours up there, Dave, in all his eloquence, unzipped his fly and gave them freaks one hell of a shower. A couple of them, he observed, actually acted like it burnt or hurt. But mostly, it confused the hell out of them.

Was it the pheromones? Was it the scent itself? We didn't know, but for even just a few moments it left them distracted enough to allow our friends an escape.

As my gifted golden shower hit them and then made landfall, I drove on. Watching in my rear-view mirror I saw them all get up from their meal and begin looking around. One freak lashed out a couple of times at another though it was broken up by one who ran between them, sniffed the air, then turned back and ran to another point and sniffed, then back to where he started.

I took the next left, chuckling to myself as I did so. The next twenty blocks or so passed uneventfully. I had travelled west from our home, and most of this area was regularly scavenged by our short-range crews. There weren't even too many infected, as the crews had adopted a thorough sweep and clear method of scavenging. This resulted in similar gains scavenging but left us engaged for longer as every sign of infected had to be met and cleaned up.

Rich even found a more effective way to neutralize the occasional brute, as well. This was the name we had given to the rarer eight to ten feet tall monsters that had come up from time to time.

Everywhere the large grayish colored freaks went, things got broken. If you became adept enough at identifying the marks, you could stumble across one bedded down at night. We'd found three. Two of them chose partially open garage doors to weasel under. They were each found inside, laid out like some kind of alien gorilla, either asleep or in some other kind of dormant state.

Another had actually made its way inside a house and either pulled up the floor, or fell through, but it seemed to have made a long-term nest in that basement, as evidenced by the piles of bones and gore strewn about in every corner.

In all three cases, the buildings were slowly, quietly flooded with whatever gas, diesel, or fuel oil we could muster in the area. An ignition trail was then poured, lit, and the beast would inevitably go on a rage until the flames consuming it finally took its toll and quenched the fire on the inside of the creature as well.

For if and when we'd encounter one in the open, Rich had disassembled fireworks and saved only the part that made them go *boom*. He then wired an electric charge for them that could be run off the long-range transmitter and receiver system for radio-controlled cars. Simply turn the five-pound pack of boom to 'ON', attach it by bolo, spike, or whatever else you could use to stick it to one of the big freaks, turn on your transmitter, and pull the throttle trigger. It always resulted in a satisfying earth pounding blast, and then the peppering of the surrounding area with whatever included shrapnel the device contained. It worked, it was dangerous but simple and effective. And the detonation system was much smoother than waiting for a mechanical timer to get done with 'Wrinkle Free'.

The smaller ones, or normal infected, were dispatched in the same ways as usual, as those proved to be the most effective. Disable the head, destroy the entire freak, or shut down its spinal column and render it useless. This went the same for the juvenile infected that were encountered, though understandably it was much more mentally taxing to do the same job. You never get used to being rushed by an eight-year-old in a baseball uniform with exposed veins and blood trickling from his eyes.

My musings continued for the next few blocks until I reached the overpass.

The southern edge of the overpass had been blackened. We'd taken to dumping our nearby dead infected over it and onto the highway. Then, to prevent the stink from reaching the compound, they were doused in accelerant and burnt every week now.

It worked two-fold. It allowed us to dispose of the bodies in a way that kept us somewhat at a distance, and the resulting cloud of smoke had brought a couple of good people here and there.

We had, however, had one small group try to strong-arm their way in. Some of our newer members made note; they recognized the woman and her scraggly group. Some Southern chick who'd taken to calling herself 'Texas Rose'.

We'd all gotten a laugh as we're in Ohio, not Texas. You could smell her as well. The small group smelled as bad or worse than the infected we were dumping onto the highway. No rose there. Apparently, she'd been run out of another place of good people that was rumored to be south of here. Much the typical story these days. Ostracized for theft, fighting, laziness, any number or combination of reasons. But as per usual, if they weren't welcome where they called home before, chances were they wouldn't be welcome with us, either.

We made mention that we should reach out to that compound, but last anybody heard, they were going under and disbanding, scattering here and there. Oh well.

At any rate, their departure from our vicinity had been hastened by gunfire when it was all said and done, leaving two of her party DOA and Rose herself suffering from a gut wound that claimed her before help could even be administered.

I guess that's the price to pay when you get turned down on entry twice, and then try to pry your way in via spud bar.

TWO

I passed the long wall to our compound on my way to the southern gate. Henry and his crew had busted their asses, and with the additional help we were getting from so many new hands, the wall was essentially complete. Rich's dry moat idea had worked wonderfully, though with recent heavy rains, it was more of a mud bog that slowed anything that found its way in.

We'd gotten a few deer that way, as well as a random pig that found its way in. They were good eating, but they also proved that the defense was solid. The thinking that if a deer, which can jump and run and climb to an extent, couldn't get out of the moat then neither could the infected.

The monstrosities themselves had proven this to be true, as every morning yielded a varying number of them. The work crews had taken to placing bets. They were taken down on a blackboard every morning before work. However many freaks were found in the man-made ravine dictated the winner. The group with the guess furthest from reality was on clean up duty for that evening, and that included burning the barrels of human waste on ground level collected by a laundry chute style system that James had affectionately named his "Shit Chutes". There was a chute at the end of each floor, and an angled gate to dump or pour into for each. It was grisly, but it's what we had living in nine-floor brick apartment buildings with no working plumbing. The mess was then rinsed down with a bucket of river water. Disgusting, but again, it worked.

I passed the wall with my driver's window down, giving a friendly wave to each of the sentries posted at freshly built guard towers as I passed. My hunting truck, painted in old school brush stroke camo, was easily recognized and waved on. My bald head, lengthening facial hair and tattoo covered arms helped too, I was sure.

Katie rolled the large drawbridge down over the moat for me, then rolled the outer gate to it open. I drove through and stopped at the second gate and waited.

It was a prison entrance type system. Henry and James designed the bridging system together. It was robust as all hell, able to raise and lower relatively quickly thanks to a large pulley and crank system. Once the bridge was lowered, an outer gate could be rolled aside to allow access. Then, you waited inside for that gate to close, and then the inner gate could be opened. It was all linked together and one couldn't move without the other in place. It made entry of multiple vehicles a bit of a chore, so we'd stage outbound and inbound and run both gates as needed, but we agreed it was worth the added security. And it was strong enough to allow loaded semi-trucks or construction equipment passage, which was a definite bonus.

Katie worked slowly but steadily. A heavy-set brunette in her twenties, she'd been an attitude-ridden thorn in my side since she showed up at our door near the beginning of our residence here. Therefore, when she got caught sneaking extra food and supplies from our supply floor, it was my pleasure to put her on gate duty.

I smiled and nodded jovially as she passed me by to roll the inner gate. She said not one word and made sure to watch her feet as she passed by. Maybe, I thought, just maybe I'll keep her here until her attitude improves. That might be a while.

Once the gate was clear, I rolled my truck through the compound, making my way through rows of houses in varying states of dismantle. The outer wall was a few blocks from the inner, which tightly encircled the pair of long nine-floor brick apartment structures. The buildings provided lots of room in little space, set parallel to each other, and made everyone and everything in view accessible with little to no relative effort.

I reached the single inner gate and gave two chirps of the horn. Noah and Parker, also on gate duty, were nearby at what appeared to be an old poker table.

Noah, having been one of our new additions from the high school, needed as much work as Parker. The thought was to pair them together, and they could watch each other and do better. This clearly wasn't a thing.

Each thin man had a couple of light snacks and a drink. Parker leaned back in his chair as Noah rose to work the gate. In the process, Parker knocked his rifle over and fumbled with it in the dirt before righting it and leaning it back up, then turned to me, offering a nervous nod.

As Noah rolled the gate back and I pulled through, I stopped.

"Parker, Noah, both of you," I ordered softly, "come here."

Both made their way over, issuing a simultaneous "Yes, sir" as they approached. Noah reached me first, running a finger through his permanently greasy dark hair and fixing his glasses.

"You boys are doing better," I commended. "However, what did I see wrong here?"

"I dropped my rifle," Parker admitted, a bit sheepish.

"You dropped your rifle because it wasn't tightly in your hands and at the ready," I admonished. "Look, I had to honk. You both should be aware. One of you always covers the other, and you both need to be more observant. You just let me right in without even double checking me, my vehicle, or to see who I was and if I was alone."

"Sorry," they said, nearly at the same time.

"I'll get Will or Frank down here to go over some basics with you two," I advised. "Whomever it is will help you clear and inspect your rifle again, Parker. You dropped it right on the open dust cover."

They both exchanged guilty glances and complied, then rolled the gate shut behind me as I entered and drove a beeline right into the entrance of the underground garage.

Henry was present and appeared to be forming a steel cage made of fencing and rebar around a wooden form of sorts.

"That's the most awkward fishing net I've ever seen, dude!" I called to him as I stepped out of my truck.

"What?" he questioned, then slapping the chain link, "Oh, yeah it would be! Nah my brother, this goes for the big trucks. And we welding the doors on 'em and putting in roof hatches."

"Sounds like work," I opined. "I'll make my rounds and come back to see if you need help later."

"Sounds good to me, my friend!" he replied in kind and returned my handshake.

•

I had scaled the steps to the second floor, our medical floor, and went straight to the first room to meet Shannon and see if Ashley was around as well.

The second floor had come around as well as the rest of the compound. It was barely even recognizable as having once been apartments. The first room doubled as an office and intake area. Each room after that was either exam rooms, short term recovery, or one of the two operating rooms we'd managed to cobble together. Nothing was exactly Grade A, and every day there was a need for this or that, but the girls did their best, and we did the best we could to accommodate them.

"Hey Shannon!" I called as I entered the office.

"Oh, hey Scott!" she replied, smiling. Shannon was short to say the least. She says five-foot, we give her four-ten at best. At any rate, she was nearly perpetually friendly and pleasant to deal with. A bit spacey at times, but that was just her personality. The girl was ungodly smart, and most of the guys didn't mind seeing her if they were sick or injured. There seemed to be an unspoken poll as to which one was better looking, Ashley or Shannon. Either way, I was happy to have them. Both were smart, hard-working, and very useful practicing medicine here.

Practicing, however, was not just a term to use lightly in this case. They each carried medical experience, but neither was a full-on doctor, and many times their work was learning as they went. Nevertheless, they made an amazing team and usually so with my wife as a third, doing her level best when she was needed or at least not busy elsewhere.

"Is, uh," I began, and she finished for me.

"Yeah, he should be awake, I haven't gone up to check," she replied.

"Okay, cool," I replied, smiling genuinely. "I'll make sure he's ready at least, maybe five minutes?"

"Works for me!" she answered before going back to what seemed to be a collection of medical seminars in print. Always learning, I admired that.

I turned and left her office and went up to the third floor. These apartments were kept mostly spartan, and two to three beds usually placed in each one, they were set up for more long-term care of patients.

I reached the last one and listened. I could hear some rustling and movement through the door, but just in case the occupant was still asleep, I pulled the door in tight before working the knob and easing it open slightly. The door mechanism made a barely audible *tsk* as it moved.

It only took a moment to regret my decision. I could make out the bed in the far room, the only one occupied here. A pair of bare legs, upon which rested a laptop. And, of course, on the laptop was the image of two very nude people in compromising positions. Shit.

Before I could subject myself to any more of the view, I quickly eased the door closed. I took a step back, gave it a moment, and figured 'what the hell', and knocked three times followed by, "Hey, dick, you decent? You awake?"

"Uh, yeah one second buddy!" came his response, and a moment later, "Okay man, I'm cool."

I opened the door and eased my way into where Tony had been kept for the last few weeks. His skin was flushed, and I latched onto that to torment him. It was a tough choice to make as I could have very easily started in on the decorative frilly throw-pillow he held tightly over his lap, pressing the covers into place.

"You look red, dude," I began, trying to mask my internal laughter with false concern. "Has she checked your vitals today? You look almost flushed, you're not having a reaction or anything, are you?"

"What?" he explained. "Nah man, just a little pain in my chest still. Still rough to breathe and all that."

"Well I mean you got lung-shot, dude," I reminded him. "You're lucky to even be alive given our resources. I'm still convinced we lost you and you're just a ghost filling in."

"No ghost here," he replied. "Hey, do you know if one of them are coming up soon?"

"I'll tell you," I began, "if you tell me how you're so lucky to have porn with no internet."

"I found a laptop that ended up being filled with it," he answered, reddening more deeply, then added a greedy, "And it's mine. Man."

"Yeah, I'm not touching it after you," I laughed. "Keep it hidden better though. And keep your little lacey pillow there tight, I'll send Shannon in."

"Okay dude," he offered. "Oh hey, they said I'll be cleared for light duty in a couple of more days. They don't know why my healing is taking so long, but..." he shrugged.

"Yeah," I replied, "just don't let the milk spoil."

I turned, leaving Tony laying there propped up and looking confused, and walked back out to the hallway where I nearly collided with Shannon and Ashley.

Ashley was a bit taller, but not by a whole lot. She had darker hair, and a similar round face with hazel eyes, instead of Shannon's green eyes, but aside from that they could have almost doubled as sisters. Both pale, round faced, pleasant demeanors and they nearly even dressed the same.

"Hey, he's up," I informed them, then said just loud enough for Tony to hear, "he did complain about some kind of sharp groin pain. I don't know if that's anything related, but he said it's pretty persistent. Might want to check that out."

Before either woman could reply, Tony's voice called out above all of ours.

"That man lies!" he proclaimed. "There's nothing! I don't need my groin checked!"

I shrugged and walked past a pair of very confused ladies and made my way to the stairwell again.

•

I'd finally cut back smoking enough to where I wasn't ready to keel over dead by the time I reached the ninth floor.

That being said, I was only mildly panting by the time I reached the command room. The whole floor, the ninth floor, was the highest in either building, and was referred to as the 'Command Floor', or just simply 'Command'. It was also the floor I lived on, my family and I the only residents here but I liked it that way, it gave us some extra separation but also allowed me to be quickly on hand if something happened that required my attention.

This space had transformed the most in the past few weeks. One whole side of the floor had been turned into a two-part command center.

One section, perhaps a third of the space, had been opened up and given seating for meetings. We could stuff every person in the compound into this room and still have room, but mostly it was relegated to department heads such as myself, Henry, Shannon, and others.

The rest of the space was accessible through a doorway in the conference room, or another near the end of the hallway. I took the shortcut through the conference area.

Opening the door, I walked into a slightly smaller space, but with much more going on in it.

The open light-giving windows had all been covered over. The inside of the windows first painted white and baby blue to reflect sunlight, then backed with jet black to block the rest of the light filtering through. This was then backed again by another coating of white to brighten the interior space and allow the bare minimum of light to be as efficient as possible.

The lights were mostly kept off as well to save power, leaving the area darkened save for the blueish glow from the banks of several monitors arrayed against the interior wall.

Two desks sat against that wall, each surrounded by a mass of monitors arrayed concavely to allow each to be viewed. One desk held a view over the main compound. The monitors screens divided into six to eight panes showing the entire main compound. The other desk held a watchful dominion over the outer wall, sentries, entrances, river, and any land between the two walls. Thanks to a couple of good scavenges, both stations were run by state-of-the-art PCs and all operations were controlled by separate twin-monitor setups. It was a computer nerd's wet dream.

Speaking of computer nerds, I had just walked in on our two best. And they were in the middle of a Nerf gun battle. Of course.

Rob, our resident computer expert, had moved all the surveillance and scouting tools off of one table and onto another and had the table flipped on its side, hiding behind it the best his squat frame would allow. Despite the wall mounted air-conditioner, he was covered with sweat, his short, curly dark hair matted to his head and his glasses slightly skewed as he returned fire to Ryan.

Ryan Boyd was one of our new additions that came into our little community. He came up as a computer hobbyist when he went through intake. Whatever that was, he was damn good with the things. He too was shorter, close to Rob's five-and-a-half feet tall, but he was much thinner. Athletic build, short cropped haircut, and a nose meant for a much larger person, but he was respectful, diligent, and worked his ass off for us.

Ryan had taken shelter behind the sliding screen doors used to cordon off the power for the entire compound and the actual command area.

They'd been brought in from the balconies to provide a divide and served him well at deflecting the foam darts.

Neither man noticed my entry in the least, and they continued on for another minute until I reached up and grabbed the tie for the blackout curtains between the monitoring stations and the rest of the area. The curtains fell and the room went dark, save for my shape silhouetted in the doorway I stood in, and their whoops and shouts at each other ceased.

I could just make out where Ryan was because the lights on the various electric equipment would disappear when he moved. Just before I opened my mouth to say something witty or derogatory, it happened. A series of soft pops broke the new silence, and it came from both ends of the area as my form in the doorway was pelted with a hailstorm of high-speed foam darts.

"DIE FUCKER!" came from Ryan's area as Rob followed with "They're retreating! Press the attack!"

I fell back around the corner laughing and yelling back at them as they rushed the doorway.

"Shit heads! It's me!" I called. "It's Scott! Cut that shit out!"

My authority was undermined by another hearty chuckle as the darts stopped flying and the other two joined me in laughter.

"We knew it was you," Ryan said through his laughter, "been tracking you since the far side of the overpass!"

"We got cameras that far now?" I questioned, a bit surprised.

"Not yet," Rob explained, beginning to calm himself, "but we've got driveway sensors across all the roads within 6 blocks approach from the wall. We knew you were there before you could even see the furthest reaches of the compound. Ryan actually set them up."

Rob motioned to the wall as he raised the curtains and pinned them back up. On the wall was a pegboard laid out with all the streets like a map. On each street was a single LED light with a label and on the bottom corner of it all was what I'd recognized as a piezoelectric speaker. I studied the board for a moment before turning to Ryan, his expression clearly seeking a response or reaction from me.

"How are they all connected?" I asked.

"Oh," he began, "they're all wireless, but they've got good range, so we sent a car out and radioed when we lost signal on one, and then set it a half block inside of its range. All the roads are covered for a half-dozen blocks in any direction, even got a couple across the river."

As if to emphasize the lesson, an archaic mechanical buzz resounded loud and clear as an LED on the board lit up for a moment, went out, then lit again and held steady. Ryan reached past me and pressed a button, shutting the warning off completely as both of them took individual seats and began inflating screen sections in the direction of the alarm. Ryan picked up the incoming traffic first.

"Got 'em," he stated calmly, then picked up his radio from the desk and spoke into it, "Southbound, this is Central, over."

A woman's voice crackled over the handset, "Southbound here, over."

"Southbound, you have incoming friendlies, over," Ryan informed the voice.

"Incoming on Southbound, copy, over," the voice came back.

I held my silence and observed. Ryan pulled up the vehicle as soon as it came into range, a long black crew cab cruised casually in our direction, with something in the bed of it and a trailer loaded with supplies. It approached Ryan's camera and passed by, where it was picked up on the next screen, then eventually to the outer gate's southern intake.

I could make out Dave driving the truck. His lanky form covered in tattoos, long dreadlocks hanging from under a ball cap made it all but impossible for me to mistake him for anyone else. I'd known the guy for years. The mop of red hair and dark sunglasses of Rich could be seen next to him. In the bed of the truck, however, was a sight to behold.

We didn't expect the level of crazy we'd get when the guy finally got comfy and opened up, but Cody was something else. Not bad crazy. Not scary crazy. But, if you wanted a friend when you were growing up that would window surf on your car at midnight on some backroads while shooting at every road sign you passed, it was probably Cody. He was currently sitting on what appeared to be a lawn mower, his feet up on the steering wheel, and a beer in his hand. A cowboy hat and a tank top that proclaimed 'YEET' in big bold letters across the front.

The vehicle passed into the inner portion of the outer compound where Ryan's cameras followed it until Rob's picked it up, then his electronic eyes followed the vehicle into the compound where it stopped. The guys in and on the truck and trailer dismounted and started unfastening supplies from both as yet more people came from different areas to help carry things to wherever they belonged.

"Okay, looks like y'all are doing well up here, keep up the good work!" I commended as I turned to leave. They both thanked me, and I departed for my apartment to grab a cup of instant coffee and head to the rooftop.

●

Jennifer was up top and busy helping a handful of others with building a rain cover over the roof of the building. Enough solar panels had been brought in and installed at this point to nearly obscure the view from all sides. Between these, screens and heavy netting were installed. We nearly all agreed it was better to sacrifice most of the view from this building after Tony fell to unknown gunfire during what should have been a celebration.

This was capped across the rooftop with a huge quilt of tarps. They'd been sewn together with everything from 550 paracord to old shoestrings, but the setup looked strong. It was all backed by steel cable looped through reinforcing rings and anchored to the roof to hopefully keep the whole assembly solid. With a little luck, it will hold tight. The real test would be the coming winter winds.

Looking at the new rooftop shelter and thinking of the drops in temperature we'd be experiencing, I started making more plans. It seemed as though there would never be a shortage of needs and wants for the community.

"Hey! Bri!" I called across the rooftop to where our supply floor lead was working.

"Oh, hey Scott!" she returned, standing and moving to head my way.

Bri was a slightly heavyset blonde in her mid-twenties. She had been appointed as the lead of Floor Eight, which was our designated supply floor. Everything we could need that wasn't earmarked for Shannon's medical needs, Henry's garage or Rich's armory went through Bri. The woman loved it and kept steady track of what supplies came in and what went out. Her and Dave had been an item since early in our adventures, though their relationship wasn't overt. They'd spend quiet parts of days together. Dave had even mentioned maybe moving into her apartment.

"What's up?" she asked as she approached.

"I need you to take some items down for future scavenging runs," I instructed, watching as she retrieved a pocket notebook and pen.

"Okay, shoot!" she directed.

"Check the storage areas of bars, mechanic shops, and private garages," I instructed. "Any kerosene heaters, or even better the tall one's bars use for smoke pits. Maybe even wood stoves if they can, we've removed a lot of trees, but that wood will need to season for a year or so first so have them watch for split woodpiles too."

"Okay, anything else?" she asked, eager to assist any way she could. I liked that quality, such a contrast from Katie and Parker.

"Just the usual," I said casually. "How are we on food?"

"Uhm not bad," she replied, recalling her figures on the fly, I was sure. "We look like we're set up until about mid-February, I'd say? We've got the three chest freezers running now but James wants to use some of

SHEOL

the new power we're making to put some more in. The hunts are really helping, so is the scavenging, of course."

"And every person we add to our home increases the strain," I observed. "I'd like to pull some people from work parties and start sending more or larger scouting and scavenging groups."

"Sounds good to me!" she replied, a grin still stretched across her round cheeks.

"Got your radio?" I asked, and nodded when she removed it from her side. "Good, call James and Rich up here, I want to get a feel for taking a run tomorrow with them."

She nodded in the affirmative and did as I instructed. We parted, her heading back to work, me moving over to where my wife was.

"Somebody actually convinced you to work?" I said, teasing.

"Oh, shut up!" Jennifer replied, reaching back and tightening the dark blonde bun on her head and wiping sweat off her forehead.

"Looks like everything is almost done up here?" I inquired.

"Mostly," she replied, then, "How was the hunt? Get anything?"

"Revenge," I stated. "They took my deer, I took their dignity."

She didn't reply, just looked at me with her ice blue eyes like she was trying to figure out a puzzle.

"Boss!" I heard a familiar voice call.

"You called?" Rich's much raspier, lower voice chimed in, and I turned to meet my friends as they approached. The two couldn't have looked any different. James's average height and lean build, his dark skin and eyes, all in contrast to Rich's shorter stature and bright red hair and pale, freckled complexion. An odd couple if I'd ever seen one, but they got along amazingly. And truth be told, I liked the both of them a whole lot. They'd been instrumental in our success thus far.

"Yeah, I did. Hey guys," I said, "I need you to pull four experienced scavengers and eight new people off work crews, I'm sending out more short-range scouts tomorrow."

"You expecting something?" James questioned.

"Nah man," I explained. "All I'm expecting is to be prepared. I want to scavenge as much as we can now before the real weather starts in a couple of months. So, we're gonna hit shit twice as hard."

"Works for me man," Rich joined in. "Is that all?"

"Nope," I smiled. "You're also going to pull in Dave and three more. You're on our team. We leave at sunup."

Smiles and excitement came from Rich and James as they departed. I could, however, almost physically feel my wife's stare as I turned to face her.

"You know I don't like you going out on runs," she stated firmly.

"I literally just got back from hunting alone, I think your priorities for worry are skewed a bit, woman," I joked.

"Yeah," she started, "where you're mostly hidden inside a vehicle that's built for it. Just, just be careful Scott. You know I worry."

"Somebody's got to," I stated, giving her a kiss before turning away. "But I've got a job to do. I wouldn't send these guys and girls out if I wouldn't do it myself."

"If you get hurt, I'm going to kick your ass!" she called to my back.

"If there's any of it left to kick!" I replied, jumping with a start as a flip flop sailed past my head.

Leaving the rooftop with haste, I went down to check on the armory Rich had been constructing. He told me the night before he considered it finished, thanks to the work detail I broke off for his purposes. I was excited to see it. According to him, all it needed was that 'lived-in' touch to feel like home for him.

I made my way down the stairs, nodding to the occasional person as I passed them. It was much easier to go down these steps than it was to go up them, that's for sure.

Stepping out of the newly built front entrance and into the spotty sunlight, I made my way to where the swimming pool had resided, nestled between a pair of driveways heading back to the parking lot.

The iron security fence had been removed, and the pool had long since been drained. The drain had then been wedged open to keep the floor dry and hopefully keep moisture from building up.

I walked down the short flight of stairs that had been dug out. The pool was a seven-foot deep affair and provided plenty of room when empty. A slightly raised sub-floor had been put in and then covered with thick plywood. The pool was in-ground, but additional walls around the perimeter added another four feet in height and were made of double layer cinder blocks packed with ready-mix concrete and capped by a peaked roof and shingled in like a standard house. It was a veritable bunker and built like that for a purpose. By Rich's logic, if anything he were working on in this armory were to 'go boom', the danger to anyone else would be directed upwards.

The interior was lit by scavenged LED lighting systems. These provided tons of illumination and drew minimal power from our little grid. They'd become standard as we found more lighting setups, and the goal was to eventually replace everything that lit up with LEDs and direct the power to other functions that drew more.

The entry stairwell dropped down into a short wide corridor of sorts. The wall was lined with seating on one side, the other side consisting of a steel door with a security window. The rest of this length looked to be a textbook armory window, a counter mostly protected and hidden with chain link save for a gap tall and wide enough to pass gear through. Rich was serious about tracking the gear, and utilizing the rest of the space for building things and living in. And damn he was good. The guy blew up most of the gang members' compound just weeks prior, full Oklahoma City-style with a truck and large fertilizer bomb.

"Hey Scott," he called as I entered, "what do you think?"

"I think you're an insane mad scientist and you scare me a little bit," I described, "and this is definitely a perfect spot for you to do your thing. Is it secure though?"

"Touch the fence," he directed as he flipped a switch on the wall by his bed.

I was expecting maybe an alarm, on the extreme side maybe another grate to drop and seal it off or something.

What I wasn't expecting was the instant blinding pain that overtook my entire arm before being replaced with a numb tingling. I wasn't expecting the crackle as electricity arced into my hand and singed the flesh across the back of my hand. I shouted and jumped back as Rich's insane giggle filled the space.

"What the fuck, dude?" I asked angrily. "You could have just told me. Or showed me! What the fuck?"

"This was more fun!" Rich admitted as he continued laughing. "Here, check it out, door's powered, too."

He flipped the first switch off and interacted with another one next to it. A solid *snick* issued from the door and it swung open just an inch before it clicked again, and a deadbolt bar extended from the edge.

"James set it up," he explained. "Check this out!"

He motioned to a hatch near his bed, which he reached for and swung open as I approached. I peered in and saw a bank of car batteries and a couple of black boxes anchored in place. He talked excitedly as he explained about the capacitors and how much power could be directed to just the fence alone, or it could all be used for backup power if the main grid went down.

"And check the floor in front of the counter on your way out," he instructed. "We had grounding issues with the fence, so it's got a shit load more nails than it needs; the extras are wired together and grounded below. You touch the fence and it completes the circuit, even with your boots on, and ZAP!"

We continued talking and hanging out through the day. Apparently, James had put a lot of work in down here for Rich, even running ventilation and getting the area ready to be heated electrically during the cold weather so there's no open flames. Considering Rich had probably a ton or two of ammo, powder, and explosives down here, that made a lot of sense to me.

Two of the mortar tubes we'd found before had been mounted on the far end, the tubes sticking through the rooftop. Rich informed me they were set to go off by trigger and contained illumination flares. Just in case, he stated assuredly.

As the day neared a close, we all met as per usual on the rooftop. It was our informal area to meet and share a meal at the end of every day. This high up, with this many solid doors and stairs between us and the outside world, we felt totally safe and secure. It boosted morale to have everyone together and sharing a meal and a laugh.

It felt safe, at least, up until Tony was shot. We had just liberated a ton of people from the hands of some real bad people. We were getting to know each other, the old and the new, and out of nowhere, one of my best friends on the planet fell to a single gunshot. None came after, and nothing since, but there he lay, spraying fluid across the rooftop every time he tried to exhale the air and blood from his lungs.

Shannon, Ashley, and Jennifer worked quickly and diligently and yet he still almost didn't make it. They got the lung to reflate but couldn't stop the bleeding. Even with their combined knowledge and skills it was touch and go. So much so that as they worked, Jennifer read out loud from medical books and coached like they were working on a class project.

They managed to keep him stable, but just barely. I was scared to death and didn't leave his vicinity for those first several days.

We didn't feel safe any longer, not even on the rooftop, and had used everything we could to build a wall of solar panels and more plywood scavenged from homes we were deconstructing. It still didn't feel totally secure, but it eliminated anyone being targeted. Can't hit what you can't see.

After a while the crowd had begun to peter out, leaving less and less of us until Jennifer and I decided to gather Gwen and head to bed ourselves.

I was again so worn out I scarcely remembered laying down before I was fast asleep.

THREE

My morning came quickly. Never one to take long to wake up fully, I was dressed, prepped, and waiting nearby a crew cab pickup as others trickled in.

There were four teams today instead of one, about six people each as opposed to ten on one crew.

The other teams already started to filter out of the compound as we loaded up our vehicle and checked our ICOMs before climbing in the truck and departing.

The truck was a standard crew-cab Ford that was then reinforced with chain link fencing bolted to the windows. Henry then reinforced the vehicle in other ways, such as welding and boxing various points across the body and frame. The truck was a tank to begin with and now felt like that much more of one now.

Locked into the vehicle, we headed out through the inner gate, then waited behind Clara's team as they departed the outer gate.

Clara and Frank were a couple, with a son and a daughter between them. They'd lived for a while locked in their apartment in the South Building, even after we'd begun making the place home. It was basically a rescue getting them out of there, but they'd been as vital to us as anyone else. Frank was a bit slow but came into his own. Clara was a tough little ball of lightning since day one, and she'd always handled the work put in front of her with aplomb, whether it be building, scavenging, or killing.

A beat later and they cleared the outer gate, which closed and allowed the inner to open for us.

We passed through the gate and Dave spoke up.

"Got me my tea!" he announced, holding up a large bottle of Arizona iced tea, "and it's mine. Not sharing!"

Dave was always a handful. Another of my long-time buddies, much like Tony. I wouldn't trade the world for either of them. Dave had a fire in him. A definitive dickhead with a true heart of gold, and truly one of a kind. There were few in the word I'd rather have on my side than him.

"Yeah?" I replied. "Well don't chug it, we aren't stopping for you to use the ladies room dude."

"It'll be alright," he assured, clapping me on the shoulder. "Where we going?"

"I figured I'd take you kids to the movies," I chided. "Maybe go see that horror flick your mother didn't want you to see."

"Sweet!" Dave replied, the others chuckling. "We going to see some titties?"

"Now you know you should cover your eyes for those parts," I laughed. "You're impressionable."

"Fuck that," Dave called back. "I'm in it for some fuckin' titties. And ass."

"You got Bri, don't ya?" I picked as I watched his face change like I let a secret out. "Anyway, we're gonna check the south, over by the school we blew up. Lot of decent houses over there, lot of businesses too."

"We should hit a hardware store sometime soon," James advised. "Shit went down during the warm part of the year. With luck, most of these people didn't think far enough ahead to grab space heaters, garage heaters, plumbing. I need more electrical. Oh, and Rich told me to keep my eyes open for stump remover? I don't know."

"Powdered sugar, too. And lots of PVC pipe," Rich's gravelly voice added.

"Yeah, that too," James added. "Not even going to ask. I've got so much of my own work still to focus on it's ridiculous."

"You been kicking ass for us, James," I awarded. "You know if you want to chill for a few days you can go on vacation."

"Can't do it man," he stated. "I stop working, my shit doesn't get finished. I been teaching Cody as I can, but we're talking a lifetime of knowledge…"

James chuckled and we conversed until Rich pulled the truck down one street and pulled up to a house near the dead center of the neighborhood.

We worked throughout the morning without much worry. The area was eerily quiet. Mention was made of the solitude, but no solutions could be found. We hadn't scavenged and cleansed this far south yet, we should have been dealing with much more infected.

We reached the ninth house of the day and approached it as we always did. Looked from afar for signs of life, and when we saw none, we stacked up six deep on the front door and breached it.

I went left, Dave and Rich hot on my heels as we cleared corners. James broke right with a pair of the high schoolers, two late teens named Jimmy and Korin in tow.

We moved briskly through a living room littered with baby toys. A smattering of stuffed animals and brightly colored objects littering the floor, a soft pink blanket laid out as a playmat.

Moving into then through a basic dining room, we quickly stacked to each side of a door on one wall. Breaching that, we moved into a garage occupied by only one car, called it all out as clear and moved back into the house.

"Scott!" James's hushed voice came. "We got something!"

We followed the sound of his voice into a large kitchen with a pantry and half bathroom off to one side. On the far side, behind an island occupying the center of the kitchen, James and company stood looking down at something on the floor.

As I moved to view what they saw, a pair of feet appeared on the floor. One bare, one covered in a patent leather shoe. The black of old, dried, infected blood was smeared throughout the area and around what seemed to be an old grey corpse dressed in a tattered and long-soiled grey business suit. The once well-fitted watch hanging loosely on an emaciated wrist as it lay in place on the floor.

"What the fuck is this, man?" I inquired. "It's a body. A corpse. I know this isn't your first-"

I let my sentence fall short as the corpse's head spasmed and jerked to face my direction.

The jaw slowly worked, and the dry raisin-skinned arms made an effort to turn the body and move to me. I took a reflexive step back, garnering protesting voices as I backed into Dave and Rich.

But the mummified freak stayed in place despite its best feeble efforts. The large torn open section centered in the lower back seemed to be heavy damage from a previous encounter with the living. The aged and encrusted bodily fluids of all likely types sticking it to the smooth linoleum like a glue. It was going nowhere. A dusty croak crept out of its mouth as it continued in vain to snack on me.

"What's your name?" I asked, eyeing the tall dark-haired girl by James.

"K-Korin," she said, her face drained of all color.

"You ever killed one of these up close?" I inquired.

"No," she replied, her voice wavering. "No, I haven't."

"Good," I replied. "No time like the present to learn. No gunshots unless we have to. It's been here a while. We don't know if there's a mind in there behind the monster that's suffering. And, it presents a threat still. Kill it."

"What?" she nearly chirped. "Kill it?"

"Yeah," I said, firm as stone. "Your boot should do. It's weak. One good stomp."

"Scott," James said, defending the girl. "It's a bit much."

"If she doesn't do it when it's easy," I observed, "she'll freeze when it's difficult. Stomp it."

"I can't," she said, grabbing the boy's hand. "I just- "

"Do it," I growled, "or I'll have you left here until you do."

She traded a look with the other high schooler and got a sigh of resignation followed by a nod from James, who actually turned his head away. She took one last pleading look at me, and before she could protest, I unsnapped the holster clasp for my pistol. I'd have never gone that far, to hold her at gunpoint, but that unspoken intention was the last push it took for her.

She let out a grunt as she brought her foot down firmly on the head of the freak. She followed with a whimper as her foot slipped on the smooth grey flesh and almost took her balance, but the girl righted herself and gave it one more.

The skull gave way like a calcified eggshell and began oozing grey matter and blood that seemed impossibly thick, and the monstrosity fell limp.

With the thud of her foot and the collective exhale from the group came another thud. This one came from above us. We all froze and looked up at the ceiling. The thud was shortly followed by several softer bumps, a thud, and then silence.

I motioned for all to be silent as I brought my shotgun to low ready and looked around. I clicked on the mounted weapon light, thankful for the extra help in the mostly shadowy home.

In the flood of light coming from my 870 tactical, I saw several large blackened streaks leading away from our new friend. Motioning the others to follow me, I followed the trail. The streaks led out of the kitchen and to an old dried puddle at the bottom of the stairway for the upstairs.

Each step bore its own markings of the freak's trespass. I followed them to the top and caught sight of the scene we were entering. The upstairs hallway was peppered with dozens of small holes from what appeared to be buckshot. Following the pattern, they seemed to have, at least in part, come from the bedroom at the far end, where a much smaller pattern was visible in the center of the door positioned dead at the other end of the hallway.

We stacked three to a side on the door, pressed firm against the wall and low, lowering our profile as Tony had taught and the rest passed on for others to learn. In the front, I tried the handle.

Locked.

So, I did the next most logical thing I could. I knocked. Once, twice, three times.

The response was the last thing I ever expected.

A soft, very young whimper responded, followed by a cry. No, not the telltale ear-piercing shriek we expected, but an actual cry. A *cry* cry. A baby's cry.

I looked back at my men, and girl, and knocked louder.

"We're friendly!" I called through the door and waited some more. Nothing.

I then called Dave up and whispered to him to boot the door open so we could see what was going on.

Dave let out a grunt as he brought his boot forward and impacted the door with it, adding his footprint to a score of scratches in the woodwork. It held, firm, but then gave way on the second try. The door swung violently inward and impacted the wall next to it as the catch and several large splinters of wood entered the room.

In the low light filtering in through bright pink curtains I could see the outline of a crib against one wall. A couple of dressers, and swinging my light around revealed a changing table, and a rocking chair.

In the far corner was the room's previous occupant. A long-dead young woman rested on the floor, her back against the wall. She wore a floral dress that was torn open at the chest that revealed an empty chest cavity. The pattern of the dress stained rust-brown with old blood. The area surrounding her covered in much the same shade with scraps of blue printed fabric littered throughout.

On the floor next to her body lay the cause of all the pellet damage in the hallway. A pump shotgun, and an empty 5 round pack of shells. Just five rounds?

Before I could any longer ponder the preposterous notion that someone would own a gun and such little ammo for it, I heard another soft thump followed by a rustle near the rocking chair. In the light streaming from my shotgun, a form appeared from the far side of the rocking chair. On sight the figure sent my soul over a hurdle. This. Now this, was too much.

The baby, not really old enough to even consider a toddler, crawled into view. A little girl, little pink T-shirt torn and ratty. She used her hand to bring herself to a standing position and turned to face us. The grey mottled skin contrasted by the red rims around her eyes, and the twin trails of blood streaming from her tear ducts. Her knees worn wide open from crawling, the skin peeled back like old leather.

She let out a final baby-like cry which turned into a thin, high, tinny screech as she took three steps toward us and fell flat on her face.

Before the smallest infected I'd ever seen recovered and we had to do something about it, I reached in and slammed the door shut.

"Nope," I said. "No fucking way. This is too much now."

"What the fuck was that?" James nearly spat.

"Baby," Dave breathed. Rich just traded glances back and forth with everybody.

31

What the hell are you supposed to do in this situation?

"Sure you don't want to stomp on it?" Korin asked from behind us, her tone and glare driving solid spikes into my being.

"Go get a jerry can from the trailer," I ordered. "Everyone else follow her out. We don't need anything from this house."

"No, yeah, I'm good on that," James agreed.

We left the house without even a word among us until we got outside. I took up the tail, and Korin was first out so she met me halfway back with the jerry can. I took it from her without a word and we turned back to the house together.

"What are you going to do?" she asked.

"Not going to ask anybody to handle that one face to face," I explained, "but we can't let it stay."

Her eyes went wide as I opened the nozzle and casually stepped into the house and began liberally pouring gasoline around the stairwell, leaving a trail as I walked it out through the front door.

"I'm sorry about what I said," she informed me.

"Don't worry about it," I stated.

I pulled a matchbook from my pocket and struck one on the cover, lit the rest, and threw it on the ignition trail. The air grew instantly warm as the fire sprang into being, leaving an angry orange trail. A larger secondary *woosh* sounded through the neighborhood as the puddled home interior caught and the air ignited with flames. In no time at all it was fully invested in consuming the house, so I turned my back, Korin in tow, and we wordlessly walked back to the truck. All eyes were on the flames behind us as they tried to exit the front door but were dragged back inside by their need to consume.

Dave nodded as I approached, and we mounted up on the truck, Rich climbing back behind the wheel, and moved a couple of blocks over in case the flames drew the attention of any local infected. We still hadn't seen any sign of them, and that worried me.

Rich pulled the truck to the end of the block then turned to the right, heading westward and deeper into the residential area.

The next handful of blocks passed uneventfully, and nobody dared say anything at all about the toddling monster. I was sure if anyone had half a similar mind to mine, we were all actively trying to forget what we'd witnessed.

We had all seen our own fair share and then some in these end days, but I think a shit-diapered little girl looking to become a literal ankle-biter was just simply more than we'd needed.

Despite the multitude of possible reasons for it, we continued onward in silence. Every eye trained on the cruel outside world as we went.

We started seeing a couple of infected here and there. A few staggering around on one street, a few more than the first on the next. They grew in number for a few more streets, always further down the road than we were.

We crept up to another junction when something caught my eye.

"Hey Rich," I called over, tapping him, "hold up here."

"You see something?" he asked, bringing the truck to a halt, but never taking it out of gear. Always ready.

"Yeah, I think I do," I relied, motioning for James to hand me his binoculars.

"What is it?" James asked.

"A whole world of shit that we're about to dive into," I replied grimly. I could feel my chest tighten and all the hairs on my body stand on end. Just the sight in James's binoculars was enough to set the adrenaline flowing through my system.

There were dozens of them. Infected. Fast and slow. Men, women, even some small figures darting around between the others. Great. Somebody there was having a Grateful Dead concert and forgot to invite any security at all.

"Jesus," James muttered as he looked at the scene and handed the optics to Rich.

"They're all around one house, we can leave it," Rich opined.

"Can't," I stated flatly. "Jennifer's going to kill me for this one, but they're around that house for a reason. Could just be a dog, or a whole community holed up in there, but we gotta help."

"He's right guys," Dave sighed. "We got to be the good guys again."

"You know I'm willing to help," James echoed.

"Fuck," Rich sighed, and the high school kids just held their silence. Both had gone visibly pale, perspiration breaking across Korin's forehead.

"Give me the glass back," I instructed, "and double check your gear and weapons. I'll craft a plan while we sit."

I had taken Jennifer's AR-15 and a half-dozen magazines. I checked that, and also checked the Sig 226 on my drop leg holster. Good to go. Bringing the binoculars back up to my eyes, I peered past the broken outlines of Henry's chain link armor and observed.

The small horde was a few short blocks away. Just enough distance to keep us safe if we didn't make a huge scene here. There was easily five or six-dozen of the freaks, estimating for those I couldn't see. They were surrounding an average two floor home, attached garage, it was even the same basic cream color as half of the other homes in the neighborhood. The obvious difference between this one and those around it was the burglar bars lining the windows, and the steel cage of the outside storm door. As hard as some of the infected were hitting the house, they weren't getting through. The most that had been done was the shattering of the glass inside the outer door.

"Okay," I stated, breaking the silence, "We drive up and say hi. Then we drive away."

"How is that going to help?" asked Jimmy, the other kid with us.

"No, he's right, that's smart!" James chipped in, "Drive kinda slow and make a scene real loud, like Pied Piper them away from the house. But, then what? We circle around and pick them up?"

"Nah man, we still got to clean this area of infected if possible," I said, eyeing Dave as he ran his hand down his face

"We can't ram them all," Rich noted. "The truck's brush guard will only take so much."

"We trap ourselves," I explained. "We get enough room to dismount on the circle back. We go in through the front and leave it open. That house is two floors plus attic. We back up to the second floor and use the steps to funnel them. Then stack fuckin' bodies."

"You're insane!" Rich nearly croaked. "What the fuck makes cornering ourselves sound like a good plan? I'm crazy. You're fucking *insane*, Scott."

"This goes against every basic instinct I have for survival," James added, "but I see your side of it loud and clear. Boss man, if we follow this plan, I trust you."

"He's right," Dave barely muttered in agreeance, "that's as solid a plan as any other we have here. Fuck. Let's go."

I visually checked each person for readiness. When all gave the good-to-go, I nodded to Rich, who pressed the accelerator and the truck lurched, then began to rumble down the street.

Two blocks away and moving at the pace of a good healthy run, Rich started laying on the horn loud and long and flashing the bright headlamps.

Just one block away, and with the attention of our swarm of greeters garnered, Dave opened the sliding rear window and hung his top half out, sitting perched on the sill. A little noise and movement from our lanky, tattooed friend, that should do us fine here.

The infected reached our truck even before we reached the house.

The first few hit head-long, the heavy brush guard doing its new job well, catching them and tossing them bodily to the side, or dragging them under the heavy vehicle to thud along the underside below our feet.

Other freaks started coming out from between homes, previously unseen and adding to the count with every hiding spot we passed. There was a lot of them, running and shambling beings coming out of ambush points all over the street. They really were getting clearly smarter, and as uneasy as I felt about our plan, I realized it was the only chance whomever we were rescuing would have at survival.

Then the screaming started. At first, I thought it was another monstrosity shrieking the dinner bell as it joined the pursuit. But it was too low-pitched for that. Not the characteristic screech we'd come to know and loathe. Then the scream came again.

"Dave! DAVE!" I shouted, twisting to see him being grabbed on the arm by a young male that had latched onto the truck's ladder rack. Then his screaming stopped.

I tried to pull his feet and get him back in the truck but was met with much resistance, then a kick.

"I'm alright!" Dave yelled inward to the truck. "Gah! Back, bitch! Boop!"

As the last, most unusual word 'boop' left his lips, he gave his hatchet a back-handed swing and buried it into the head of the monster that had him, causing it to fall over the side back to the street and taking his bladed weapon with it. He started yelling again as we reached the house, at the top of his lungs.

"WE'RE CIRCLING BACK!!!" he called to the house. "HAVE THE FRONT DOOR OPEN!"

"Rich, give it more now, get ahead and lead these assholes," I directed, then turned to Dave as he slid back inside the truck. "You think they heard you?"

"I sure hope they did," James breathed. "The madman risked his life for it!"

"They did," Dave confirmed. "I saw a chick on the second floor, not infected, she was nodding and waving and shit."

"Okay cool. Good," I offered, then, "Okay Rich, part two. Everybody get ready, we'll have to haul ass. Be ready!"

Everyone confirmed as Rich cleared the monstrosities on the street and started to slow to pace them.

"We could just outrun them and come back alone," Rich suggested.

"Scott's right," James disagreed. "We don't get rid of them now, they'll get someone else in the future, maybe be a problem for us for all we know."

The idea was so outlandish that I was happy to have people on my side, it reassured me that I hadn't completely lost it.

Rich's acquiescence was apparent as he sped up, then used the next intersection as a cul-de-sac and swung wide to bring the pickup truck and trailer around. The impacts started almost immediately again, and despite his best efforts to swerve, the front of the truck was taking damage and the wipers were run at full blast as thick blackish blood from the infected covered the windshield of the truck.

Everyone was shouting directions while Rich reimbursed them with assurances. The scene was pure chaos. The yelling, the laboring truck engine, the whole vehicle rocking with each *thud* and *bang* as it took another creep to the pavement.

Finally, we cleared the tail of the herd that was on our back, the runners, at least. Rich hit the throttle and rocketed forward for the final one block back.

Then, truck, followed by trailer, bounced the curb and slid to a jack-knifed stop in the dead center of what used to be an immaculate front yard, now waist-high with summer grass and overgrown flower beds. We came to a rest near the now-opened house door, and both of our front doors opened as I shouted to everyone.

"DISMOUNT!" I shouted, nearly falling out of my side of the truck before turning and seeing the back doors of the crew cab were both dented out of shape and refusing to open. I didn't even waste time to yell for help, and instead grabbed the handle and yanked with all I had, snapping the plastic handle right off but failing to get anywhere.

"FUCK!" I bellowed. A glance over my shoulder showed the freaks approaching way too fast for comfort as Dave nearly flew out of the front of the truck opposite me.

He turned and reached for Jimmy and yanked him over the seat and out of the truck as I extended my hand to James. James grasped it tight as he tried to clamber over the front seat. A solid yank from me put him nearly on his feet as a loud *crack* sounded right by me. I felt the slickness of the infected blood on my back as one near me fell to rifle fire. Dave loosed another burst from his AK and dropped a couple more.

"Let's go!" he shouted, firing another burst. "THEY'RE HERE!!!"

Dave fired one last burst and ducked back as he was almost blindsided by one. The freak nailed the door jamb and bounced as Dave filled its chest and neck with rounds, dropping it. Then he disappeared into the house as I ran, James hot on my trail.

I had just crossed the threshold into the house in time to see Dave disappear around a far corner. At that moment, a hand locked into the back of my T-shirt and pulled me, nearly taking me out of the doorway backwards. I turned and realized in horror it was James.

He was pulling me as his face twisted into a mix of sheer terror and pain. Looking just past his body as his arms stretched to their length, I could make out the stark white and grey face, just as it sunk its teeth through the windbreaker he wore, drawing an instant gush of hot blood like the juice of a fresh tomato.

I used my free hand to draw the Sig and place three 9mm rounds into the bitch's face as I drew James inside, the heavy door swinging closed on its spring and latching.

I began to feel shaking in the hand holding James's shirt across his chest. As I turned to look, I realized it wasn't my hand, but James himself shaking. His head was already starting to snap back and forth. The vessels in his eyes began to darken and I pulled him near me then slammed his back flat against the wall. It was too late for him.

"Sorry, buddy." I spoke solemnly as I brought my pistol forward, drawing down square into the center of his forehead.

Just as my hand started to tense on the trigger, he broke his convulsions long enough to lunge forward. The move took me by surprise and caused him to hit the gun just as I squeezed, causing it to go out of battery. Pulling the trigger yielded no result.

"Fuck!" I growled as I redoubled my efforts. I barred my whole forearm against his upper chest and leveraged against the wall behind me in the narrow space, forcing him back and into the adjacent wall again. This time I used enough force that the drywall behind him cracked and caved. Drawing the pistol up again, the trigger broke cleanly, expelling hot gas and full metal jacket into the cranium of what was a good friend to us all just a moment before. The shot in that instant became louder than a supernova in the vacuum between us.

The round perforated a neat little hole just in line with his eyebrows, dead center. The exiting round found the drywall ahead of the wash of blood and grey matter that covered the neatly hung portraits behind him. The weight on my arm went limp, and I released my pressure, allowing him to fall to the floor with a thud. The last noise our buddy would ever create.

As the first sting of tears fought its way to my eyes, the world started to come back into focus. The pounding and shrieking coming from outside. The yelling coming from the interior of the house. Even the way James's freshly smoked thoughts tainted the otherwise sterile scent of the home.

"I'm coming!" I choked out. "James is gone!"

A series of replies I couldn't discern came back to me. It was so loud in that house. Fuck was it loud. And the ringing in my ears from the single gunshot did nothing to ease the auditory tension. I whirled as I felt something brush my back. An infected arm reached its entire length into the home from the gap between the storm bars in the door.

Thinking quickly, I reached for James's backpack, removing it from his body and reaching in to retrieve the container of ammonia. Twisting the cap off and ripping out the foil seal, I forced it into the grasp of the freak's hand. It withdrew with the bottle, stopping and turning it this way and that until it forced it through the bars, flooding the chemical out of the bottle and onto the stoop.

I pulled the bleach out of my own pack and squished the bottle through the bars, hoping for the reaction that was sure to come.

In short order, the freaks pushing closest to the door started to rasp, some of them outright choking as they issued short rasping barks. Using this opportunity, I kicked the latch to the door, forcing it open and knocking a few demons backwards.

"Dinner's UP!" I called to the horde, moving back toward the door and reaching down just long enough to wedge it open with the foot of the nearest fallen infected.

I turned and ran to the stairs bellowing *"IT'S ME!"* just before I rounded the corner. Leaping up three steps at a time, I nearly literally ran into the arms of the remining members, backed by a pair of clearly frightened strangers. After repeating the news of James, the first infected hit the bottom of the staircase.

It careened into the staircase, actually. The infected man, looking much like everyone's favorite barbecue father, burst around the corner, hit the first step, and carried his momentum right into the wall. The sheetrock cracked and broke free in places as he rebounded and scrambled for purchase on all fours, nearly pulling off a Looney Tunes cartoon burnout as Dave and Rich opened fire.

"Controlled bursts, make them count, we're gonna need all our ammo!" I instructed, then turned to the two newcomers. "There any way out of this floor?"

"Windows are barred, mate," the man replied in a strong British accent.

"On the second fucking floor?" I asked, incredulous. "Who the fuck bars the second floor?"

"Well," said the woman in a matching accent, "there was a robbery, and- "

"Where?" I asked, incredulous. "Here?"

"Well, no," she dragged, "down the street but it still bothered me."

"That's why you get a *gun*, lady!" I spat to her. "Something besides that ancient double barrel pops here is holding!"

"Well I'm sorry I'm just not comfortable with-" she started.

"Later," I shot, moving to check the bedrooms. All the windows were barred. Shots rang out from the hallway as I peered out and scanned the mass of freaks gathered in the front yard.

Christ there was a lot of the fucking things. A crowd rung in like a horseshoe pushed and fought for access through the front door, while others tried the windows despite heavy burglar bars. They were ravenous, and completely determined to gain entry one way or the other.

"They're coming!" Dave called in as a new fusillade of shots flew down to the first floor. I ran to join my friends.

The man came to aid, loading new shells into the aging side-by-side. He was dressed in such a way that it appeared as if he were about to go on a fox hunt. A matching jacket, trousers, and bowler cap all woven in the kind of brown that looked like it would be better suited to furniture in the mid 90s. His round face flushed as he brought the shotgun up and dumped both barrels into the upper half of a teenage boy in track shorts. The boy fell and added to the eight or so bodies already piling up as the remainder of the pellets from the massive old cannon found another freak behind that one.

More infected tried to hit the gap for the stairs and missed their entry by a margin. So much blood and body matter pooled at the bottom of the steps already that even the carpet was slick. The air hung thick with the coppery scent of them, infected B.O., ancient feces, and gun smoke.

I joined in as the swarm tried to make their way upward, none making it further than halfway as they slid down to trip up the next one in line. As the ones from the front fell, they pushed back those below them.

I'll be damned. Funneling them was working like a charm.

More freaks could be heard infiltrating the house as they clamored through the open front door, shrieking and knocking loose everything in their path on their way to a meal.

I cycled through the rest of another magazine and swapped it out for a new one, readying the weapon again.

"Rich! Dave! Korin!" I ordered. "Take the windows, get what you can hit for sure! Jimmy! On me; help keep them downstairs!"

They barely spoke a word as they broke contact at the stairs and rushed away. In a mere moment later, I could hear them shattering glass elsewhere on the floor and opening fire. The cacophony continued as what seemed to be a never-ended flood of the infected followed the commotion we were making

Somewhere between the bursts of weapons fire and all the other commotion I heard a new noise. Very familiar, yet alien, I felt it as much as I heard it. A moment later it came again.

BOOM!

The sound split our entire world in one large concussive blast.

"What the fuck was that?" Dave shouted from a nearby room.

"I brought toys!" Rich shouted back.

"Is he gone mad?" asked the woman.

"No!" I shouted back. "He's crazy, probably only mad that he's here!"

"No, I meant mad as in-" she started. "Oh, no bother."

I shot a look at her as there was a sudden lull in the action from the stairwell. She was unremarkable in most ways. A rather short, and shapeless individual but what stood her apart from other people would have been her darkly dyed red hair and green eyes. These features were framed with an almost perfectly square chiseled jawline and a pair of bushy dark eyebrows that reminded me of wooly bear caterpillars in the autumn. It gave her a nearly comical appearance at any angle, almost a caricature in profile view. I turned back to focus on the work at hand before a chuckle left my lips. My God, what a pair!

Just then, the entire environment shattered for a moment as one blast, followed by a second, then a third much, much larger one that shook the entire house. Hell, it shook the *air* in the house, followed by a loud crash from the front.

"Everybody okay?" I called out and was met with the right number of 'yes' answers in one form or another.

Just as these calls came back to me, the bottom of the stairwell flooded with a redoubled number of the freaks. So many new faces showed up to join us, upturned eyes and mouths barely taking themselves away from the sight of us even as they clamored for position to be first in line at this glorious buffet.

"Back to the stairs!" I shouted.

"They're all inside now!" Dave yelled as he came flying into view from the bedroom. He turned to face down the stairs and unleashed a full magazine from the AK down the steps, shredding everybody in sight, moving or not. He drew his pistol forward, allowing the rifle to fall limp on its sling, informing me, "Out of ammo for the big boy!"

"What about Charlie Chaplin over there? Trade him!" I instructed.

"I'm low, too!" the guy answered, then, "And it's Ash, you wanker, not Charlie Chaplin!"

"You're kidding me, right?" I answered, perplexed.

"Sorry? It's a common name!" Ash informed.

"No, it's cool," I replied. "I just thought a guy named Ash would do better in a house surrounded by monsters!"

Catching my reference, he actually chuckled, grinned, and dumped two more loads of buckshot downstairs while saying something I couldn't quite catch.

In the proceeding moment, Rich appeared, holding a section of steel pipe the length and diameter of a man's forearm.

"You guys should go to the attic!" he informed us, his frosty blue eyes flashing in the low light from outside, then eyeing the device he held, "The, uh, far side of the attic."

"Oh god he's back on his bullshit," I stammered. "Okay y'all heard him! Upstairs! MOVE!"

We scrambled upstairs. Starting across the uppermost floor of the house, I stopped and watched for just a moment, and took a headcount to make sure we still had everyone.

The last thing I could hear after that for several minutes was the flick of a Zippo, a soft hiss, and Rich's footsteps as he bolted upwards behind us. Then the world ended. Again. But, just for a moment this time.

The sound hit with physical force greater than any we'd felt before. I could have sworn the floor of the attic *jumped* with the concussion, and nothing was left to behold but a ringing in my ears. A ringing so deep it was as if my own brain had turned into an old dinner triangle.

In the silence, the first form appeared after us, bursting through the doorway and into the attic. I unloaded an entire magazine into it from the Sig, my rifle on its last magazine.

A second and third form broke into the dark of the attic, falling silently to more gunfire, then nothing. Nothing but the ringing in my ears as we scrambled in perceived silence to check each other. The first sounds I heard as my ears found their places were my friends. Everyone's okay. Then immediately, the woman started in.

"Look, I appreciate the rescue, really," she began, her voice coming from miles away, "but I don't like you just barging in and acting like I was wrong for doing something because my windows were barred. It's not nice and ordering us around is just, well, it's controlling!"

"What's your name?" Dave asked her, trying to distract and diffuse, but I was having none of it. We just risked everything to rescue these two, and she was bitching about how we talked to her?

"My name?" she asked. "Oh! I'm Lara!"

She gave a beaming smile at Dave that somehow did nothing but highlight the premature wrinkles on what should be a youthful age. I guessed her to be about my age, give or take, and a good fifteen or more younger than Ash.

"Lara?" I interrogated, echoing her attitude. "A British chick who just happens to be named Lara? What are we, *fifteen*? You don't even like guns, and I highly doubt you've been raiding many tombs in your shape."

"Alright, alright," Ash interjected, offering a prize-winning smile. "Let's stop this. Just now. Her real name is Lauren, Lauren Dennis. I don't know why she chooses Lara, either."

"Guys," Rich added another two cents. "This is ridiculous. We still aren't safe, and James is dead. Please."

"I agree," Korin added. "James was nice to me, he helped everyone."

"And I'm not letting his sacrifice go to waste," I stated firmly. "Let's get ready. Mr. Chaplin? Groucho Marx? Get your things. We're leaving."

Ash chuckled, and Lauren glared at me like I'd kicked her dog, but she kept her mouth shut this time and in a moment they were ready.

"Rich, you're still driving, you'll go first. We'll follow," I ordered to all present. "Jimmy, you have the good shotgun, follow Lauren, you'll take the rear. Let's go, guys. I only see a couple slow ones outside. We can make that. I'll carry James."

All responded to the affirmative and we departed the attic. Each person with a gun out, ready, and covering their own unique direction. Most of us, at least.

We swept through the second floor, finding only one lone straggler. She looked around aimlessly and didn't even seem to notice us as Rich pushed a round through her skull and kept the line moving forward.

We moved as quietly as possible until we hit the stairwell for the first floor. It was a mess of bodies, fluids, and broken building material, and was difficult to pass through in the least. Rich did his best to use his foot to roll infected corpses aside, but they were so piled up he could buy almost no extra room. This resulted in an awkward passing for all leaving a few, myself included, to slip in the thick stew of remnants left over by whatever the hell Rich threw down there.

The entire back of the first floor was blown out, showing a backyard unpopulated by our tormenters. The floor closest to the gap had been blown clean through to the basement. A pool of thickening gore followed the dip that now warped the floor and ran into the basement of the house, leaving thick splashing sounds as it fell to the floor.

The place reeked, as well. Burnt hair, carpet, and burnt infected flesh all did their best to assault my nostrils, leaving my stomach on the edge of retching. Others did their best to keep composed as we each stole a chance to peek at a very proud Rich Lester.

The smell didn't seem to bother him at all, neither did the gore, as the insane Irish fuck took in his handywork, very likely already planning improvements.

We made our way around, then out through the front door and into the sunlight that was beginning to break from the cloud cover. I decided as I passed that I'd leave James where he lay for a moment and make sure we were clear before retrieving him for a proper burial.

That decision was ideal, as I was about to learn. The few shamblers that resided in the yard were evicted as we broke cover, and the nightmare came back home to roost.

Rich appeared first into the sunlight. No sooner had his heel breached that threshold, the first high-pitched dinner bell shriek sounded, and my heart nearly turned into one of Rich's explosives.

"RUN!" I cried so loud my own breath hurt. "Rich, drive, lure them! Guys go with Rich!"

The first half of our line broke free and sprinted for the truck as the rest of us started to fall back.

The infected were still horde strength as I could now see. They spilled from the sides of this house. They came from cover across the street. They even came from inside of other houses. A couple of dozen in number at least.

As Dave and I fell back to the house, following Jimmy and Lauren, more shrieks sounded from within the home. Before I could process what was happening, monsters from all angles inside rushed forward. A shot load of freaks filtered between and over furniture as even more came in through the gap in the back of the house.

The first one hit Jimmy before he could even react. It came perpendicular from the front room, the momentum carrying them both out of sight as one shrieked and the other screamed.

"TRUCK!" I shouted, and we all reversed direction a second time and sprinted, the infected already darting around within reach of us, testing us, and feeling us out. Dave and I hit the bed of the pickup just as it started spitting sod and soil from its tires, grasping for purchase towards our escape.

I felt a fresh, hot round from Dave's pistol breeze past my ear as it found the throat of a nearby infected. Likely, it blew out the spine because the creature crashed face first into the lawn, nearly impacting one spinning truck tire as it slid to a pause. Then I heard a yelp that was half squeak, half bark as a linebacker-sized infected pummeled Lauren.

It hit the small woman from behind at a dead run that was nearly twice her own speed. They both hit the dirt half the distance from the swaying trailer where she had been a mere heartbeat before.

The truck began picking up speed and it hit me that this was it for her, the woman was gone.

"Hold Ash back!" I yelled to Dave, just as the man lurched forward yelling for Lauren. Dave grabbed him in time to keep him from going over, and we departed the scene in a cloud of smoke and spray of topsoil. The entire back end of the truck jumped and shuddered as we found pavement and began to gather momentum, then it started to even out.

Deciding to try for mercy, I turned to face the scene behind us. As runners gave chase, Lauren and her new friend finally stopped their momentum.

The bruiser of a monstrosity perched over her, nearly insect-like in his posture. Just as she rose to flee, tearing clear two of her fingernails in an attempted escape, it buried its face deep into her back just below the shoulder blades. The monster brought its head back, a sickening snap and crunch issuing forth from the scene, audible over even the vehicle's noise. It swallowed its prize nearly whole and swiped at her, rolling Lauren to her freshly wounded back.

She no longer moved. Her gasps and screams told us the woman still lived, yet she ceased any further fight against the freak that held her captive to the surface of the planet.

Somehow, her fight had left her already, but her screams of terror only grew. It soon became apparent to me. The *why*, that is.

His first bite paralyzed her, I thought.

"I'm sorry," I muttered as I stood and braced myself with the ladder rack over the truck bed. I brought my rifle to my shoulder and squeezed the trigger. The weapon bucked just a little in my shoulder as it let out a bark.

Miss

Her shrill screams continued as the nearby smaller and also the slower infected moved in, calling their first dibs on the fresh meal. They began low, each taking a section of leg and digging in, lower on her flaccid form than the big guy had perched.

As more and more freaks dove in, and the distance grew, I began to get a hopeless feeling deep in my gut. Christ, she knew she was being eaten and couldn't do anything. Couldn't even feel it. Could do nothing but watch herself be consumed. Helpless.

I squeezed the trigger several more times. Again, and again. The moving vehicle adding its own factor to the shots, and each missed. Rounds kicked up dirt and debris, they winged monsters and dug into infected, but none hit their true mark.

"FUCK!" I shouted as I started firing all I had left. I had hoped to at least hit something. Something vital, something keeping this poor woman alive, but it wasn't happening.

My rifle clicked on empty, and the distance grew. The crimson puddle around the feast expanded. Encircling them like a bullseye. The buck stops here, kiddo.

The only thing that diminished with the distance was the pursuit that was against us, and the volume of her screams.

Ash's screams for Lauren finally began to fade as we lost sight of the area. They were replaced by silence as the man stared blankly at the houses we passed. Only occasionally would a new tear fall to forge its own path through his scruffy long cheek stubble.

The only thing that was said for the rest of the ride home was by Dave. He asked Ash, in sympathy, if Lauren was his girlfriend or sister or something.

"Cousin, mate," Ash spoke softly. "Favorite cousin. I was here on holiday to visit her."

No suitable words could find me, and so none left. We watched as the neighborhood passed, each person in the back of this truck stuck in their own thoughts. We had all lost somebody, mostly in the first days of the end, but the hits and losses never seemed to stop coming. There was always somebody hurting, somebody dying, and I had a feeling in my gut that we were nowhere near the end of it.

We nearly coasted through the neighborhood as we went. I had just about had enough to force my thoughts away from James when the radio on my hip chirped, and I touched my earpiece and spoke the go ahead.

"Should we circle back and grab what we'd staged? Over." Rich's gravelly voice crackled in my ear.

"Negative," I informed him as a pair of freaks broke my line of sight and stopped as if trying to figure whether or not we could be caught. "Look around us. These neighborhoods were practically empty. Now they're everywhere. Over."

"Solid copy. Straight home then? Over," he questioned.

"Yeah buddy," I agreed. "I'll send a larger team with more guns for retrieval tomorrow. Shit shouldn't be going anywhere by then. Unless it grows legs and becomes sentient. Over."

A word of agreeance from Rich and the conversation died.

Before long we were in line with the southern gate. The mismatched wall stretching out in both directions. It had been capped off at nearly ten feet in height and fastened together with such an eclectic mix of everything it was comical in the least.

Some sections even appeared to be made from entire pieces of roof from a home, complete with attic vents and skylights now backed with plywood. Others were bare panel wood and studs; I even could make out the hood of a car in the distance. Road signs had also been used to bolster or patch certain areas, save for the stop signs that had been placed on each side of the entry gate. They may have been the only part of the wall that actually meant something legitimate.

As we neared the compound, I tapped Ash on the shoulder and motioned ahead.

"Welcome home," I said flatly, then, "If you'll have it, that is."

"This is where you boys are from?" he asked, nearly in shocked amazement. "Lauren and I, well, we've been over here before. Didn't get too close, though."

"Didn't?" I asked. "What, didn't want to risk it in case we weren't the good guys?"

"Pretty much buddy," Ash resigned. "You saved me, tried to save my cousin despite, well, despite her shortcomings. I owe you for that, and I'm grateful. That wall looks like my best option for safety now."

"It is for all of us," I agreed as we stopped before the gate.

Katie was once again on duty. She remained in her own world and bad temper at the sight of me and said nothing as she rolled back the outer gate for us. Her brown eyes changing from spite towards me, to confusion at the sight of Ash, just for a moment before she averted her eyes to the ground.

"Well she's a cheerful looking lass," Ash commented softly after she passed to work the front gate.

"Busted for stealing a shit ton of food," Dave assuaged. "She's out here on outer gate duty for a while."

"She has both her hands still," Ash joked, "that speaks volumes of fair leadership."

Neither Dave nor I laughed along, but we both forced an amused grin for the man's benefit.

We cruised the few blocks to the inner gate and repeated the dance, but on a smaller scale, for this entry as well. I only partially paid attention to Ash as he muttered words of amazement at the things he was seeing. Okay, so apparently, we were doing quite well for the world to be over.

As we pulled the truck around to the motor pool and parked it, I instructed Dave and Rich to get the department heads up to the ninth floor so we could discuss James.

"What did you do for a living, Ash?" I asked, a part of me wanting to know for our benefit, part wanting to find a way to distract him from recent events.

"I was a handyman in general," he began, "mechanic, cabinet builder. I'm sure I could be of use to you."

"Oh, I'm sure you can. We just lost our guy today," I said flatly, considering the sad irony and eyeing Ash as he began taking a second look at his surroundings. "James was a carpenter and handyman as well. He had some mechanical and electrical engineering knowledge, too."

"Well, what's your plan?" he inquired.

"Use you," I replied. "I'll introduce you to Cody. He's a smart guy, he's become James's best right-hand man in the weeks he's been here. Actually…"

I broke my speech off and called Cody to the ninth floor command with my radio.

"I'll have you two meet right now," I finished. "Follow me."

Without a word, he followed me into the front entrance. The area, having been recently rebuilt after Tony smashed a car through it, reeked of fresh latex paint. I caught a glimpse of Bri disappearing around one corner as Jennifer approached from the same area.

"What do you think?" she asked, motioning around, then noticing Ash, "Oh! Hello! Who's this?"

"Ash, Jennifer," I introduced quickly. "Jennifer, this is Ash. We're on our way up, I think you should come along."

"What happened?" she asked, seeing my expression, I was sure. "Scott? Did something happen?"

"Take Ash up to the ninth floor," I said flatly. "I'm going to make one more stop, and I'll be up there, too."

"Scott, did we lose somebody?" she asked as we reached the third floor landing in the stairwell. "Who was it?"

"James," I spoke as I opened the door and passed into the hallway, leaving the two of them behind as my own thoughts swam. As I walked, I fought the tightening of my jaw and burning in my eyes. I won't cry. Not yet.

Having learned my lesson previously, I stood at the door near the end of the hallway and pounded three times with my fist. A beat later, and a voice ushered me in from the other side.

"What's up dude? You good?" Tony goaded as I entered the area.

"Shannon said what, three more days for you?" I asked, direct in my approach. Tony grew to appreciate this, I never spoke around the bush with him, it was always to the point.

"Yeah, she said she'd release me for light duty then if I felt up to it. Why?" he asked in turn.

"You're cleared now," I directed. "I need you on the ninth floor."

"Okay," he responded. "Let me get some fresh clothes on, I'll be right up."

I gave my farewell and turned to leave, then back down the hallway to the stairwell.

FOUR

Tony found his way into the meeting area on the ninth floor, Henry tagging along with him. They both found a seat, and the chatter between everyone in the room increased for a moment as I watched. Clearing my throat and removing my feet from the table was all it took to bring it peacefully down to silence, save for Henry.

"We about to begin, brother?" he inquired, looking around. "Where's Mr. James? Brother James should be here too, he's his own department head."

"James is the first order of business to discuss," I said quietly, and paused until the confusion in the room quieted. "We lost James today. He was lost in the line of providing aid to Ash here, and his cousin. It's safe to say James died a hero."

"Oh, no, no, no," Henry muttered softly, a tear forming as his eyes began to well.

The reaction was much the same around the room. James had been a friend to all of us. Always a team player, and we wouldn't be where we were without him. A few, including Jennifer and Shannon, outright sobbed. All but Ash, who did his best to shrink into his seat.

"Everybody, this is Ash," I introduced without waiting for the commotion to settle this time.

Ash exchanged a nod and a few quiet handshakes with the others and returned to his seat. I nodded to Cody as he finished the last handshake with the man, and he spoke.

"What's up, boss man?" he asked me, returning the nod to me.

"You and Ash are together," I instructed. "You're now in charge of setting up and putting together all the kinds of projects James was always working on. I trust between the two of you, we should still be okay."

"Sounds good," Cody agreed somberly.

"Yeah, sure thing mate," Ash added.

"Tomorrow morning, I need everybody available for scavenging duties," I ordered. "Rich will take you there. Take double the normal number of vehicles and make sure to keep heavy security details. The area is crawling with them, and these ones seem smart enough to ambush you. Once you have the supplies gathered up, both trucks and trailers filled, I'd like you to try to retrieve James's body. If there's no body left, or he's too gone to transport and bury respectfully, then seal the front door of the house and burn it to the ground. I'll not leave our man without some form of interment."

Everyone exchanged glances and words with each other. Cody was the first to speak up.

"What do you need us to do?" he asked.

"Go over James's work plans and get together with Henry," I instructed. "Get a solid idea of what needs to be done, and we'll plan accordingly the next day. Use the rest of that time to get Ash acquainted with things around here."

"So, you still need me to be here?" Henry inquired.

"Yeah, yeah I do," I explained. "Henry, Cody, and Ash, you're all together. Halt outside construction tomorrow, skeleton crew to keep stations here filled. Everybody else outside of Tony and Dave fills a role or meets at the trucks at sunrise. Medical exceptions only."

"What do you need us for?" Tony asked, as he sat forward.

"You two, and Jennifer, actually," I said, watching the surprise on my wife's face, "We're gonna take that load of goods in the riverside shed up to Hashman."

"You want me to go?" Jennifer asked, nearly astounded.

"If that's okay by you," I replied. "Boat seems to be the safest mode of travel, we haven't seen these fuckers swim."

"What about Gwen?" Jennifer asked.

"I'm sure Carolyn wouldn't mind watching her for a bit longer than usual," I suggested, eyeing Carolyn as she perked up in her seat.

"Yes, that would be completely fine!" Carolyn replied, her heavy French accent sounding so out of place here, even with Ash present.

"Takes care of that," I noted, "So, you good?"

"Uh, yeah! Sure!" Jennifer responded, shrugging.

Just as Bri raised her hand and was about to speak, a mechanical *buzzzzz* sounded from the next room. Within a moment, Ryan poked his head into the room.

"It's down on high, heading toward the south gate," he informed.

"Get it on camera," Rob said calmly as he stood up and made his way to the command room, nearly squeezing his squat frame past me.

I turned and followed Rob into the room and was tailed by Jennifer, Rich, Tony, and Dave.

Ryan was already tracking what appeared to be several vehicles on one camera looking down the street from the gate. Rob was sitting in his seat, having wheeled over from his own station.

The vehicles approached the gate in even step with one another. As they drew closer and the image sharpened, I began to make out some very familiar shapes.

"Tony, you seeing this?" I called over my shoulder.

"What do we have, man?" he questioned as he snaked past and peered at the monitor. "I'll be damned."

"Hey, uh, command?" several radios crackled, Katie's electronic voice permeating the room. "There's a bunch of trucks coming. I think it's... I think it's the Army!"

You would think the entire command center would be buzzing with activity. The Army? Here?

But instead of panicking, or going into some kind of frenzy, we just stood there for a moment. Each of us in our own kind of world and wonder. Finally, Tony was the first to speak up.

"Well, I guess we should go say hi," he opined.

"Yeah," I agreed, snapping forth from my own thoughts. "Yeah, we should."

"How do we know they're military though?" Jennifer inquired.

"What do you mean?" I asked her.

"She's right mate," Ash offered. "Look at them. Ryan, was it? Can you...?"

Ash motioned to the screen in front of Ryan.

"Oh! Yeah, I got you," Ryan replied, turning the camera slightly to keep the vehicles in view as he zoomed in and refocused the lens.

"1025, 1096, three of them, and two Oshkosh trucks," Tony started. "The problem is, they don't match up."

"What do you mean?" Ash interjected.

"What I mean is look at them," he replied flatly. "Two Army. I also see Marines, Navy, and National Guard. Same for the handful of men that are actually in some kind of uniform."

"You're sure our comms can't be picked up, Rob?" I asked.

"No, not those ones. They're bound together," Rob answered, confidence in his voice.

"Good," I replied, then spoke into my handset, "Everybody that currently has a gun, meet me at the outer gate. South. Everybody else, get a gun and fill the windows of the homes closest to that gate with your bodies. We have visitors. Over."

A chorus of replies mixed with questions came through, then the communications started smoothing as people began directing each other and everyone started moving.

"That means us, too," I instructed. "Ryan and Rob, keep on the surveillance feeds. Let me know if you find anything at all that I can't see. Everyone else, come with me."

Now it was time for the command center and the remaining people listening from the next room to get into motion. I checked my pistol and readied it before replacing it in its holster on my way in to grab my rifle from the next room. The little .300 Blackout SBR always felt amazing in my hands. Light, comfortable, even with the suppressor attached it didn't make the weapon even a bit unwieldy.

No sooner had I retrieved and checked my own rifle, Jennifer appeared in the doorway. As she approached, she released the bolt on her own rifle and put it on safe before placing it over her shoulder on its sling.

"What are you doing?" I asked her, nearly accusatory.

"You said everyone with a gun," she noted. "I have a gun."

"No, you stay here. Stay safe," I said plainly.

"You just said you're taking me on the river tomorrow, now you want me to wait here today?" she challenged.

"Okay, fine," I conceded. "I'll meet you by the black crew cab."

With that, I turned and left the room, heading for the truck that I fully intended to leave in before my wife made it that far. I loved the woman, and I admired how adamant she was about helping but I had a hard time believing she realized how vital she actually is, safe and sound, and away from the firearms and teeth of this new world. I liked her hands on deck in medical, helping any sick or wounded. I loathed the thought of her put into any form of danger.

On the other hand, I thought, I seemed dead set on being in the middle of things. Ironic.

I was just about to float on to another of my walking thoughts when Jennifer's voice delineated any further hopes of keeping her relatively safe again.

"All of this walking these days is doing wonders for my butt!" she laughed as she pushed past me, swinging her backside about as she pushed into the stairwell ahead and began following them down.

I sped up and planted a hand on her ass and squeezed.

"Eh, not bad for an older lady," I retorted, jokingly.

"Watch it," she replied. "You're the one in your thirties, not me!"

"Yeah, okay," I laughed. "Fair. So, I was hoping to beat you to the truck and leave without you. I don't like you going on this shit with us."

"I know," she informed. "Why do you think I grabbed all my things first?"

"Fair again," I replied.

We continued our small talk all the way to the truck, never letting it get to be more than just small talk. Neither of us were the greatest at opening up to the other, and more often than not, in-depth talks were sparse. Somehow though, that never made a difference to us. We were intertwined so closely that we just *knew*. There was never any need for regular in-depth conversations.

Finally, we reached the truck. Jennifer slid into the passenger seat, and I took the driver's side. Dave joined us and Tony appeared from around the nearby corner of the North Building, flicking out a cigarette and watching it as it sailed into the nearby tall grass.

"Hey fucker!" I called to him through the open truck window. "You're about to pick that up, dude."

"Does it really matter?" he replied, almost sleepily.

"It does to me, dude," I scolded. "Let's try to be better than we were before. I thought Shannon told you to stop smoking because your chest is still all fucky. Plus, you start a grass fire here and we're fighting. It's safer for you to just quit."

"Yeah," he sighed. "I'm trying, dude. It's hard."

"Should just take them from you," I opined, only half-joking. "Send you after a horde with a hand axe every time you start having a nic fit."

He grumbled something and then joined Dave in the back of the crew cab pickup truck where he was met with a bit more playful scolding as I started the vehicle and sped toward the gate and the small line of vehicles departing the main compound. We were met with more along the way, presumably wall crews and cleanup crews, and they fell in wherever there was room.

As I turned the next right-hand corner and began heading directly to our southern gate, I picked up my radio.

"Fan out when you get close," I ordered as we approached. "Half of you dismount a block out and find cover or concealment. Be ready for a fight but return fire only. Over."

"Whoa, wait a second," Jennifer began. "Why be ready for a fight?"

"We don't even know for sure if it *is* the military," I explained, "and if it is, we don't know for sure that they're here to be friendly."

"Anything's possible," Tony stated offhandedly as the mood in the truck dropped and became somber.

We slowed as the vehicles in front and behind did so, letting off seemingly every type of human on the planet so they could scatter and filter like water into various doorways and behind vehicles. Each person equipped with an equally diverse array of small-arms, we really did carry the image of every rag tag militia to have ever called this world 'home'.

As vehicles fanned out to each side, I weaved my truck through and pulled right to the front, just shy of our side of the gate.

As we dismounted and toward the gate on foot, calls started filtering into my earpiece announcing various parties were ready.

Ready for what though? The alleged military vehicles sat there, idle, with minimal movement visible inside. They had fanned out much the same as we did, though I was certain their vehicles and doors would provide the superior cover to ours. Maybe some kind of mild armor would be something to speak with Rich and Henry about, if the healthy were going to tie with the infected on the threat scale.

"So," Jennifer spoke up, "now what?"

"Don't know, woman," I replied. I really didn't. This wasn't exactly a situation I had a lot of experience in. And they still weren't budging from their armored vehicles.

Dave spoke up. Okay, actually, Dave shouted. His voice booming from behind me, causing several of us to jump.

"YOU'RE GOING TO HAVE TO GET OUT TO TALK!" he projected, then, garnering several chuckles from all around, "MY PHONE'S SHUT OFF! COULDN'T GET THE BILL PAID!"

Still, nobody moved for several moments. Then, an electronic crackle sounded, followed by an older man's voice, Southern and carried deep but carelessly through the airwaves.

"This is Colonel John Parker with the United States military," the man spoke, his casual voice amplified through the P.A. system mounted on one vehicle. "Open your gates, and step aside."

We exchanged concerned glances among ourselves until Tony's voice approached me from my left.

"Don't do it," he stated, his voice dead flat.

"Wasn't planning on it," I replied, then turned to the military vehicles positioned on the other side of our main gating system, announcing, "No. No, I don't think we will."

Another few beats of tense silence ensued. I could feel my heart thudding in my chest, every hair on my body standing at attention. I did not like this in the least. Nothing about this meeting felt right. Before I could communicate as much, the rear gate of one of the larger trucks swung down and clanged into the open position. Then, the other followed suit. Following these loud mechanical reports was the sound of shuffling, and orders being given. From the backs of these vehicles spilled soldiers from seemingly every branch, some of them not even remotely recognizable as soldier. Not a scrap of uniform was within regs, I was sure.

Then, as the men and women filtered from around the backs of the Oshkosh trucks, between what I knew to be "Humvees", the doors on the truck closest to us opened. Two more uniformed men dispensed from the vehicle and took position as a man I presumed to be the Colonel exited the back of the vehicle.

He left his door open, stepped around it, and proceeded to walk directly to our gate with the other two men pacing him at his sides.

The man was tall, but not much more than me. A narrow character, I was certain he'd been called 'bean pole' by an aunt or grandparent at some point in his life. This was carried to the rest of his features. His face was sharp and lined, cheeks gaunt and a well-defined jawline. He had a head full of close-kept white hair despite not truly looking a day over fifty-five.

His face was that of a vulture in human form. His gaze neutral, but ice cold as he strode purposefully to the gate at his end of our intake box, halting just his side of the chain link. Even at twenty yards distance I could make out the diamond grey of his eyes.

"Mornin', folks!" the man beamed, clasping his hands in front of him like he had some pleasant news. "It sure would be easier to talk if we could do so directly!"

"Katie!" I called to the thorn in my side, "Open up our side only. Close it once we've gone through. Do *not* open their side. Lock the weights."

Without a word, Katie lowered the six-by-six beam that effectively locked the outer gate firmly by immobilizing the pulleys and weights. She then turned and came to our end to turn the crank and get the inner gate opened. I thanked her quietly and watched as she scowled and walked back to the makeshift guard shack attached to the boxed entry.

We walked through and into the main acceptance area for our compound, the gate then rolling shut behind us. I glanced and saw Jennifer still just a step behind me and inwardly sighed. If this all went bad, she would be right up here in the heat of it.

"I didn't catch your name," I spoke as six of us approached the far end of the entryway.

"Parker," he informed. "Colonel Parker."

"Good to meet you, Parker," I replied, enjoying the momentary pause in his features as he processed this, then, "How can we help you?"

"Actually, Scott, we're here for you," he replied, his tone levelling, the last words becoming gravelly as if expelling them brought some form of relief.

"Me?" I mimicked, now it was my turn to be lost. What the hell? And how did he know my name?

"Yes, you," he replied, his eyes now placid yet somehow piercing into me. "A number of you, actually, but since you're the 'big boss' around here... Well, take a look."

He produced a device that seemed somewhere between phone and tablet, but thicker, as if it too were overbuilt for the military. On it, my old driver's license photo, name, although anything else I could have made out on the screen was taken as he turned it back away and began, presumably, reading out of the device.

"Mr. Pfeiffer-" he began.

"Scott," I stated; I hated being called by my last name. It always felt like it made the situation feel so impersonal.

"Scott," he began, drawing it out just slightly to convey his annoyance, "Under FEMA guidelines and regulations we are here to relieve this compound and its people of all things that we deem fit and useful to the rebuild of the United States of America. It is your duty as a citizen-"

I cut him off again as murmurs of protest sprang forth from just about everybody on my side of the fence.

"Bullshit," I replied. My single word bringing the world to a halt for a breath. "I'm a citizen and I've paid a lifetime of taxes. Your theft from me and my friends stops here, Uncle Sam. We gathered this shit to survive. We aren't just entitled to it, it's not just stuff we want, we *need* it. I have children here. I have families here. These people need to eat, to live and sleep in safety. You can't just show up and say 'it's mine, gibs me dat', you fuck."

Colonel Parker forced a faint smile, as if to put his mask right while he gathered himself and continued.

"Furthermore," he continued, "the people residing within these walls will be transferred to one of twenty-six camps spread throughout the country, designed to sustain the remainder of the population and provide them with safety and all of their daily needs, free of charge."

He beamed as he clearly anticipated the rush of people stepping forth to follow him to the safe promised land. Nobody moved, at least, not initially.

"Twenty-six? That ain't shit!" Dave spoke from over my shoulder.

"He's got a point, John," I explained to the Colonel. "How many did you start with?"

"That information is not public, nor is it relevant, Scott," he replied, his eyes now burning into each of us like laser beams. "Especially not to you. You're our number one guy in these parts for warrant collection."

"Warrant collection?" I asked, confused. "What warrant?"

He proceeded to look into his device again and appeared to be scrolling.

"Scott Pfeiffer," he announced, then read, "You are hereby to be arrested and processed for charges against both man and country, including, but not limited to; murder, kidnapping, grand theft, and treason. These warrants extend to your wife Jennifer, your friends, former Staff Sergeant Tony Harris, one David Caster, and several others, those are just the ones of you I can see present."

I gave no response. I could hear my friends near and far, a mix of protest, fear, and speculation. I'm sure they were wondering the same as I.

Was this the end of our compound? Was there about to be a fight? Then, Katie happened.

Look, you've been following my tale for this long, you know she doesn't do things, she *happens*. So, Katie happened.

"Scott's under arrest?" she asked the Colonel. "Then I'm coming peacefully."

"Katie!" came Wayne's shout from behind me, "Stop!"

It didn't work. As soon as she opened the man-door nearest John's men, the door was wrenched from her grasp and she was thrown to the ground despite her instant protests. A single gunshot rang out as Wayne began another shout of protest.

Turning, I could see the man clearly. He'd left his spot near the front row of vehicles, and was now falling forward at a running pace, one arm still extended holding the pistol he'd aimed at the men taking his wife, the other hand already moving toward a small hole neatly placed in the center of his button-up shirt, looking nearly like another button itself.

The next moment was a blur of everything. Katie, realizing the sound was a shot, began wailing for Wayne as he continued his fall. The Colonel immediately began bellowing for his men to 'CEASE FIRE'. My own crews were all hunkering down, a few blasts of gunfire already being returned from our side, dropping two of the closest from the Colonel's crew before I could bellow my own cease fire. It lasted mere seconds. Longer than Wayne had in him, according to Clara, who perched at his side, tears breaking the edges of her eyes.

"What. The. *FUCK!?*" I roared at Colonel Parker. "What the fuck kind of twisted diplomacy is this?"

"Excuse me, Mr. Pfeiffer," he shouted in return, "but your guy made the first move!"

"How many shots did he fire, then?" I returned, then motioning to Katie, who lay still gripping her nose that they had busted. "And could you blame him if he did? Release her."

"Alright, alright," the Colonel retorted, palms forward. "Jacobs, let this young lady up, that was entirely uncalled for."

The young man eased his grip for a moment, then released it as Katie looked around wearily then found her feet, nearly shuffling back to our side. Her nose ran with blood and snot, her eyes leaked with tears as she cried, each breath shaking her still fairly large body. I disliked the woman, but this was pitiful. And he was right, uncalled for.

Fuck it, I'm going for broke, I thought.

"Give me your pistol," I ordered Tony firmly. He complied and placed a worn .38 revolver into my hand, which I then checked, closed the cylinder back, and handed it to Katie.

"What?" she muttered, confused, eyes searching my face for answers.

"Colonel Parker?" I inquired. "Kindly instruct the gentleman who shot Wayne to step forward."

"Oh, now Scott, you know we can't-" he began, and once again, I cut him off.

"Do it," I offered, leveling my 9mm at him and watching his eyes light up with surprise. "Or I'm blaming you directly. Jennifer, Tony, Dave, Rich, Henry, all of you, follow my lead. When I give the word, or if they shoot me, Johnny here dies before any of them."

Somewhere from behind an Oshkosh came a yelp as a medic worked on a man we'd just wounded, followed by frantic muffled conversation.

"Come on Scott," Colonel Parker urged. "This isn't a solution."

"You've given me none. No solutions," I stated firmly. "Not one. Bring him out, or you die instead. Your men can open fire, but you'll be the first to fall. Don't *fuck* with me. I'm not in the mood today, and you just made me inconsolable."

"Very well, Scott," he resigned, nearly grumbling. "Mooreland! Front and center!"

I didn't expect what I saw. A nondescript brunette in uniform was shoved forward, looking like a beaten dog with her arms folded and shoulders hunched. She couldn't have been more than her earliest twenties, and she appeared as filthy and low rent as the rest of them. By the looks of it, we were all just simply surviving.

"You shot our buddy Wayne?" I asked her, my tone pointed. "You pulled the trigger and put that round in his chest?"

The girl sobbed as she nodded her head in the affirmative.

"Let me hear it," I instructed. "Let Katie hear it."

"I shot...I shot the man named Wayne," she spat out between sobs.

"Katie?" I asked, Katie's heavy brown eyes settling on mine before going wide at my next order. "Shoot her."

"What?" Katie questioned again. "Her?"

"Yeah, she fucking shot Wayne, Katie. Your husband, your children's father," I reminded her. "You shoot her, or I will."

"I-I don't," she stammered, "I don't think I can."

I turned my pistol from the Colonel to the girl he had called Mooreland.

"You shoot her, or I will," I explained. "At least if you do, you can say you avenged your husband. It'll make it easier in the-"

Wham

The small caliber pistol bucked in Katie's hand, sending ripples through the ample flesh of her arm as a flame leapt forth from the end of the barrel. The round hit the girl low in the abdomen, and she clutched at the spot, issuing a forceful retch as she dropped to her knees.

"Again, or she'll suffer," I instructed, trying to hold myself together. Sure, the infected looked like us, because they were, or are, us, but it never got easier to see a 'normal' person go down.

"She should," Katie muttered as she dropped the small revolver and found her own knees, beginning to dry heave over the pavement.

"Fuck," I muttered as I turned my gun, and attention, back to Mooreland, three shots in close succession barging their way out of my 6906. The rounds perforated neatly into the girl's middle and upper torso, causing her to slump back onto the ground and begin gasping her last breaths.

"While we're at it, Colonel," I grimaced, "Which one of you shot Tony those few weeks ago?"

"Sorry Scott, that I do not know," he answered, his gaze calmly on the girl as she took her last breath, shuddered, and fell limp, then he added, "I really like that pistol, Scott."

"Not for sale," I offered, then to my friends, "Take a truck, get Wayne and Katie back there. Put a few of the kids on outer gate duty in her place."

"Oh, I'm not offering," he intoned, "but it will be mine soon enough, regardless."

"You'll have to take it, John," I threatened. "I don't recognize your form of government in my neck of the woods. Best to just stay away, for your own sake. You've got this one chance. We're even for now. But, just for now. I hear Florida's nice this time of year."

As if on cue, the soft patter of rain began to fall around us. I turned, putting my back fully to him and motioning for my friends to follow as three of our older teens moved past us to grab the revolver and work the gate. It rolled with a creak and groan as we passed, then slammed shut.

"Catch you later, Scott!" Colonel Parker's irritatingly calm voice lulled after me.

I gave no reply. I merely spoke the order to clear out and secure our perimeter, and to get a portable awning up. We'd bury Wayne as soon as he was cleaned up and his effects gathered. Jennifer called into Shannon in medical and she assured us she'd be ready to make him presentable. Henry already had a radio to his mouth as well, setting up the grave digging detail like it was any other day.

It was amazing how quickly you became nonchalant about death when you lived surrounded by it. I'm not saying it had zero effect but dealing with it now compared to on day one, things would never be the same.

Wayne did his best to remain little more than a useful backdrop item. He was one hell of a shot, a disciplined and diligent worker, but he spoke little and made friends even less. He seemed to be happy that way, and, I supposed, after spending some years with Katie, I'd be happy to enjoy every minute of solitude I could achieve on my own as well.

As we rolled towards the North Building, the rain grew in intensity. It was a steady shower by the time we got in and wordlessly made the climb up to command, the detail carrying Wayne and consoling Katie breaking off for the second floor in our wake.

I walked into command and plopped heavily into my seat and lit a cigarette. No sooner had I taken a long draw of the acrid smoke was I interrupted.

"Hey, why didn't you answer your radio?" Ryan asked from behind me. "You need to see this."

"I never got your call, dude," I said, checking my radio and realizing why. It was turned all the way down, the quietest setting next to 'off'.

"Shit," I projected to him. "Sorry, man."

"It's cool, but, look," he said as he led me into the security center, followed by Tony and Jennifer. "We recorded it when we couldn't reach you."

I watched for a moment as a loop played through several different frames onscreen and then repeated. A pair of small black inflatable boats sliding upriver, the same CRRC craft civilians know from video games and movies as a 'Zodiac'. On the next frames were more light vehicles stationed and waiting, just blocks from where we just were. On the final screen, an M2A3 Bradley. A large, tan-colored, box-shaped armored personnel carrier bristling with weapons. It seemed to lie in wait just at the edge of our furthest camera's range, on the far side of the nearby overpass. The same route we originally took on our first arrival at this safe haven.

"There's more, but it was perceived and not witnessed," Ryan continued as we processed all of this new information. "We had our driveway sensors go off on nearly half the roads we cover, and there seemed to be fighting right about, well, here."

He stated this as he brought up another panel on an upper screen, where across the river to the northwest of our position a pair of small black smoke columns rose lazily against the darkening sky.

"My best guess is there were more there, but they got attacked and held back from staging," Ryan opined.

"So, we were surrounded," I observed.

"That Brad worries me." Tony motioned to the screen where the lumbering vehicle still resided on the playback loop.

"Yeah I know. Me too," I stated. A fucking armored vehicle waiting to tee off against flesh and bone people. Our people. Fuck, it was positioned to attack our home, regardless of who lived here.

"I really don't fucking like this guy," Dave growled from behind us.

"Tony, get people. Right now," I barked. "Go. Full coverage, double security teams, day and night, and watch the riverside. I don't want so fucking much as a new *fly* entering our walls without being noticed."

"On it!" he called over his shoulder, already on his way through the doorway to get new crews put together. Then I proceeded to call Rich and Henry upstairs via radio and went back to my seat to sit down and finish my smoke.

"What are you thinking?" Jennifer asked, taking the seat nearest mine.

"Arby's," I stated, offhanded, as I drew in a breath of tobacco smoke and exhaled it into the air over the table.

"You know what I mean," she intoned.

"Yeah," I agreed, she was never one to let me bully my way out of talking. "This guy is a problem. A big problem."

"He has a tank," she said, her voice still as a pond, as if pondering our situation.

"Technically," I started, "a Bradley is an IFV, not a tank. Either way, they can be beat, but that's not something I even want to entertain if I don't have to. My first hope is that this is the last we'll hear from him."

"Do you think that's likely?" she inquired.

"Not at all," I confided. "Last thing I want is another fight, especially here, but I doubt he'll leave us be just the same. Maybe a deal of some sorts could be worked up. I don't know just yet."

At that moment, Rich and Henry came strolling into the command room.

"We got, ah, we got Mr. Wayne's burial set up," Henry informed me. "We can start it soon before the rain really gets here."

"Doesn't seem right, does it?" I opined. "Not even so much as a true grieving period these days."

Nobody gave a direct answer, but we all seemed to agree. This world is fucked, and it showed no signs of getting better anytime soon.

"Alright," I began, "Ryan and Rob have something to show you back in security. This new group, the military, allegedly, is bad news. Worse than what our meeting this morning would lead us to believe."

Both men disappeared into the doorway behind my seat, emerging a few minutes later.

"Well this is some shit," Rich proclaimed. "What do you need from us?"

"Henry, you're motor pool," I observed. "You're our best guy with all things mechanical. Rich, you're weapons. There are a few major ways to disable a vehicle like that Bradley. I'll tell you what I know, you find me solutions, and don't be afraid to go overboard with all of them."

We spent a few more moments in conversation about the vehicles. Basic things, at least. Getting in close to the Bradley would be tough, but necessary, as we had nothing long range capable of penetrating reactive armor. We were, technically, still all civilians. Disable the tracks, finding a way to block the exhaust, throwing paint over the periscopes, damaging the array of sensors or the huge air conditioning boxes mounted to the outside of the vehicle. There was still a number of things we could do to at least have a better chance against such a behemoth of a vehicle.

The plan appeared to be much the same for the rest of the vehicles, as well. In little time, Rich and Henry were beginning to bring the conversation more toward each other and bounce defense ideas back and forth.

"You guys may want to clue in Tony, as well," I observed. "He probably has some kind of experience with them. Where did he go, anyway?"

Nobody seemed to know.

"Anyway," I continued, "let's go. We have another friend to lay to rest today."

The mood of the room dropped back into place with those words. James by lunchtime, now Wayne. Jesus. When would the hits quit coming? Would they ever? I didn't think so. The world had ended. Everything else just kept rolling. Death included.

FIVE

We shed the protective cover of the North Building and went left. Jennifer, Tony, and Dave followed me as we approached the scene.

Nearly everybody was present, save for Carolyn and the children. We had all agreed to spare the kids when and where we could. There was enough to protect them from in this world, and while it was clear we couldn't keep them from most of the things all of the time, we could do our best to limit their exposure. Death. While I wished we could keep it from our young ones full time, we did our best.

We approached the area chosen for Wayne, placing him just past Chris's resting place. And Melissa. The dead accumulated and were buried in the grassy portions immediately near the North Building. Our own, our 'closest' people were greedily lined up, and right up front.

The rain fell soft but steady, pattering across the stubble where my hair should be. The only area no drops fell was under the blue portable awning that had been placed over a large hole in the ground. Above this hole, a simple frame of two-by-fours supported a simple wooden box containing the body of our friend, Wayne. Surrounding this was an inconsolable Katie, and many of our friends, Henry being the closest to a man of God that we could think of in this wasteland. He would lead the service, and a small work party would lower Wayne into his final resting place by ropes tied to eye hooks on his casket.

Clara noticed us approaching and went and stood nearby.

"They had children," I whispered to her, "where are they?"

"Katie said no," Clara explained quietly. "Said she'd think of something to tell them, but they've been through so much."

"Wow," I muttered, and the talk ended as Henry began speaking, reading a passage from a worn leather-bound bible.

In a way, I could understand the choice to have no kids present, even Wayne's. Yet at the same time I felt they should be. Children needed closure too, to some degree, even if it wasn't the same as that of the adults.

As my thoughts progressed, I found myself looking at Jennifer. My wife. My buddy. Her mess of never-neat dirty blonde hair was left to fall loosely around her shoulders, splitting to run its course over her chest and upper back. She wasn't even invested in the current proceedings. Instead, I followed her gaze to the small makeshift headstone for Melissa. The first one interred here. The first of a growing number now, and James to be joining them tomorrow, hopefully.

Friends and family buried together, but friends and family buried also within spitting distance of the driveway at an apartment complex I had only ever driven past in what felt to be a previous life. What a world it had become. I found myself wondering if normal would ever come back. If normal even existed anymore. My brain tried imagining things as they were. A school bus, perhaps, pulling in to deliver children at the end of a day of learning. The school bus passing the spot where one of our own lay resting for eternity.

An earth-shaking rumble of thunder brought me back to my senses as I looked around at everyone. Henry had just finished speaking and asked for a moment of silence. We granted this moment together and before Katie could take a place to begin speaking, Jennifer looked my way.

"You okay?" she murmured, likely noticing my expression and lack of attentiveness.

"As much as you are," I replied softly, and motioned with my head up to Katie. She was beginning to thank everyone for showing up but broke into tears and was quickly unable to complete her statements.

"Ten bucks says she milks this," came Tony's voice from directly behind us.

"First," I replied to him, "that's kind of a low thing to say right now. Second, money is worthless. Bet liquor instead. Third, you're probably right."

We regained our silence as the short service cleared up and the rain really began to fall from the sky. Henry stood by with Katie as she continued to sob, the work crew slightly raising Wayne's new condo a few inches so others could remove the braces and he could be laid in place.

●

The rest of the evening was spent in relative silence. The rain coming and going in spurts, the humidity hanging somewhere around one thousand percent, nobody seemed to much feel like carrying on as usual. Adding on the loss of two of our members, our friends, family even, and the entire compound was essentially on rest.

The exception was Tony. Rather, Tony's now-strengthened work crew. He seemed content in the driver's seat of one of our remaining Smart Cars, making rounds where he could stay dry and comfortable.

Henry had stolen Dave, Rich, and Bob for some kind of special project on the first floor.

Myself? I found myself with my wife and child, sharing the couch and the floor near our sliding balcony door. The falling rain traced a lazy trail here and there down the large panes of glass. As we talked quietly, mostly about those we'd lost, Gwen contented herself by scribbling in an old coloring book.

Well, it was closer to half of an old coloring book. Jennifer felt bad about the thought of Gwen coloring over another kid's work, especially if the kid might no longer be around, so she carefully removed and saved those pages.

At any rate, at some point during the evening our conversation lulled. An empty corn chip bag sat on the floor nearby, several empty bottles of water, and the rain kept on. At some point after, I fell asleep. Make all the jokes about dads you would like to make, but that stuff really happens. I pressed my head back against the couch and ended up resting my eyes until just slightly before dawn the next morning.

SIX

I awoke nearly stuck in place by sweat. Wiping a stream of it from my forehead, I immediately found the cause. Jennifer must have decided to sleep out here after I lost consciousness. The woman was putting off a heat that no blanket could match. No, she wasn't sick, that's just how she was. My heat rock. Impossible in the summertime, great in the winter. Unfortunately for me, it was mostly in the warm weather still, and the building was only allowed the air conditioner in the computer room.

I started to peel the heap of heated woman off of me, and as she woke up, I explained that it was time to do so in order to get ready to spend part of the day on the water. She replied with a groan, barely even opening her eyes.

"Come on, woman," I chided. "Let's go!"

"No," she groaned. "Let's just stay in and order a pizza."

"Get up!" I laughed as she groaned and righted herself. "Pizza shop's closed anyway, it's a holiday."

"What holiday?" she quipped.

"Uhhhh," I began, "Thursday? I think? I don't know but let's go!"

"Ugh okay," she conceded, rising from the couch. "Fine."

Not long after we woke up, Carolyn showed up for Gwen. After her hugs and kisses from us, Gwen went happily babbling away with Rich's wife, and soon they disappeared through our doorway and on their way to wherever.

•

"Y'all be safe!" I called after the last truck, Rich's truck, as it pulled out of the compound.

Once waves were returned, Jennifer and I made our way down to the water's edge. Dave was busy bringing boxes and small crates to the boat from the riverside storage shed that had been erected. Tony, on the other hand, was doing his best to make sure the boat went nowhere.

"Are you going to help?" Dave grumbled at him.

"I stacked the boxes, man," Tony replied. "Shannon says I still have to take it easy, remember?"

Trade had been fairly steady between our complex and the one a little way upriver.

The other compound was led by a man named Mike Hashman. He was a younger man, and though we never asked, we figured him to be somewhere in his very early 20's. He'd been pretty much forced into his role of leadership much the same as I'd been. His compound was an eclectic mix of people, but heavy on the side of metal heads. There were a number of buses trapped on the highway heading to a music festival near Cleveland when the world went to shit, Hashman got them out of where they were and saved the majority of them.

They had taken refuge in a small gated community on the river's edge. A horseshoe of cookie-cutter homes surrounded by a wall and fencing that, unlike ours, was already in place when the end came.

At any rate, they held their own quite well, and were well supplied. They even had control of that section of the river by way of mounting a small guard tower of sorts right by the boat tie-ups. A heavy wooden frame topped with a salvaged MCTAGS turret containing an M2 .50 caliber machine gun. Capping this setup off was a pastel pink patio umbrella, allowing it to be manned in comfort, rain or shine.

"You two bicker like you're married," I commented as I approached, then, "Tony. Get off your ass, bro. Let's get this shit show on the road. Or river, or whatever."

"Shannon said," he replied, shrugging.

"Get off your ass," I repeated, showing my impatience this time around. "She's under five foot, she's only half a doctor anyway. Start loading fucking boxes or I'll use you as an anchor."

"Fine," he replied sharply and made his way slowly out of the boat as Jennifer and I both grabbed a crate each full of various liquor bottles.

With all four of us working, it didn't take much longer and the boat was brimming with supplies. Each of us were in, backpacks loaded, and rifles slung, and the craft sat startlingly low in the water. I untied the tether holding it to the shore and we shoved off.

Once behind the wheel, I got the motor fired up and we began our lazy way up the slow-moving river to the Hashman compound.

•

The first couple of miles of the trip went well, although slowly. The river wasn't exactly a raging body of water, but we kept our pace slow as to keep down engine noise.

The infected weren't as much worry on the water. Mostly, they stayed to the shoreline. Screeching, biting the air, sniffing and barking their calls as the boat would pass. We used to get tense seeing them, but really, they were more similar to cats. Sure, an occasional healthy freak would make it into the water. But none ever followed it in and once it had made entry they always slowed down. Those were usually easily dispatched by a boat hook through the skull.

Even the lumbering behemoths scattered throughout the area steered clear of the water, which struck me as odd, because at an average height around eight to ten feet tall they could have easily touched the bottom in most places along the river.

One cloudy afternoon a boat had come down with supplies from Hashman, displaying a large dent in one side. According to the men on board they had learned a valuable lesson. Ignore the big ones. Taking pot shots at one on the riverbank had pissed it off, and after several futile attempts at reaching the boat with its arms, it had given up and thrown an entire riding lawnmower at the passersby.

I sat behind the helm of our small vessel enjoying a bag of M&M candies from one of the MREs. Though, admittedly, the enjoyment was minimal. After having been packaged away for so long, the flavor was halfway between stale and cardboard. But I slowly ate them nonetheless.

Twice I had used them offensively. On both occasions, Tony had begun nodding off at the bow of the boat. Both times I sent a candy flying in his direction, one successfully striking him on the cheek, the other bouncing off the metallic hull of our vessel. It worked anyway, making a loud series of clangs like a rock had been thrown, instantly bringing him back around while the other three of us laughed.

Somewhere around halfway to our destination, another *twang* resounded from up by Tony, causing him to jerk and spin back to look at me.

"What the fuck man?" he cried. "I wasn't even sleeping this time!"

"That wasn't me, dude," I called over to him, but any further conversation was cut off.

Another series of twangs and pings hit the boat, blowing straight through into the small interior cabin where shattering glass bottles could be heard, and the resulting sound of liquor covering the floor.

"Everybody DOWN!" I shouted as my crew of three ducked and hid to make themselves as small as possible.

As I issued the command, our assailants presented themselves, a couple of whom I recognized from a recent encounter, their various United States military uniforms easily distinguishable through the haze of humidity. They kept low, presenting enough of themselves for us to see who they were but not really enough to get a shot on them when combined with the suppressing fire they were issuing.

"Parker!" I growled, shouldering my weapon and hoping to catch a glimpse of him through the incoming hail of bullets.

The sound of gunfire drew closer and the intensity increased as I reached for the throttle of the boat and cracked it wide open. More rounds splashed down into the water around us, some just grazing the hull of the boat with loud *snaps* and whistles. The boat pulling forward under its newfound breath I had given it had caused just a bare moment's lull in our attacker's accuracy as Dave opened fire in return. His AK47 running its first magazine dry as it barked out 7.62mm projectiles, sending themselves ahead of hot flame into the direction of the attack.

Tony and his M1A joined him, a pair of .30 caliber weapons bringing thunder and kicking up rocks or piling into low cover as they tried to seek out our antagonists and put a stop to their reign of terror over us. Jennifer joined as well, which surprised me because she really hadn't seen any action to this point aside from helping Shannon in medical.

She had taken refuge in the doorway of the cabin. Whether by design, or by accident, the small bulkhead probably provided the second-best protection on the entire craft save for the small V8 engine itself.

I watched between shots, my ever-present Mk18 just a quiet clap normally, now completely drowned out by the unsuppressed gunfire on both sides.

Jennifer didn't put down the volley of fire that the others were. Her civilian AR-15 only even capable of one bullet per trigger pull. Her whole body shook, likely from adrenaline in overdrive but she did put a few shots downrange. I managed to witness at least one man fall to her, taking a round in the leg, the next one finding itself high in the man's plate carrier as he screamed for help.

As we passed, my friends and woman firing steadily, myself switching between returning fire and steering the boat away from the banks of the winding channel.

I'm unsure what caused the fire. Maybe a round penetrating the hull, striking something to set off a chance spark. Maybe a tracer, though I never saw one. What I did know for sure, was what fueled it.

The interior cabin leapt to life with a rush of heat and light as the spilled liquor took control of the blaze, breathing it into being in a flash and woosh.

"FIRE!" Jennifer exclaimed, stumbling away from her protective doorway. She brought one foot forward but the other caught on the bulkhead and she fell face-forward where she lay for a bare moment before crawling behind a seat for concealment.

"Keep shooting!" I shouted to Dave and Tony as I moved past my wife, telling her, "Take the wheel!"

I grabbed the fire extinguisher from the side of the wheelhouse, pulled the pin, and aimed a stream of dry chemical toward the floor of the compartment, quenching the first of the blaze.

"Yahtzee!" I heard Tony shout as he fired, then another burst erupted from Dave's AK.

"I finished him, doesn't count!" Dave returned, as his rifle continued to buck in his hands.

By this time, Jennifer had begun to turn the boat around a small right-hand bend. I got the inferno under control and stepped out of the small cabin. My throat burned like hell itself, involuntary coughs making it feel as if it were tearing open, but my rage took over.

Not the slow-building rage of frustration, but a white-hot flash of pure thermite had raised itself until it came forth in, perhaps, too ballsy of an open display to be considered safe.

"PARKERRR!!!" I bellowed, my throat threatening to turn itself inside-out as I shouted. "YOU JUST MADE AN ENEMY WITH THE WRONG MAN!!!"

I opened fire, the rifle coming back to life with rejuvenated vigor as I sent everything I had in their direction.

Then, it hit me. Just as we were disappearing around the bend. Not an idea, not a realization, but a freaking baseball bat. I whirled to face my friends, the shock on their faces apparent as I felt something warm on my shoulder. Looking down at my shirt on that side, I could already see what was very clear to me to be blood. I said the only thing that came to my mind.

"Oh no," I stated, somewhere further away from myself than I was previously. "Where did that come from?"

"Oh baby, no!" Jennifer spoke as she rushed to my side.

Placing my hand in the blood on my neck, I traced its pathway upwards until I felt what seemed to be a bit of raw bacon hanging from a spot just above and behind my left ear. A hair higher, and I felt something that kind of struck me as the texture of wet chalk.

"The wheel!" I heard myself tell Jennifer and watched as she turned to Tony.

"You drive!" she instructed him, then, "Dave, find me a med kit and a couple bottles of water!"

"Find her the meds," Dave told Tony, gripping his shoulder and pulling him back to take his place. "Last time you drove, we ended up inside an apartment building!"

Tony began to protest, and Jennifer barked at them both to get things in motion.

"Trauma pack," I spoke to her. "Left cargo pocket."

Jennifer retrieved the pack and ripped it open, spreading the contents on the seat next to her with one hand, leaning me over on my side with the other.

"This is gonna suck," she stated firmly as she punctured a small hole into the lid of one water bottle and began squirting the liquid into the wound.

Instantly, reality lassoed me back to Earth as a deep stinging burn spread out across my entire skull, causing me to call out in pain. I was quickly met with immense pressure as she pushed a clotting gauze onto the wound with both hands, trying to staunch the flow of blood.

"Jesus fuck woman!" I blurted as she renewed pressure with a new Quick-Clot bandage.

"You'll be fine," she stated hurriedly. "Head wounds bleed a lot. I think, I think you've been shot."

"I sure as hell would hope so!" I told her, seeing the confusion on hers and Dave's faces and adding, "Because if not, we've got one big fucking mosquito problem."

"A mosquito with a 5.56mm sucker," Tony noted as he handed a small pack to Jennifer, from which she produced a Celox syringe filled with the powdered clotting agent. I braced myself as she removed the gauze and did her best to pack the wound with the powder before pressing the gauze back into place.

"Okay," she stated, "we'll get some tape in place to hold this, the bleeding should be pretty much over until we can get this taken care of."

"We're here," Dave informed us as I felt the boat slow.

Coming around one final left-hand bend in the river, we approached the Hashman compound. Their sentry was clearly on duty, as no sooner had we come into view did the turret they kept for the river swing in our direction. Upon recognition, the barrel of the machine gun sought the sky as its operator released it and returned Dave's broad wave. Moments later, we were pulled alongside and throwing ropes to the shore to be pulled in and secured in place.

Jason, Hashman's right hand man and constant river sentry, dropped down out of their short guard tower. The stout wood frame supporting an MCTAGS armored vehicle turret had practically been his home through the end of days. He took note of my blood and bandages and doubled his pace, speaking into his radio for Hashman to get his ass down here, Scott's hurt, and a series of other short orders.

"Fuck dude, what happened to you?" he approached, halfway out of breath already. "Are there others injured?"

"No just me," I replied to him, wincing a bit as the world threatened to go dark with the movement of departing our vessel. Jennifer and Dave stuck fast to my side, helping me up onto the short concrete pier along the river.

"Do you need a medic?" Jason inquired, and before I could give my compulsory 'No, I'm fine', Jennifer jumped into the conversation.

"He does, he needs this cleaned out and patched up," She informed. "He was shot."

"Shit man!" Jason exclaimed, reaching for his radio again and barking more orders into the device.

"It was kind of a hit and skip," I explained. "My reward for visiting a new friend on our way here. I'll explain once we get settled here. You all need to know about these guys."

"Can't take this guy anywhere without him causing problems," came Hashman's voice from behind me as he made his way down the stairs to water level to greet us, his hand outstretched and taking mine in a shake. He paused for just the barest of moments and I watched his eyes widen slightly at the sight of my wounded head.

"Some of the supplies were lost," I began, and then seeing the damage and number of holes now littering our watercraft from the exchange, "we were ambushed along the river."

"That's no good," he replied thoughtfully and began ordering the men that followed him down to start unloading and cleaning our boat.

"No, it's not," I answered, then began getting him up to speed on the Colonel.

"Jesus man," was all Hashman stated at the end of his informal briefing on the subject by the three of us, Tony having stayed back with Jason and the .50 cal, likely trying to catch a free buzz and skip anything that might be considered work.

We crested the top of the stairs and onto the open field that Hashman's commandeered housing complex encircled. The horseshoe of cookie-cutter homes encircled a large open area, which was lined now on each side by makeshift housing as Hashman's population also grew.

What else occupied the space was something I didn't expect. Row after row of brand-new Ford and Toyota vehicles of various types sat positioned carefully, so as to be able to fit so many vehicles here.

"Starting a business, Mike?" I asked him as he chuckled in response.

"Dealerships," he intoned, motioning across the rows of cars, trucks, and SUVs. "The Toyota dealership was nothing. Walk in, fill up with fuel, jump batteries, and drive away. We had issues with infected, even lost a guy. Fucking runners, man. There was a dozen of them that surprised us in the back lot."

"And you said the Toyota spot was the easy one. What about the Ford dealer?" I asked, wondering what sacrifice could have made losing a guy in a runner ambush the easier option.

"The old general manager," he answered, already pinching his nose and beginning a hearty laugh, "It was the big dealership over on 18 out near the mall, ya know? Okay, so check it out."

"What's so funny?" Jennifer asked as Hashman broke into more laughter, joined by the Marine that was walking with us; Mason, if I remembered his name correctly.

"This dude was fucking cracked, bro!" Hashman exclaimed, letting out another big laugh before explaining, "Okay, we were a lot quieter going into this place, but I don't think he'd have heard us anyway. Or seen us, bro, he had all the dealership windows blacked out with like some latex paint, you know?"

"Yeah man, for sure," I assured him, already a little weary. Hashman was a good man, but he had the energy of a speeding tanker truck and loved to talk. That's fine, though, not like we had many places to be these days.

"Yeah so we figured it was occupied and snuck in around back and popped the back door," He continued, only taking enough of a breath to suppress his laughter and begin the story again in spurts. "Mason hangs a blackout curtain over doorways so if we can get in quietly, we don't make a big light show, it's helped before, ya know? Real slick shit, right?"

"Mike," I nudged, mild impatience seeping in.

"Right! My bad brotha!" he snort-laughed and began anew. "So we snuck in. Dude had generators running and some of the lights were on, and on every surface, like, even computers and desks and shit, he wrote 'Jeffy is a good boy!' Like, fucking *everywhere* bro. It was intense, like some creepy movie shit. So, we hear old music playing, some old swing, ya know? Anyway, we sneak to a corner, and this motherfucker is ballroom dancing in the showroom, completely alone!"

"What the fuck?" Dave spoke up as we all began laughing along with Hashman.

"I know, right? But it gets better!" he continued. "He was dancing with a pillow. Like, one of those Japanese cartoon girl pillows, dude. He was all kissing it and shit, so Johnson threw a bottle in his direction. Dude heard the bottle and looked straight at us instead. Then he pulled a knife and, like, fucking rushed us, dude."

"Oh!" I interjected. "Nobody get hurt, or did he get one of you?"

"We just moved aside." He laughed yet again. "Like, we stepped aside and he kind of fell through us, slid across the floor, and knocked himself out. So, a couple of the guys tied him up and he stayed asleep for most of the time we got vehicles ready to leave with."

"What did you guys do with him?" Jennifer asked, curiosity not at all hidden.

"We…well, shit," Hashman stated nervously as he whispered to Mason, who then departed. "Some of my guys are going back to untie him right now."

"You forgot?" I chided.

"Yeah, shit just gets so busy, I don't always remember-" he was cut off as another man clapped a hand onto his shoulder.

"Mike here took us once to take a fuel truck," the man began, "we loaded up on gas station foods, and left without the fuel truck."

I said nothing as Jennifer and Dave hid their laughter. Instead I just looked on. I watched Mike Hashman nearly visibly squirm from the ribbing while he kept his composure outwardly. He was too good of a guy for me to let this go on for very long.

"Hashman here," I returned, "he was also the first one to jump to our aid with the gang bangers not too long ago. Risked his own life and that of his people to help our new world lose another problem. I don't recognize your face though, have we met?"

"No, no we haven't," he answered, taking my hand. "Wilson. Ray Wilson."

The guy was huge. I was an inch over six-foot, and Ray Wilson had an entire head and neck on me. He wasn't in shape, not in the least, but he was still built like a freaking double refrigerator. His hand enveloped my entire hand as he shook it.

"Well, Ray," I replied. "Your boss man here is good people. He's given more than I could ever ask for, and I don't even have a clue who you are. So why don't you back off a little bit?"

"Talk to me like that again…" Ray spat as he crept closer to me.

I stood my ground but caught movement out of the corner of my eye. It was the motion of nearly every person present in our small group leveling their firearms, but all pointed at Ray. Everybody but Hashman, who clapped Ray on the shoulder in return.

"Keep it up, big guy, and I'll send you back with them to shield the bullets in the next ambush," Hashman said, softly but dead serious. Ray turned and stormed out of the area. I had assumed he was going to find a small village to terrorize, or city to eat.

"He's been here a week-and-a-half," Hashman explained, "and a problem since day one. Always at odds or in an argument with one person or another. He'll be finding his own path soon; sooner if he keeps his shit up."

"Where to?" Dave and Jennifer questioned nearly together.

"Fuck, I don't know," Hashman shrugged. "Anywhere but here. Big man is bad for morale. Even when he's trying to get along, he still comes across as a dickhead. Bad juju, man. Anyway, shall we?"

He motioned forward and led the way to the smaller outdoor structure near the middle of the field. The building looked like a Viking longhouse made out of modern scrap materials. We walked inside at Hashman's request, and after a few moments of idle conversation, several more people, most of whom I'd recognized, entered the space and took up seats at the same long table as us.

Mike Hashman and his people had adopted the same council-driven form of politics as we had. A representative from each department of sorts.

This was also the group which surrounded us now and listened as we recounted everything we knew, and every time we encountered Colonel Parker. They sat, listened, asked questions, and even took notes.

Wasting no time, we got into the details about our encounters with Parker thus far.

Then the questions came spilling in. What did we intend to do about this? What *should* we do? Where is he now? Does he have a base of operations? How well set up are they? Does the Bradley even work? All this and more flew at us from across the table, and we did our best to keep up. I will say, though, I appreciated the repeated use of the word 'we'. Not 'you', but 'we'. We'd helped them by giving what we could out of our scavenging supplies, in part to offer assistance, and in part to offer repayment for helping with the group at the old high school.

"But you guys haven't seen them?" Dave questioned. "They haven't bothered you this far up?"

"Nope. Haven't seen 'em," said a squat, older gentleman with graying hair. He'd been introduced as Seely. Pete Seely, and we were told he was basically the gate guard captain. He ran the gates and kept the walls clear and safe for the entire complex.

"That's good," I stated flatly. "If they haven't come into contact with you guys, they might not know about you just yet."

"That works then!" Hashman interjected. "They don't know you guys got reinforcements up the river!"

"I'd rather keep you guys upriver though," I intoned. "I'll send some people out here and there to look for these guys, get a feeling of their capability, but if they are all I think they are…"

"Do you think we can take them?" Jennifer asked me directly.

"Maybe. Maybe not," I answered. "I'd just as soon load up our shit and send it up here until they get tired of us. But I doubt that will happen; these bandages tell me this fucker wants to fight."

"Well, we're down to help where we can," Hashman offered. "I know my guys agree with me. You dudes have been more helpful than I ever asked for, we got you bro!"

We carried on conversing, lightly, and hashing out a few basic plans. I couldn't tell if we were in that tent for only twenty minutes, or for three hours. At some point, we were interrupted by a man in his early to mid-twenties as he casually opened the door at the end of the large tent. He had dusty blonde hair and wore tattered fatigues under a medical coat that was one size too large.

"Mr. Pfeiffer?" he asked upon locking eyes with me.

"Ahhh..." I started, "are you a bill collector?"

"Funny," he said as he made a beeline straight to me and began checking my head. "You know, usually when I get a call for medical, I don't find my patient taking walking tours and hosting meetings. Especially not when they're leaving a trail of blood behind them."

"I stopped bleeding a while ago, didn't I?" I asked, before looking down and realizing I was sitting in a large spot of my own blood. It must have gone unnoticed by the others because of how much of my own fluid I already wore.

"Doesn't look like it. Corpsman!" he called to the open door of the tent, and another young man pushed a wheelchair through the door.

"I'll walk," I stated flatly as both the doctor's hand, and Jennifer's glare, set me back into my seat.

"I've got no clue how much blood you've lost and neither do you," he explained. "You're rolling, not walking. If you pass out, I'm not picking your big fucking ass off the ground."

"I'm not that big!" I began to argue, but the chair had reached where I was seated and grudgingly, I allowed myself to be seated in it.

"If you're taking me out on the town, I demand to know your name at least," I offered. "My mother told me to never accept a ride from a stranger."

"It's Keane," he stated, then turned to my wife, "Is he always a pain in the ass?"

"Oh, you have no idea." She grinned in return.

•

Outside of the tent we were immediately enveloped once again in mild sunshine, and the smell of several wood fires burning at once. Somewhere in the mix was a hint of some kind of meat cooking nearby, the scent wrapped in spice and hardwood in its delivery.

Keane went on briefly berating me for being a poor patient. I should have stayed put, blood loss this and that, and, much to her dismay, mildly berating Jennifer for having allowed me to be so mobile. Dave chuckled, and was met with his own end of the conversation.

"Once we get this guy patched up," Keane started in, "we're going to take a look at that hand of yours, chief."

"Nah," Dave replied, half hiding his hand behind him, "it'll be okay."

"Really?" the doctor asked as he stopped the wheelchair and reached out to take the offending appendage, "because it looks pretty fuckin' infected to me. See this? The red? The swelling? The red lines? That's infected. I could damn near cook a meal with the heat coming off of it, too."

He turned Dave's hand to show us. There was a partly still-open gash from Dave's wrist nearly to his ring finger knuckle. The skin around it nearly glowed with an angry red hue, and in a few places, it had some more faint red lines emanating from the injury, as Keane had just detailed.

We heard a short lecture about the dangers of blood poisoning as we reached the end of a row of shining new vehicles and took a right.

We had finally reached what was apparently the medical offices here. Keane piloted my wheelchair up a long-sloped ramp that had clearly been built post-apocalypse, if you will. The railing changed heights in relation to the ramp along its length, and the surface seemed to be patched together out of several types and thicknesses of plywood.

Moving through the front door, Keane giving some instruction to others inside and Dave and Jennifer conversing quietly about something I couldn't quite catch, we entered another world it seemed.

The interior of the two-floor home was immaculate. Even in the entryway, the paint was startlingly white, on the walls, ceiling, and even the floor. Carpet had been torn up and likely repurposed elsewhere in the compound, replaced with a heavy coat of the white paint and what seemed to be a six-inch layer of epoxy resin.

In each of what were formerly rooms, there was a drain placed in the center of the floor. The walls had been stripped, the load-bearing wall through the center of the house had also been stripped of all form and left as a series of pillars to open the space. Curtain rails could be seen crisscrossing the ceiling, and each one ended in heavy vinyl curtains made of shower curtains sewn together, and, also painted white.

We disappeared into one of these areas and I found a massage table in the center, over which a corpsman was draping a plastic painter's sheet. I had been instructed to find a horizontal position here and I did so.

Keane pulled up a chair, removed my wife's makeshift bandaging from my wound, and began cleaning it. He spoke as he worked.

"Damn buddy, you got a fuckin trench here. I can see where the bullet gouged your skull, no fucking wonder you were bleeding like you was, even with all that shitty Celox in there."

"Does it look as bad as it feels?" I asked, wincing. Christ it felt like this guy was at work with a belt sander on my cranium. It started hurting inside, too; the headache that had been mild, but constant, turned on me like a beat dog and started to burrow itself deeper and deeper into my mind.

"Probably, but we can fix both of those," he stated offhandedly, almost completely distracted by his work.

His hands left me for a moment, then returned. I felt myself being wiped with something dampening a cloth, then he spoke again.

"Okay, little pinch and shit, you know how this works."

Why do they call it a 'little pinch' in the medical field, by the way? It's never a pinch, little or otherwise. Sometimes, it can feel like little more than a small insect bite. Like a mosquito. Other times, you get an angry wasp. The dentist? Three angry wasps, and it won't take so you get it twice more while he packs your face with enough lidocaine to make a horse go limp.

Luckily, Doc Keane gave me the mosquito bite. A large one, but still nothing compared to the pain I was already in. In moments, that would slip away as his needle's payload kicked in.

Keane worked, and talked, then worked and talked, and in no more than 20 minutes, he had me good to go. Dave was next.

Dave surprised me. I expected some stoicism from the man, and that was exactly what I didn't get. I don't know if Keane didn't numb him right, or not enough, or what the issue was, but Dave squirmed like a college girl getting a tattoo as Doc drained the infection and essentially reopened the wound to clean all the nastiness out. Another 30 minutes of work, and he had Dave patched back together as well, and a nice shining white bandage on his wounded paw.

He then handed Dave a bottle that was half-filled with some kind of gel capsules.

"One of these twice a day for a week," he instructed him.

"What is it?" Dave asked, naturally.

"Do you really want to know?" Keane asked, his youthful smile glowing. I decided I didn't want to know.

"Yeah, if I'm taking it, I'd like to know," Dave intoned, and Keane chuckled and tossed each of us a box from a lower shelf nearby.

The blue and yellow box had pictures of fish with various things wrong with them on the label. Bacterial infection, mouth fungus, red sores, all kinds of apparent waterborne ailments. Across the front, in bold black letters, it read 'E.M. Erythromycin'.

"Fish medication?" I queried, nearly in time with Dave's "What the fuck?"

"Yeah, fish antibiotics," Keane echoed. "Erythromycin. They give it to people who are allergic to penicillin. While everybody that was left after the start was killing each other over whatever they could carry from the local pharmacy, I pretty much walked right into this fish shop down on State Road. Biggs, Boggs, whatever the place was, yeah."

"So, it's a crossover?" Jennifer asked.

"Yep, pretty much," he replied. "These packs are two-hundred milligrams each, but I like five-hundred milligram dosage, so I just measure them out and dump them into herb capsules. Like, GNC supplements and stuff. Dump the junk out, refill with this shit, boom. Apocalypse antibiotics."

"No shit," Dave said, trailing off as he mused over the little clear capsules full of white powder.

We spoke with Keane a while longer, exchanged goodbyes, and walked back outside just as the sun was being overtaken by light clouds. The sun shone through one such cloud, high in the sky. I was thankful it had been gradually cooling down. The brunt of the summer usually wasn't too kind on me, as I could just sit there some days and still be drenched with sweat.

We made our way through the cars and flagged down Hashman again. He stood tall among a group of what appeared to be mostly young teens, talking them through some kind of work he needed done.

"He got you together, eh?" Hashman inquired as we approached, and the talk was mostly light. Of course, then it became much less light, and we spoke briefly again about a plan regarding the Colonel. A plan that we all felt very good with, which involved Hashman, with all his resources, doing pretty much nothing.

We reminisced for a bit about days before everyone was trying to eat everybody else. We even speculated about the big guys. The behemoths. Hashman had no more inkling as to their origin than we did. His medical team had made mention of capturing one, which was, quite literally, laughed off. They thought about bringing in a dead one, but they were heavy, tipping the scale at an estimated one-thousand pounds. And further, Hashman explained a few of his men even had superstitions of bringing anything dead back, let alone a behemoth. Some of them feared the dead were never really dead, and also questioned how we could be sure the dead couldn't infect anybody. We had never thought of that, but suddenly I was very thankful we'd never attempted to keep the deceased around, outside of the scattered graves around our compound. We buried deep, and the areas were carefully tended to by a few of the younger members of our crew. Flowers were planted, shrubbery relocated, the gravesites were slowly becoming shrines of sorts, though the rough wooden markers were left.

We carried on conversing with Hashman as we moved among the rows of cars and toward the area where we'd come in from. As we neared the top of the steps, he stopped and turned to me.

"Hey, I saw how fucked up that boat of yours was when you were with Keane," he intoned.

"Yeah, they got it pretty good. It's a miracle we weren't hit," I replied.

"Aside from, you know, getting shot in the head, bro," Hashman responded casually. "Look, your shit's fucked up, I want you to take my boat."

"The electric one?" I asked, kind of surprised; that was his baby. A bit smaller than our little cabin cruiser, it had been a shallow-bottomed fishing craft somebody converted over to an electric outboard. It was nearly silent, fairly quick, and Mike's personal craft.

"Yeah, but you're just borrowing it," he cautioned. "And you better not fuck it up, too. My guys will pull yours out of service and fix it up for you, good as new."

"Why are you so good to us?" I asked, only half-joking.

"You kidding?" he shot in return. "You guys have given us ten times more than what we could have asked for. What was supposed to be just trade turned into a full-on supply line, brotha! We're more than happy to help!"

"But Mike," I admonished, "you lost guys in that raid. Good people. And equipment, morale, all kinds of irreplaceable things."

"And that was entirely my choice to help," he shot back. "Look, don't worry about it. I've had no problem telling people 'No' before, if anything is going to stretch us thin, I'd tell you the same. Now, take my boat before I change my mind."

That was all he really needed to say, because in a few minutes time, we had his belongings unloaded from the little vessel and were underway.

The little craft barely made a noise as it glided over the water, and neither did we.

All four of us, even Tony, kept our eyes glued to the riverbanks and beyond, in a constant state of readiness for an event that never repeated itself. I still don't know exactly what gave our presence away, and that drove me a bit mad. I hated not knowing these things. Especially since knowledge was the best preventative for failure.

Did he hear the engine laboring to push us upstream? Did he see us? Follow us? Was there some kind of sensors?

Nonetheless, we were met back at the base by Henry. Mike's craft was well known at our compound, and gave no reason for alarm, so the crew meeting us at the water was minimal.

"Good Lord my brother, what happened to your head?" Henry interrogated.

"Parker shot me," I replied levelly.

"Parker?" Henry asked, astonished. "When did he do that? Last I saw, brother Parker was at the outer gate on duty!"

"Not our Parker," Jennifer informed him, laughing, "the Colonel."

"Oh! My word!" Henry exclaimed as he joined the rest of us for a round of laughter.

"Yeah, we gotta find something else to call Colonel Parker," Dave suggested. "It's gonna get confusing having two Parkers."

"How about C.O. Dickbag?" Tony offered.

"That he is," I returned, "but we'll just leave it at 'the Colonel', I guess. Either way, he's become a thorn in my side even quicker than the end of the world did."

"Has for all of us," Henry added. "He has for all of us."

"Anyway," I stated, "my head's pounding. I'm going to go take a nap."

"Sounds good to me my friend," Henry agreed. "I'll hold the fort down."

"Put Tony to work," I instructed, "don't let him slack off. Dave will find something I'm sure."

"What?" Tony asked, sounding disappointed. "I don't slack off."

"Oh, boohoo Shannon said," I mocked as I walked away, hearing Dave and Henry laugh at his expense as Jennifer followed me.

I had just gotten out of earshot of the others when she started in. My faithful wife, and faithful anchor.

"You said nap?" she asked after me.

"Christ woman, you too?" I asked, joking with her.

"Well, we did just get done being shot at today, a nap sounds nice," She stated. "But, before you lay down, you're going to go see Shannon. Then we'll nap."

"I'm napping," I replied, "you're going to make sure Shannon doesn't need help, and then Bri. I can't play favorites, you know."

"Fine, I'll make a deal," she persisted. "You go get checked out by our doctor, and I'll go be useful or whatever."

I grunted in reply, and she took my hand in hers and began pulling. Within minutes, we were in Shannon's office on the second floor where I was essentially shoved into a chair.

After removing my bandage and replacing it with a new one, she gave me some mild painkillers and instructions to keep it clean. She also requested that she meet with the doctor who patched me up, and maybe they could compare notes. I agreed, if for no other reason than to placate her, and left to make my way upstairs. Before I knew it, I was on our couch and dreaming, of course, of cheeseburgers.

We're going to need to find some cows and a meat grinder at some point.

SEVEN

I was awakened by yelling. I had not the slightest clue how long I'd been asleep, but clearly it wasn't enough, because my head screamed at me with every pound at my door and every movement I made.

"Scott!" I heard familiar voices call, "Scott wake up! We have casualties!"

That was all it took to set me in motion as I threw the covers back and bolted out of bed, ignoring the pain that ripped through my every thought and nearly clouded my vision.

Without further thought, I grabbed my MK18, clasped my drop leg holster for my pistol to my thigh and ran straight into the door of my apartment. I was already reaching for the knob before my brain told me how stupid I was, at which point I burst through the doorway and into the midst of a half-dozen people, Tony and Ryan at the forefront.

"Whoa!" Ryan exclaimed, shielding his eyes. "Calm down, Scott! All of you!"

"Huh?" was the only intelligible syllable I could manage.

"Having some nice dreams there, buddy?" Tony chimed in, chuckling.

I looked down and realized my folly. In the excitement, I had rushed through arming myself and never considered getting dressed. I was about to run into whatever fight might be present with a raging sleep-boner and nothing to hold it back but threadbare plaid boxers. Shit.

"What's the emergency?" I asked, playing it off. "Is it the Colonel? Is he here?"

"I mean, it's an emergency, but not that big. Get dressed first," Ryan stated, then, "For all of our sakes."

As I eased my way back into the apartment, I caught the gaze of the older, early twenties girl that was with them. She grinned. Double oops.

"No. Bad!" I pointed at her as I closed my door and went to search for my pants.

Once I had recycled and improved my exit method, I left through my door again.

"You should be proud of yourself, dude," Tony chided.

"One more word about my junk from you, and you're getting slapped," I shot back at him. "So what's going on?"

"The crew that left this morning got the supplies, then made contact on the way back with a small hostile group," Ryan informed. "Quick exchange, left five bad guys dead, rescued two hostages, one critical, we have one dead and one wounded on our side."

"Whose bad guys?" I questioned. "The Colonel's or someone else's? Who did we lose? How's our injured guy?"

"They don't think it was the Colonel," Ryan offered. "Two Akron cops, three other unknowns, no military far as we can tell."

"Cops, eh?" I asked, then, "And our guys?"

"One of the kids from the high school," Tony started. "Xavier. Another survivor we have named Jonesy, three rounds in his hip and upper leg; Shannon expects him to survive but doesn't know how or when he'll ever walk right again."

"Xavier have friends or family here?" I interrogated. "I'll check on Jonesy. What about the survivors they rescued?"

"Two girls," Ryan spoke again. "One, early twenties, she's rough and they don't think she'll make it. She's slipped into a coma."

"And the other?" I replied as we entered the stairwell and began descending. "What the fuck happened? And did they find James?"

"Clara's waiting to get you up to speed on all that," Tony suggested. "The other girl, well, she's different."

"We're all different," I scolded, descending the stairs in double time. "What the fuck is different?"

"Blind," came his single word reply.

"Blind?" I echoed. "Like, she can't see things?"

"Like a bat," Tony replied, his voice level.

"Bats aren't actually blind," I replied, offhandedly.

Blind. A blind girl. How much help could she be for us? I mean, the end of times did a fairly thorough job of eliminating the weak, the elderly, much of the young. It's hard to get away from a hungry running freak when you have physical limitations, or imminent medical needs to take your life when outside aid stops. But *blind*? This chick was already an anomaly, but to survive like this. Wow.

I hit the second floor doorway and burst through the door into the hall, then stopped.

"Tony, give me your radio," I instructed, and he handed over his Baofeng before I continued, "All of you, thank you, but there's still work to do. Go help offload the supplies and get things in order."

Most left in compliance, the dark-haired girl left with a smirk.

"You!" I called after her.

"Candace." She turned, smiling.

"Drop the crush. I'm an asshole, and I'm still married." I returned the grin as I watched her face fluster before the girl departed behind the rest of them. I heard Tony ribbing her as the door closed behind them but couldn't quite make out the conversation.

Then, naturally, Clara was present before I even turned all the way around.

"Scott," she started, "it's all fucked up."

"Start at the beginning," I soothed. "Where's James?"

"Gone." The word left on the head of a sob. "It was such a mess. He was *everywhere*, Scott."

Her sobs broke into full-on tears as I extended an arm and drew her into a friendly hug.

"Hey, you did good," I tried to console. "We were prepared for this, you couldn't help any of it. It's okay."

"We burnt it," she expelled between more sobs, one of the toughest women in the compound, still, just human.

"That's good. You did great, exactly what was right," I continued. "Now, take some deep breaths, there ya go, just close your eyes and breathe."

I pulled away from our embrace enough to look into her eyes as tears fell. Christ, she was a mess. I put a hand to the side of her face and wiped back a tear with my thumb.

"Hey," I kept trying to ease her, "you're a fucking star, okay? You're one of my best here, and you did as you should have. James died on *my* arm. Technically, I'm the one that killed him. It hurts, I know firsthand, but you did amazing. Never think otherwise."

"It's not just James," she caught another sob and visibly pushed it back. "Scott, the place we rescued those girls from…"

"Bad?" I asked, as she broke our coupling and wiped her face on the sleeve of her jacket.

"Worse," she said ever so softly. "It was a rape den."

"A fucking *WHAT?*" I shot, immediately regretting the outburst as she jumped.

"Here," she said, motioning to the empty room next to us, and I followed her inside.

"Take it slow," I urged as she closed the door. "We've got time, I'm sure."

"Okay," Clara began, "we spotted a guy guarding the outside of a house. Just, standing on the porch with a shotgun. So, me and one of the teens, Xavier, dismounted and approached from a couple of blocks away while the rest circled around to come up from right across the street and watch."

"Just a guy?" I questioned, trying to kickstart her brain as she took a short breather, the tears still wet in the dirt and grime on her face.

"He was dressed like a cop, but we aren't sure," she continued.

"How so?" I urged.

"Well," she explained, "these days anyone can grab a uniform, and if they were cops, wouldn't they have changed their clothes after this long?"

"You have a point," I concurred. "So then what?"

"It went south quickly," she informed, after regrouping her thoughts. "We approached, acted lost and in need of help, and he almost immediately grabbed me and turned his shotgun on Xavier, the kid...the kid didn't stand a chance, Scott. I killed him with my knife, but he already got the kid."

"Okay, nothing you could have done, right?" I asked, watching her eyes flash. "I mean, how could you expect that, right? But you got him back, so, is that how the rest started?"

"Yeah," she said, looking down at her feet for a moment, then, "Then someone from inside started shooting, from both floors. That's when Jonesy got hit. We rushed the house as soon as the gunfire started, they got him in the doorway and Frank threw one of those pipe bombs Rich makes into the front room."

"Did that get the shooter?" I asked, never ceased in my amazement at Rich's propensity for destructive devices.

"Mostly, we finished him as soon as we entered," she explained, then her voice dropped again, "When we cleared the house, the downstairs was empty, but there were three more upstairs. Two dressed as civilians, but, Scott, that's when we found the girls."

"It's okay hun," I stated. "Take a breath, take your time. What happened?"

She shook her head and pinched her nose as she breathed in deeply and exhaled, several times.

"The third guy was in the far bedroom," she began anew. "All six of us shot at him, seemed like it at least, and he was dead before he could get his pants up all the way. He had the younger girl, the blind one, Scott he had her tied to the bed, and-"

"No, no, no," I paused, "I can probably guess, we can leave that part out. So, you guys killed him, which is less than he deserved, but then what?"

"We freed her," she said, beginning to sob again. "Scott she's blind, and he was doing *that*. Fucking *blind*, and so young!"

I could feel my face flush, and the rage spread through my neck and down my back. It became a physical presence, yet I did my best to remain as stone, if anything for Clara's benefit. Before I could urge her to continue, she did of her own accord.

"So, I started cleaning her up the best I could," Clara detailed. "We found some clean rags and bottled water, got her dressed from the dressers in the house. We found a drawer full of trinkets and IDs. The other girl, we think her name is Jordan based on the IDs. Jordan Townsend, early twenties, but she's so beat up Scott we can't hardly tell for sure."

"Hey, you guys did great," I encouraged. "Look, we lost someone, someone got hurt, but where would those girls be without y'all? It's always worth sacrifice to do the right thing, provided that sacrifice can't be avoided. And I think you all did great."

"The basement," she carried on, barely even here anymore, so much distance in those green eyes. "That must be where they put the ones they were done with. The spare room, where we found Jordan, it was like a holding cell. All boarded up and secured. But, the basement, Scott, there was at least a dozen dead girls in there. I just, I don't-"

"You need a rest," I confirmed. "Go talk to Bri, tell her to give you some of my scotch. And go do your best to relax. You're off guard duty tonight, too, I'll cover."

"Scott, I-" she protested, but I cut her off with another hug. A big one.

"Go take care of yourself," I stated. "That's an order."

She nodded and made her way into the hallway, then the stairwell.

Previously focused on Clara, and still only half-awake, I hadn't heard all the commotion until I re-entered the corridor for the medical floor.

It sounded like a legitimate hospital here now. Several voices, loud and strong but not quite yelling, emanated from the first emergency room. I approached the door and merely cracked it open an inch, not wanting to disturb whatever life-saving procedures were going on.

Shannon and Ashley worked feverishly on the leg of a young black man, Jonesy. Jennifer held a place at his head, one hand on his pulse, the other holding some kind of medical device I did not recognize. Frank, and the rarely seen Fred, both held a limb of the man they worked on. Just as I was about to close the door, Jennifer's head turned toward my direction.

"Whoever that is, get in here!" she fairly spat, the heat of the emergency room keeping her nerves frayed.

"It's me, wife," I answered, opening the door a bit wider so she could see.

"Good!" she replied, seeming relieved. "Chloroform, or any inhaled anesthetic; check the closet in the next room in this hallway."

"I told you," Shannon said to her, "we're out. We don't have anything for him. Just hold him while we work."

"Won't hurt to check!" she returned, then, to me, "You going to look, or stand there figuring out which of our asses you like better?"

"It's mine!" Ashley called over her shoulder.

"Yeah, I'm out," I replied. "I'm looking for chlorophyll!"

"*FORM! CHLOROFORM!*" Jennifer barked as I left the vicinity before they ripped me apart.

Walking to the next door in the hallway, I grabbed the knob and pushed my way in heading straight for the pantry and digging in, checking bottles on every shelf and coming up empty.

"Hello?" came a girl's voice from the next room.

"Just a second!" I called back, then brought my borrowed radio to my mouth, "We need chloroform! Anybody? The med staff needs some kind of chloroform, or analgesic!"

"Dammit Scott! Anesthetic!" Jennifer scolded through her channel.

"I don't have any," came Rich's gravelly voice, "but I can whip some up for next time, or later, it'll be a few hours at least. Over."

"Better than nothing," I replied. "Wait, you can do that? Oh, over."

"Yeah, is Bri on?" he replied. "Bri! If you're hearing this, switch to my private channel. Over."

"Switching!" Bri replied through the microphone. "Over!"

Well, that sounded handled, so what next?

Oh! Right, somebody had said something!

My head still throbbing, I made my way to the nearby bedroom. On the single bed, arranged at the head of the room, lay a thin, filthy blonde.

"You called?" I said from the doorway, and the girl eased herself onto her side, then pushed into a sitting position. She was thin, and young. I placed her age at maybe fifteen, sixteen years old. She had short, nearly platinum blonde hair that framed a pale face. From what I could see of her arms, legs, and face, every inch of this girl seemed to be a maze of bruises, scratches, and filth. I assumed this must be one of the girls they just brought in.

"You okay?" I asked, knowing the likely answer.

"N-not really," she said sheepishly, her eyes finding me, but seeming to look right through me.

Okay, I thought, this must be the blind girl.

My heart immediately fell upon this realization, and the brunt of what Clara said seemed to weigh it down even further. Ah, shit. This is her. This poor girl.

Even under her dirt and oversized clothing, her battered exterior, the young girl radiated a wholesome, clear, glow. She would grow up to be a simple beauty, if this world let her grow up.

"What's your name?" I asked her, not sure of what else to say.

"Hannah," she stated, then almost physically closed herself back up.

"Hannah," I continued, "I'm Scott. And you don't need to worry, okay? You're as safe here as you can be."

"As I can be?" she asked. "You don't sound so sure."

"Well," I replied, grinning slightly at how clever this kid was, "nowhere is totally safe, but we're probably your best shot. We're the good guys."

"I hope that's true," she said with all the force of a field mouse. "I'm thirsty."

"I'll get some water," I offered, "and some other things."

"Okay," she nearly whispered.

I left for the apartment's pantry and grabbed one of the gallon jugs of water we kept purified and refilled from river water. I also grabbed a bottle of water and the largest bowl I could find in the kitchen cabinets and stopped by the bathroom for some washcloths and a towel. Then, I returned to her room again.

"Here you go," I said as I handed her the water bottle, then turned to place the rest of the items on the nearby dresser. Opening the gallon jug, I poured the entire thing into the bowl, and began to array the washcloths and towel on the dresser. As I worked, she spoke up.

"You said Scott? You must be important here," she observed. "They all agreed you needed to be found and brought down here. And, that woman, Clara? She was scared you'd be upset with her because one of your people died."

"No," I replied, nearly offhanded. "She did great. We saved people that needed it from people that were bad. They all did great, and our guy gave his life helping others."

A scream came from the next room as if it were on cue, Jonesy, I assumed, then quieted down on its own.

"They're fixing our other friend," I explained, seeing her mouth part in a panicked expression. "Heard he took a couple bullets to the leg."

"Hey guys?" Henry's voice crackled as I observed Hannah taking another sip of her water. "I have some nitrous in my garage, if it will help. Over."

"Bring it, NOW!" Jennifer called back. "You guys are easier to work on unconscious! Over!"

Henry complied and the radio fell silent again.

"Hey, I set some things up here for you," I spoke to Hannah, "so let's just get you cleaned up, I guess. I'll, uh, I'll let you take care of it, but let me show you where it is."

"Okay," she said, she was so quiet and timid. Christ, I felt horrible.

"I'm going to take your hand," I instructed loud and clear.

"I'm only blind," she informed me," you can just talk."

"Right, sorry," I said, my turn to sound sheepish.

I led her to the edge of the bed and let her stand before leading her cautiously to the dresser. She wasn't much more than a wisp of a girl, her entire frame narrow and she stood just a bit taller than my shoulder.

"Here's washcloths, two of them, on a dresser," I showed her by placing her hand on them, then carefully collected her left hand, "on this side is a towel to dry with. There's a large bowl of water here, it's clean. Just, uh, I guess try to get yourself the best you can, we'll get you taken care of better later. There's a few gravity showers around, it's kind of still primitive here."

"Thank you," she stated, then, "Why?"

"Why what?" I asked her, careful not to sound harsh.

"Why save me?" she questioned. "I'm clearly not going to be much in a fight, or much of a help in general."

Wow, so this one didn't pull her punches. It seemed to be the theme around here now. You see enough shit hitting the fan and you just kind of quit caring about what offends, or how to tip toe sensitive subjects especially when time was usually at a premium.

"Right thing to do. What more reason do we need?" I countered. "Not a single one of us was going to let that continue to happen to you if we could stop it."

She just shrugged meekly and stood still.

"Okay, well," I began, "myself or one of the doctors will be around in a little bit, I'll at least give you time to clean up and get dressed again. Then you rest. I'm probably already in trouble with Shannon for having you out of bed."

"In trouble?" she chided. "I thought you were the leader here?"

"That's what they call me," I laughed, "but at the end of the day, we're all equal, and all boss of our own areas."

On that note, I left. I headed past a now much quieter emergency room, only glancing in to see them hard at work, Henry standing by, a Nitrous Express bottle standing near his feet.

I turned for the stairwell, went down one flight, and guided myself through the poorly-lit first floor, and out into the overcast day. As I walked across the lot, to the entrance to Rich's bunker, the sun managed to filter through the gap between two clouds, just for a moment, but even that little bit felt refreshing.

Reaching the door for Rich's armory, I pushed my way in, only to be met with his nearly glowing ice blue eyes staring at me over the top of what resembled a chemistry set and still combined into one.

"You know," I issued, "just because the world is over, doesn't make that shit legal in my house."

"Shut up," He chuckled. "It's not meth. Different process. I'm making chloroform."

"Making it?" I asked in amazement. "I thought you were joking."

"Nope, chill and drip the gases from a couple of household items and you have rough chloroform."

"What, ahhh, what chemicals?" I asked, genuinely curious.

"Bleach and acetone," he stated proudly.

"You scare me," I replied in earnest. He did, at times. The things this man knew were startling, if not mind-boggling. He looked every bit the opposite of a mad scientist, yet he was very much exactly that.

We were momentarily interrupted by a radio vote for dinner; it seemed most preferred to dine on their own tonight. I couldn't blame them, especially Shannon and the girls. She'd been at it longer than most of us had today.

Rich tossed a beef ravioli MRE on the counter and a bottle of water.

"Looks like dinner is on me tonight, if you'll stay," he beamed. "On the house for you, of course."

"You gave me one of the good ones," I noted. "What's your angle?"

"Let me test explosives from inside of the outer wall?" he implored.

"Fuck no." I burst out laughing. "No way, dude! I'll give you a crew and you can go east of here, you're still not testing inside. Besides, we don't want to show our hand to the Colonel, and he always seems to be nearby lately. Fuck that."

It was well after dinnertime before we broke our conversation.

I bade Rich goodnight, though I knew he'd likely be up much later working on God knows what.

I made my way back up to the second floor, where I met with Ashley.

"Hey! Scott," she greeted, "Shannon and Jennifer are upstairs, on the roof for their dinner."

"Jonesy?" I asked.

"He's stable, lost a bunch of blood but not enough to have to worry, we think. He's asleep in recovery."

"Hannah still next door?" I asked, genuinely curious.

"Oh, you two have met?" she inquired. "She's such a sweetheart. Blunt, but so kind, I can't believe it. Poor thing."

"Yeah I know," I confirmed. "Did she get cleaned up? I may give her room on the ninth floor with us."

"Aw, that's so nice!" Ashley replied. "But are you going to have time? She's going to need a lot of adjusting and probably patience."

"I know, but I'm sure Jennifer will help," I suggested, "and either way, I wouldn't offer if I didn't mean it."

"Well, I hope it works out!" she replied as I turned to leave.

"Oh, and Ashley?" I called from around the corner. "Your ass is flat, Jennifer wins."

I departed on the tail of a sarcastic scoff from her, smiling the whole way.

I neared the door for where Hannah was located, one down from the main office. I listened for a moment, and heard nothing, so I knocked three times in quick succession. The last thing I wanted was to walk in on her. Tony was one thing, he was damn near family, this was…a little different.

A moment after my last knock, Hannah's soft voice floated to me through the door.

"It's okay!" she called, and I entered the room.

"How ya doing, Hannah?" I asked.

"Oh! Scott, hi,," she replied, then, "I'm fine. Your doctor, Jennifer, she got me cleaned up the rest of the way and found me some new clothes to wear. She's really nice!"

"Yeah, that's my wife," I chuckled. "But listen, where we've got you, right here, it's just a recovery room, and really not much better than a janitor's closet as far as accommodations here. I want you to come stay on the top floor with us, if that's okay."

"It's nicer up there?" she asked, sounding a little uneasy.

"It's the command floor," I explained. "It's also where our apartment is. Me, my wife, and daughter. It's a monitored floor, there's somebody awake and on-duty there twenty-four seven. And you'll have your own room, a nice one, and I'll lay out things so you can always find your way. Rooftop access, too, if you want fresh air."

"I won't be in anybody's way?" she wondered. "Like, I won't bother anybody?"

"That's not what any of this is about, Hannah," I stated. "You're one of us now, which makes you family, more or less. It's a big family, but you're welcome here if you want to be. There's a ton of people here and it's the safest place any of us know of. And, we'll help you, with whatever you need, or whatever amenity you need. It's not a problem."

"If you're sure," she agreed, biting her lip. I couldn't tell if it was a conscious move or not, but dammit this girl just simply looked helpless.

"I'm sure," I reassured her. "We'll set it up however you need, make sure it's comfortable. You can always join us for meals, and being the command floor, there will always be someone there for you to talk to if you like, no matter the time of day or night."

"We can try that, it sounds nice," she agreed, forcing a small smile.

"Jennifer," I spoke into my radio, "Recovery Room One when you can, please. Over."

No answer came back, but, before I could say anything to Hannah, or try again, the door to the apartment opened.

"I'm here already," Jennifer called as she entered the space. "I was just walking by after checking on the other girl, and Jonesy."

"Jennifer is my wife, as I told you," I spoke to Hannah, then, to Jennifer, "Meet our new roommate. I need you to get her settled into the spare room, just kinda get acquainted, help her around. Tomorrow I'll go through and set everything up with her."

"Um, okay," Jennifer agreed after a pause. "Come on Hannah, let's go upstairs. There's a bunch of stuff in that room but we'll get the bed cleared off and get the covers changed for now."

"Thank you, wife," I called as she departed, albeit slowly and carefully, Hannah's hand in hers.

Amazingly, somehow in over thirty years of life, I have never encountered anybody with an impairment like this. What are you supposed to do with a blind person? This girl has been through hell, and that's only what we knew of her. None of us had any idea to this point how she had managed to survive in the apocalypse, or even what kind of life she had prior to the end.

I continued pondering things as I left this apartment and entered into the one across the hallway. These were usually for severe cases, people the girls needed to monitor frequently, so I didn't give the courtesy of a knock this time.

In the first room, Jonesy appeared to be sleeping. The rhythmic rise and fall of his chest, and soft note of his breath told me as much as I'd find out. He was fine, and whether just sleeping or out for a long while was beyond my immediate ability to tell, I decided to leave him.

I checked the adjacent bedroom, again stripped of all but a bed and dresser which was likely full of basic care supplies. Here lay the other girl we brought in. Jordan, they thought her name was, but her face was too battered for them to tell.

I approached her bedside and confirmed this myself. The poor girl looked like she'd been through several automobile accidents. One whole side of her face was puffed and swollen, and a mass of heavy purple and angry red hues. Her body showed thin as a rail, even under the stark white sheets she was covered with.

They had her hooked up to a machine, one of only a couple the crews had managed to liberate from the local veterinary clinic. I didn't understand the numbers, but they all seemed much lower than they should be.

Not wanting to mess anything up, I watched her for a moment.

We tried to save everybody we could. Some people, you could just simply tell they were going to be trouble. Even then, unless they showed outward hostility or aggression, we'd help. If not by offering them a place to stay, then by handing over a simple backpack from the collection stocked at every gate.

Each pack had some water, a few power bars or small bag of beef jerky, and a simple change of clothes that were as close to 'one size fits all' as we could get. Usually, sweatpants or basketball shorts, and an XL T-shirt. Better than sending someone away empty-handed, at least. We were doing well, amazingly, even, but we still just didn't have the supplies to stock every soul we encountered.

As I drifted into thought, what I perceived as movement brought me back to the real world.

I stood in stark amazement as something moved, just where the girl's legs parted with the rest of her being.

No, not movement, something spreading. An irritated red glow began to pool across where the blanket lay lowest, against the bed, and between her legs. As I watched, frozen to my spot, the entire mood of the room changed.

The pool of viscous blood continued to spread, tainting the sheets like the spread of oil from a damaged car. The machine that had previously managed a low, periodic *beep* began a long monotonous tone. This, I knew, was not a good thing.

"*ASHLEY!*" I bellowed over my shoulder as I watched, completely panicked and without a clue as to what to do. I fumbled for my radio, finally managing to find it, and pressed the button to make the stupid box work.

"Shannon!" I barked into it. "Shannon, Recovery Room…fuck! The girl by Jonesy!"

"Four!" Ashley directed as she rushed past me and immediately began checking things left and right.

I didn't have time to call again as Shannon rushed past, still in her pajamas with her hair flying in as many directions as she was. I took several steps back and watched as they worked. It felt like a real emergency room, and though I didn't fully have a grasp of what they were doing, I was impressed, as they sure looked like they knew.

As I pressed myself against the wall, things took a turn for the worse. The girl, Jordan, arched her back and took in a tremendous shuddering gasp, and expelled a spray of crimson blood from her lips that stretched out to cover the bed as far as her toes.

I had no clue how to react, so I drew my sidearm and pointed it straight at her.

"IS SHE TURNING?" I shouted over the commotion.

"No, Scott!" Shannon fired hastily, then calmer, added, "She's not turning, she's dying."

"Shit," I muttered, holstering the pistol again. The single syllable was less in disappointment, and more resignation. So many had died to this point, but seeing it happen to the living was never as easy as, say, taking down an infected. We had moved as far as possible from thinking they were ever human. Some instances, like the young, never got much easier, but mostly I was able to distance myself from reality and view them as little more than figures on a television screen.

"Scott!" Shannon shouted, bringing me back. "Main office, get the bottle of nitrous and the mask attached to it! NOW!"

I turned and ran out of the apartment and down the hall, nearly bowling over Clara in the process.

"You're off duty!" I ordered her as I ran by, and she turned to follow.

"I just needed some Ibuprofen," she informed me. "Is everything okay?"

"Nope! Now go home, rest!" I ordered again as I grabbed a bottle of Motrin from Shannon's desk, dumped a half dozen of the pills into Clara's hand, and ran back out with the nitrous bottle in my free hand.

"Shift starts soon!" she yelled after me.

"I'm on it, two minutes! GO HOME!" I replied, nearly skidding back into the room and standing the tank between Shannon and Ashley.

Shannon immediately grabbed the mask and instructed Ashley to hold the girl down as she pressed the mask over her face and cracked the bottle valve fully open.

"Can you fix her?" I asked, watching as Shannon's frantic eyes found mine.

"No," she asserted, "but, if she can breathe enough of this in, we can help her pass as gently as possible. We knew she had internal bleeding once we couldn't get her heart rate up."

"Do you know where from?" I asked, trying anything to keep Shannon's mind in step.

"Not exactly," she admitted. "We're not much for invasive surgery here, but she has several broken ribs, and, uh, damage elsewhere. I don't have a delicate way to put this."

"We're all adults," I calmed, "what 'other damage'?"

"We think she may have gotten a perforated colon," came her response, and I could read the uneasiness on her face.

"Oh," I replied, softly. "Do you need me anymore here?"

"Not unless you want to stand and watch, that's all any of us can do, keep her comfortable and wait," she explained.

"I've got guard duty to cover for Clara," I stated, knowing full-well it was a cheap excuse, but I felt so helpless. At least I could keep an eye on our home.

"I'll call you," she replied. "And, thanks, Scott."

"Yup," was all I could say, and I was gone.

Back up three-million stairs.

I reached the top, thinking I was less and less out of breath each time. I'd been smoking hardly any at all lately, at least, compared to before. This was in part by my own doing, but also due to the ongoing scarcity of cigars and cigarettes. And mostly, what we had now was stale and dry anyway. What better time to quit than when the only thing you can get is garbage?

I reached the ninth floor and began walking toward the opposite end of the hallway to take the next flight of stairs.

Stopping to walk through the conference room, I peeked into the command center long enough to see two of the younger teens against the far wall with a monitor, going through what appeared to be recon photos from the array of digital cameras.

Rob was standing behind two older teens, instructing them on how to use the camera systems. I didn't intrude and turned to quietly leave. The irony didn't miss me, that the man with eyes on an entire compound had no idea he was just being watched.

I passed slowly, and extra cautiously, past my own apartment. Again, not wanting to intrude, I could hear Hannah and Jennifer quietly talking from the couch, while Gwen could be heard playing, presumably in her bedroom.

I made the rest of my way to the stairs and climbed the single split-flight to the rooftop. Here I was greeted by the last bit of red across the horizon, signaling the sun had gone down and the daytime was over.

From time to time, I had covered nighttime guard duty, and when I took it from this rooftop, I had a stool I always sat on at the end of one row of plywood and solar panels. I was delighted to see it standing proud, as it always had. But, between myself and my little guard seat was an entirely different scene than I was expecting.

I cleared my throat and watched the two previously embraced figures separate, and instantly felt a little guilty at intruding. It was Bri and Dave.

She had always been a little on the plump side, even this long after the end of everything, but she appeared twice as wide, and twice as short, as she pressed up against Dave's long, lanky frame. I laughed internally, thinking to myself that if I'd approached them from behind her, the silhouettes would look like a straw in a beer can.

"Scott!" Bri was the first to speak.

"You guys each have an apartment," I chided, "and locking doors. A towel. A bed, floor, kitchen counters, even a couch."

My guilt left, if only momentarily, as I watched Dave cover his mouth as he laughed. Bri, on the other hand, turned a shade of red that glowed, even in the pale lighting of the few tiki torches and LED patio lights.

"I'm kidding," I responded to the silence.

"It's cool buddy!" Dave laughed, openly this time. "I was just about to see if she wanted to smoke one with me. You can join, if you want."

"Right, you don't drink," I mused. "I always forget that."

"I…" Bri started. "Well, I have to go do some figuring and tally up some supplies, see what we're running low on."

"It's nighttime though, you're off-duty, Bri," I offered.

"Please," she rolled her eyes playfully. "My boss is such a slave-driver!"

"Oh, oh, I see!" I shot back, grinning. "Well, library, and country."

"Sorry?" she asked, eyeing me like I had just had a stroke.

"We need a team to hit any library they're nearby," I explained, "the focus being music, and audiobooks. And, it's a strange request, but get me the nicest earbuds we can find, too."

"Planning on shutting out the world?" she asked, still playful.

"For Hannah," I corrected. "And, the countryside. I need fuel, our two strongest pickup trucks, one trailer, and a strong team. Oh, and lots of rope and ratchet straps."

"What's in the countryside?" she asked, now at full attention.

"The day after tomorrow, I'm going to alleviate some of your food concerns," I grinned. "We're going to go rustle up some livestock."

"Oh!" she exclaimed. "Okay, so my boss is actually pretty sweet."

"I figured it'd take some of your worries," I confirmed, "and bolster our food supplies with fresh meat, hopefully boost morale and give more jobs to any idle hands here. And any manure could be stockpiled for whatever crops we plant in the spring."

"Okay!" she chirped, then, grabbing Dave's hand and letting go after a moment, "Well, you boys get some private time up here. I won't interrupt like some people."

"Go do your thing, smartass," I joked, then, to Dave, "A smoke, you say?"

"Fuck yeah man!" Dave smiled, producing a cigarette pack and pulling a joint out of it.

"I'll take one of those, too," I said, pointing to the pack, which he turned on its side and allowed me to draw a single stale cigarette.

We walked over to my stool as he lit the joint and took a long drag, before fixing a run that had formed already and handing it to me.

"How do you always have pot, even when the rest of the world struggles for anything at all?" I asked, genuinely amazed. "Like, we could live a decade underground in a cave and I think somehow you'd still have some smoke."

"Magic, buddy." Dave exhaled and passed the leg back to me. "Fuckin' magic."

I laughed and took my own hit before passing it back and declining any further.

"Just a couple for me," I explained. "You know I only like being leveled out, plus, guard duty and all."

"Yeah, true," he replied. "So what's up with this chick?"

"What chick?" I asked as he drew another hit.

"The blind one," he nearly croaked as he again breathed out a plume of smoke.

"Hannah, bro," I intervened, "her name is Hannah. I don't know much else, but she's staying with Jennifer and me. Which reminds me, I need you to grab me some rope before tomorrow. A fuck ton of it. I have an idea. And some eye hooks."

"Rope and eye hooks. Got it," he confirmed, then backtracked to Hannah, "How do you think she survived for so long out here?"

"Damn sure didn't take many walks, I'm certain," I replied, and we both laughed before things became somber again. "Truthfully, man we don't even know how long she was with the alleged cops. She couldn't tell us, not like she could say when was day or night, or how many had gone by."

"Didn't think of that, either," he said thoughtfully. "Chick's been through some shit, eh?"

"Yeah," I agreed. "More than any of us, too. Besides the obvious things, where is her family, ya know?"

Dave nodded solemnly and we both held a short silence as we stared out over the landscape.

Between the two walls, both of which could be seen at night due to being covered with solar-powered garden lights, was the old neighborhood. Nearly a full third of it had been stripped to bare ground. The remaining foundations were filled in with trash, then eventually buried in with what was left from digging the dry-moat or what had been dug up to fill them from yards beyond the outer wall.

We could have left the exposed foundations open, it's not like there was anyone to care, but we didn't need anybody falling into one at night. It also bought us more open, flat land for farming, and it simply just felt safer. No giant holes in the ground half-filled with busted dressers and other varying debris meant less places a possible infected freak or marauder could take up residence.

Some homes were left, those that had been inspected by James, rest in peace, and Henry. The ones left were deemed to need no work in the near future. The roofs were new, or at least recent. The interiors well-kept and cared for, the foundations solid, and so-on. Those would be essential, and probably sooner than later, for bunk houses. I estimated our population to be around 180, but I wasn't sure. That was Bri's department. Someone else always managed numbers and figures for me, despite all I knew, I was completely inept with such things.

"How long do you think we'll last?" Dave asked, breaking the silence.

"We're human," I answered. "If we continue working together, and the outside world learns to stop fucking with us? Shit, dude, this could be the new heart of civilization. Our ancestors had less to work with and did it. We really just need to do two things."

"What's that?" he inquired.

"Manage resources," I explained, "and mitigate risk. Keep the people safe and fed."

Before we could continue, we heard a series of distant *pops* and *bangs*. We continued listening, and soon enough the radios came to life. The furthest west guard post on the outer wall, a couple of early-20s guys that had come in recently, began reporting gunfire.

I eyed Dave for another ten seconds or so as he did the same to me, and we listened.

Sounds like a ways west of here, the radio crackled. *Command, please advise. Over.*

The responder was Rob's voice, instructing them to hang tight. Listen to the action but draw no attention and don't get involved, but to radio in ASAP if they got closer or if contact was made.

The gunfire seemed to bring an impossibility to the first priority I'd spoken.

Keep the people safe.

People were a handful at the best of times. This was clearly not the best of times. And winter was approaching. Keeping them warm was also keeping them safe. There was another challenge.

"Knew I'd find you up here., came Jennifer's voice from behind me.

"Hey!" I called. "Join the party. How's Hannah?"

"She's a wreck, but, she's asleep finally," she responded. "I found melatonin in the cabinet and gave her some. That poor girl."

"Did you find anything out about her?" I wondered aloud.

"She survived the end with her father," Jennifer started. "Her mother never came home. Her dad kept scavenging for supplies, then, maybe a week ago she guesses, he just never came back home."

"Probably a lot of that going around," I surmised. "How'd the scumbags find her?"

"Said she heard someone breaking in and hid," Jennifer continued. "Clearly not well enough, but the guy that found her convinced her he was a cop and going to take her somewhere safe."

"Sounds like a perfect setup for pieces of shit like them," Dave offered.

"Yeah," I agreed, "pretend to be a cop, earn trust, break that trust. Probably all in short order, too. Though not much different than 'real' cops always did."

"We can't save the world, though, Scott," Jennifer opined.

"No," I stated flatly, "but we can save our part of it."

I brought Jennifer up to speed as the night carried on. Explained to her what I wanted to do for Hannah, and about the livestock. She expressed her admonitions about traveling so far away for something that may not even be there. Or, that, even worse would be there. I agreed, but it had to be done. We had mouths to feed and the number of mouths seemed to grow without influence.

It hadn't seemed like midnight was already there, but before long, a middle-eastern man I recognized as Mo had come up to relieve us.

I didn't think I'd ever get used to so many names and faces. I had my favorites, and my original crew, of course, and kind of kept my distance from the rest. Not out of any kind of contempt or anything else, but I was just simply as bad or worse with names and faces as I was with numbers. My two weaknesses. Usually, I'd forewarn someone. I'd explain that I may 'meet' them another half-dozen times, and it's no offense to them, I'm just terrible with names and faces.

Just as I was about to leave my post, I glanced over the edge again and saw what looked remarkably like Tony, holding hands with another, taller person. I couldn't quite tell, given the provided low level of lighting, but it was almost certainly his figure. I'd known the man for over a decade. But I couldn't recall having any women taller than him here though I could possibly be wrong.

I led Jennifer down to our apartment, moving in utter silence as both Gwen and Hannah were asleep, last either of us knew.

We crept through the apartment, and wordlessly switched into our night clothes. I drew Jennifer in and gave her a soft, quiet kiss and a tight hug before we lay down in bed.

EIGHT

The next morning came quickly, and before I was even awake enough to know what was happening, I was already dressed and seated at the kitchen table with my morning cup of coffee. I'd just started pulling on a clean pair of socks when I heard a soft rustle coming from the hallway.

I lifted my eyes in time to catch Hannah feeling her way around her doorway.

"Shit!" I said in a whisper, then a little louder, "Hannah? I'm coming, one second."

"Oh, okay!" she replied, slightly startled, I thought, then, "I have to pee."

I squeezed past her, instructing her to wait just a moment, and checked to make sure the camping toilet was clean. It was, so I returned and took her hand to lead her to the bathroom.

"Here you go," I instructed. "Seat's down, lid's up. It's all ready. I'll, uh, I'll wait outside. Call me when you're finished."

I waited a few moments down the hallway until I heard her voice calling.

"Mr. Scott?" she spoke through the door before opening it. She was wearing an oversized T-shirt that I could see. I didn't even know if she had shorts on under it, and I wasn't asking.

"You're going to need clothes for today," I observed.

"Got a big pile of stuff in her size we rounded up yesterday after I took her up here," Jennifer called after me. "Everything she'd need."

"Okay cool," I replied, then set to thinking. A pile? She can't exactly see to figure out what's what, and I didn't like the thought of forcing her to dig through a pile of clothes and figure it out on her own. Then an idea struck me. It was perfect!

I led Hannah back into her room and checked the dresser. It had been emptied. Great!

I sorted through the pile and found what I figured would work. She was so thin, and although Jennifer just said they were all in her size, the clothes felt so tiny in my hands. Nevertheless, I rummaged and found her some brand new underwear, what appeared to be some kind of sports bra, jeans, a belt, and a long-sleeve T-shirt with the logo of some band I'd never heard of.

"Okay hun," I spoke, "we got you covered! I'm going to have you go back into the bathroom to change. I've got an idea for your clothes."

She thanked me, and I led her into the bathroom and closed the door behind her.

I then returned to her room and began sorting. One clothing type per drawer, as to eliminate any confusion, and even a drawer for her shoes and a pair of new house slippers we had found. By the time I'd finished, she had finished as well, and found her way back to her room.

"Mr. Scott?" she asked.

"Just Scott is fine." I smiled. "Here, check this out."

I took her by her hand yet again, the offered appendage so much smaller and softer than my own and helped her feel her way around the dresser as I explained what clothes were in which drawers, certain that she'd get the hang of it soon enough on her own.

She thanked me, and after some brief small talk, I took her back into the kitchen so Jennifer could help her with getting some food. At this time, I turned and noticed that at some point during the night, Dave had gathered what I asked for and set it all just inside my apartment door. Nice!

I grabbed the coils of long, thin rope, closer to paracord than rope, and set to work.

•

Better than half the day had passed before I was finished. The entire length of the ninth floor, the conference room, and the stairwell to the roof were all lined with various lengths of the cording. Each end was secured with an eye hook, and just before each end was a specific number of knots. One for 'home', two for 'roof', three took her straight to the nearest bathroom, and so-on.

For her benefit, the roped walls also all wore signs now as well. Each sign declaring that there should be no objects placed near or along that wall, as to eliminate any tripping hazards.

Admittedly, I wasn't quite sure if this was overboard, or just right, but it felt great to me to be helping someone that needed it in a way that didn't deal quite so directly with how badly the outside world had gone to shit.

I called her and Jennifer out, and took her hand to show her the new system. Almost immediately, tears formed at the corner of her pale blue eyes and she threw her arms around me.

"Stop being awkward and hug her back," my loving, dear wife instructed, to which I complied.

After a moment, I explained that I'd be adding another rope that would lead to a stash of snacks and water for her to access at a whim, as well, within the apartment.

We continued talking, and I asked her what else we could do to help make her stay more comfortable. She kept declining to ask for much, and I didn't push, but I had some more ideas.

After a few more minutes, Jennifer offered to stay behind and introduce her to our daytime computer nerds, Rob and Ryan, and I departed for the first floor.

•

As I broke into the outdoors, I immediately wished I'd brought a jacket. Inside, it wasn't too terrible, but today seemed to be the coldest one yet, and the wind did little more than enhance the drop in temperature. Additionally, there was a light drizzle of rain coming from the low cloud cover. Fall was here. Or, at least, coming soon. Not cool.

As if a sign, meant to assuage my worry about the coming cold season, two trucks pulled through the inner gate and into the central area.

Henry was already out directing them and had ordered both vehicles to be backed up against the first ground-floor apartment in the building. They did so, and after a few haphazard attempts to back into place, they succeeded. Not having anything better to do today, I decided to pitch in and approached the scene.

"Brother Scott!" Henry offered, extending his hand to take mine in a half-handshake, half-hug. "Good to see you my friend!"

"You too, man!" I returned. "What do you have going on here?"

"A thing of beauty!" he exclaimed. "These people were kind enough to rustle up a couple of woodburning furnaces, and as much seasoned firewood as them there trucks can carry. We're getting set up before mother nature dips her cold-ass hands into our home."

"It's like you read my mind, Henry." I grinned. "I'll help."

I nearly regretted my words as they removed the tarps from the heating units. They were both huge, easily the size of the biggest double-door refrigerators I'd ever seen. Each wood-burning furnace stood taller than me, and wider.

"Oh baby!" Henry exclaimed, rubbing his rough hands together, and in moments they were both unstrapped and ready to move once the various firewood and pallets were pulled free and stacked inside the far apartment. We had perhaps two-dozen people and made a pair of human conveyor belts into the barren far apartment.

"Now, I can't guarantee we ain't about to be bringing all kinds of bugs and such inside," he noted, "but, that's on my list. They grabbed these from the local hardware store, brand-new, and a slew of home pest control. We all the way good, my friend."

I concurred, nearly as excited as he was, but before I could even finish my statement, he was already issuing orders. We were to take them in on their sides and bring them into the first apartment through the sliding door, where he'd begin setting things up today to run the ductwork and 'all matter of other bullshit we gotta do to get these puppies working', as he put it.

It was a beautiful feeling, and, damn it sure took a load off my shoulders.

As Henry had informed me, these units wouldn't be enough to make the entire building jacket-free, but it would keep the place well above freezing. And, over the next few days, he intended to get more furnaces. Maybe one more for the main building, at the opposite end, but definitely two or three more for the south structure, as well. We had people living all through that one as well, plus, that's where Carolyn and now a couple of other ladies had the daycare section. Nice and safe, and away from the hustle and bustle that painted a larger target on the North Building.

"Mr. Pfeiffer?" spoke a younger guy I didn't completely recognize.

"Scott's fine man, what's up?" I queried.

"We hit a local library on the way. I was told to give you these," he stated as he swung a large blue storage tote from the backseat of the black crew cab pickup. It was stocked to the brim with what appeared to be mostly audiobooks of nearly every kind imaginable.

"No shit?" I asked, eyeing him carefully.

"No shit, sir. Scott. I'm sorry," he stated, almost visibly sweating as he pushed his glasses back up over his nose. His dark skin nearly shone with it.

"Loosen up, man, you're cool!" I chuckled, then, "Hey, you look like a pretty smart kid. You want to get a couple of friends together on a special project for me?"

"Sure!" he beamed. "What is it?"

"Take these," I handed the tote back to him, "Find somewhere quiet. Use one of the books you found on braille, and find a way to label them for me, please?"

"There's, uh, there's no need to, sir. Scott, I mean," he said in return.

"Sorry?" I questioned.

"Check them out!" he glowed again. "The library had a standard practice of labeling all audiobooks in braille already. I guess they're popular with the blind?"

"And they will be yet again," I congratulated. "Thanks. Hey, what's your name by the way?"

"Harrison," he stated firmly and shook my hand.

"You did amazing work, Harrison," I acknowledged. "The world isn't kind, and y'all are out here kicking ass in it. Keep it up, be proud of yourself."

The kid, who I assumed to be possibly only 18, glowed at this.

He returned the tote of compact discs to me, and I immediately took them into the building and began lugging them up the stairwell to the Eighth Floor.

Okay, this time I was out of breath. As much as I preferred to call on Bri by name, I didn't have it in me. I'm also, possibly, getting too old for this shit, but we'll see.

I rang the bell on the desk in her hallway and received no answer. After a second try, I still got nothing in return. Finally, I had gathered my lungs just enough to speak.

"Bri?" I inquired down the hallway, and still got no reply. Figuring she was busy, and not wanting to bother her with something so mundane, I pushed past her desk and retrieved the notebook she had tucked neatly into a cubby and found the location of the section she'd titled 'Electronics, portable'.

Her organization was so on point that barely a full minute later I had retrieved an old-school CD player, an MP3 player labeled 'full, modern music', and a handful of batteries.

There was also a small bundle on her desk that read:

Headphones- give to Scott

I took those as well and left my own note in its place, listing everything I had taken and where I was taking it, in case that mattered to her.

I put my haul in the top of the blue tote and took it all up one last floor where I found Jennifer and Hannah together on the bed in Hannah's room, talking.

"Check it out!" I stated proudly, placing the tote on the bed. "I didn't think they'd get this so quickly but *damn* those boys are good!"

Jennifer noticed the contents of the box, and her eyes widened, and her jaw dropped before forming a beaming smile.

I gently took Hannah's hand and ran her fingers over the tiny bumps on one cover, and she slowly repeated what she had read with her touch.

"Run," she stated, loud, slow, and clear, "by Rich Restucci. These are books? It's a CD, an audiobook?"

"A whole tote of them!" I grabbed her with one arm in a hug, not even thinking with my excitement, and she shied away at the quick grasp but then embraced it for a moment.

I also showed her the CD player and MP3, unsure of how to help her work them, but she assured us she would figure it out and thanked me again.

This, I thought, *this is one of those moments that makes surviving worth it.*

No, I couldn't reach into the past and bring her parents back. I couldn't undo the horrible things that had been done to this girl already, but I could make her here and now the best I could. And I could do my level best to shield this young girl from any more wrongdoings in the future. And, I tell ya, to see that smile on her face? Like seeing a happy child at Christmas time. It made it work, somehow. A bit of paradise in Hell.

I left Jennifer and Hannah again, but this time I didn't go far. Just to the next room, where Gwen played, home with mommy today since mommy was here for our new friend.

"What're you doing, turd?" I asked her, cheerfully.

"Nothing, dork!" she returned in toddler. She still wasn't fluent in English, but these days it seemed like she was advancing daily, at an astonishing rate for someone her age.

"Got your blocks again, huh?"

"Yeahhh, got blocks," she confirmed, holding one in front of my face.

"That's very nice, baby," I agreed. You always agree that it's a nice block with a young one, no matter how many tooth marks are in the damn thing.

"Love you daddy," she spoke in her endearing tongue.

"Aww, love you too baby," I returned and squeezed her in a big hug.

Just then the radio broke our moment to inform all that there had been injured. I urged Jennifer to get out of the apartment, I'd stay with the girls, as she was more medically useful than I.

"Okay, I'll let you know how bad," she said before kissing me and rushing out the door.

I led Hannah and Gwen to the couch in the living room so I could watch the windows. Hannah followed, her new audiobook already playing in one ear, the other left free so she could use her most important sense. I had a feeling she'd never leave herself totally unguarded after what she'd been through.

Gwen took out a pad and retrieved several crayons and began scribbling at my feet on the floor.

While I watched the rain come down, Hannah curled up against the opposite end of the couch, engrossed in her new story. Her pale grey eyes looked out over the balcony into the weather, despite not seeing a bit of it.

The radio came to life again; it was Jennifer informing me that she was coming back up, it was a work incident and not completely severe. Head injury from falling sheets of plywood, just some stitches.

I had fallen asleep before I heard any more of it.

A burst of full-auto gunfire shook me awake. From inside the compound, no less.

"What the fuck?" I exclaimed, jumping up before my eyes could even focus. "What the fuck was that?"

I looked out of the sliding glass door in front of me and over the balcony but could see nothing.

"Anyone got a location on those shots?" I barked into my radio, forgetting the customary 'over'.

"It's us boss, it's cool! Over," came a gravelly response. Rich. The little shit. What was he thinking?

"Are you in your bunker? Over," I replied hastily.

"Ah, yup, one minute I will be. Over," he replied casually.

"I'm going to go choke that fucking leprechaun," I said to whomever was around, then turned to see Jennifer, Gwen, and Hannah staring at me wide-eyed.

"He, uh, well, you were asleep," Jennifer explained, "but Rich did announce on the open channel that he was going to be firing a burst before dinner."

I immediately felt foolish.

"A burst from what?" I asked.

"Don't know." She shrugged in return.

"Well, maybe I won't kill him, but I'm still going down there," I said before checking to make sure my pistol was still on my thigh and grabbing my rifle to sling it over my shoulder on the way out the door.

I pushed my way through the door of Rich's armory and right up to the door by the counter. I tried it, and of course, it was locked.

"Try it now mate," came Ash's voice from the other side as the door popped open a crack. I opened it and proceeded through.

"What the fuck, man? Scared the shit out of me," I informed Rich, who only grinned. "I was asleep when you put the call out."

"It's not 100%," he began, "and I've got Henry making a rolling, swiveling mount for it, but take a look. Its timing is off, I only managed a short burst before it stopped on its own, but we should have it working good before the end of tomorrow."

"I almost forgot about this, honestly," I confessed. "The 240."

"M240E1," Ash corrected. "She's a beaut. A real machine gun, haven't seen something like this since my time in the service."

"I've never seen one in person," I admitted.

"Thought you Americans were-" he started, but I cut him off quickly.

"You thought we were all gun freaks and had RPGs just sitting in our living rooms?" I shot. "Yeah, I know. But reality is a long way from our world perception. Over half the people in this compound had never even seen a gun before the end."

"Sorry, I didn't mean offense," Ash relented.

"It's okay. I get grumpy when I first wake up sometimes," I replied in excuse. "Anyway, you said a rolling, pivoting something for it? Wouldn't it be simpler to mount it in the bed of a truck, like a technical?"

"It would," Rich observed, "but I was thinking of like a house."

"A house?" I questioned.

"Yeah, like, mount it on the second floor of one by the main gates," he explained. "That way it can just be rolled from window to window and shot wherever."

"I like it," I admitted, "but what about the main building?"

"You mean here?" Ash and Rich asked, nearly in unison.

"Yeah," I answered and pointed vaguely upwards. "Right up on the east end of the ninth floor, the conference room. Run the track on the balcony, cover it from the weather. Be a good ace-in-the-hole for if there's ever big trouble and we get pushed back to the inner compound. Gate's right there, too."

"By big trouble," Ash began, "you mean the Colonel?"

"Yup," I replied.

"Not bad, actually," Rich agreed. "We retreat, he thinks he's got us on the run, we show him our cool new toy."

"Get on it in the morning," I instructed. "It's dinner time."

I left Rich's bunker without much further back and forth and looked up into the still-drizzling rain to see the rooftop lit up. A lazy haze of smoke encircled the top of the building, given life by the flickering torches and likely small rooftop bonfires we used to light the space. So, this became my destination, and upwards I marched to the top, across the ninth floor, and then up to the rooftop.

Here, I was greeted with what seemed to be a sea of people. Every seat had been taken, save for a few around my table. People were standing everywhere, and around the small fires in the cooling night air. But there was another thing that struck me as odd and explained why everyone had shown up. The smell.

I could smell *fish*. Okay, well, to say I could smell it was an understatement, the aroma was so heavy in the air that you could damn near walk through it. And there was more; the smoke hanging above the rooftop gathering spot smelled of onion, and garlic, and so many other things I couldn't even begin to tell where to begin the rest of my description.

"Scott!" called Bri, excitedly. "Go! Sit! I'll bring you a plate!"

I complied, and pulled up a seat at what I still considered to be the 'main' table, and before I had even gotten properly scooted in and seated by my family, Bri had returned with a plate for me and set it on the table with a smile.

"I wasn't hallucinating," I noted. "This is real fish. Where did all of it come from?"

"Fresh protein is essential," she explained. "So some of our boys have spent the last two days on the river with nets! Another team found a house with a pretty sizeable cellar and brought back tons of canned veggies in those glass mason jars."

"How'd they keep the fish fresh for two days until they caught enough?" I asked.

"Said they had waypoints or something," she said. "Some kind of floating totes on the river where they'd put fish they caught so they could stay in the water and alive until they came back through."

"Nice!" I agreed and began to check out the fish and vegetables with my fork.

"It's a few different kinds, we all got a little of each," she continued. "They said pike, bass, something called a steelhead? I don't know. But it's super good!"

"Yeah, steelhead's great," I confirmed and began shoveling bits of food into my mouth as Bri left to go join Dave.

After most of my plate had been cleared, and my wife, daughter, and our new friend broke into conversation for a while, I sat back, brushed off my chest and face, and rang my fork against my drink glass.

I'll be damned, it worked! The entire rooftop went quiet and turned in my direction.

"No worries, everyone," I said, feeling instantly uneasy as I had so many eyes on me, "I'm not giving a speech. I need my department heads for a moment, plus Fred, Frank, and Parker."

Most of the dinner party went back to their food, though heads started popping up here and there as those that were called up to my table made their way over. I held my words until all were present.

"Rich, Ash, Henry," I called, though mostly a formality, as they were already right there, "You three have a machine gun project to work on. I want it up and working ASAP, as I don't know when or how we'll see the Colonel again, or what he's going to do."

All three men spoke in the affirmative and went back to their respective seats and tables.

"Tony, Dave, and Frank," I continued, "I want to know about the Colonel. Where he's operating from, how many people and how much equipment. Just like we did for the gang bangers. But, being military, keep your distance. If he's got guards a mile from wherever he is, stay on this side of them. Don't endanger yourselves."

"What if we're spotted?" Tony asked.

"Return fire only, and run south, then find the river and come back up the opposite side of it," I instructed. "Whatever you do, don't get yourselves killed, and do NOT let him know you're from here. With a little luck, if you get found out, he might just think you're nosy scavengers."

"What if we get caught though, boss?" Frank broke in. "Like, what if running doesn't work?"

"I have had you all implanted with cyanide capsules in your teeth," I advised, and watched as Dave grinned, and Frank took a visible step back. "I'm kidding, and I can't believe you even considered that, Frank."

I could see Clara, his wife, at the nearby table watching and snickering. Frank was a good man, but we didn't much credit him for having a big brain.

"Look," I continued on, "we don't have much for backup plans. So just don't get caught. And if you do, figure out an exit strategy. The whole world is just kind of playing things by ear, so we'll do as the Romans."

"Rome fell," Tony said flatly.

"Yeah," I agreed, "but it lasted a hell of a long time and did many great things before that."

"This is true," Tony confirmed. "So, what are we taking?"

"Your time, first and foremost," I ordered. "But also, one of the hybrids. No noise, room for your packs. You're pure recon, no scavenging unless it's worth it. Take a scout pack from the command room, cameras, batteries, et cetera. You three know the drill by now. Finish dinner and get some rest."

"Sounds good" Dave concurred.

"I suggest, by the way," I began anew, "locate their general vicinity during the day, rest through the afternoon, relocate them at night, and do your recon the best you can from the darkness. And always, always, always, watch out for the infected. Be safe, guys."

"Always." Tony grinned as the three of them left together, likely to go plan, or whatever it was that they did.

"Rob, Ryan, Bri, and Carolyn," I started back, "you four don't really leave, and I'm not asking you to, but keep the best eye out that you can."

They concurred and departed as well.

"Okay. The rest of you," I began, my tone dropping and the conversation being heavier than it already was, "get some rest. And round up two teams of five. I need two trailer trucks, and one hooked with our longest trailer. We're going to get some pets and supplies tomorrow morning."

"Pets?" Parker interjected.

"Livestock, my boy," I grinned. "I want to find where they are, and maybe another trailer, but if we have to lead them all back on foot and by hand tomorrow, we will. Cattle, pigs, goats, sheep, chickens, whatever we can, and as many as we can."

"I like that." Fred nodded.

"We'll need a lot of shit," Cody suggested, having come with the others.

"Like?" I asked in return.

"Food for the animals. Bedding. Room to roam," he started listing things off, his head cocked to the side as if he were thinking. "I mean, you can bring back every animal on the planet, but that's work. And a lot of maintenance."

"And we've got people passing the days away for a single meal's worth of fish, Mr. Freeze," I reminded him. "It's too late to plant and we could scavenge our hands and feet raw and not find enough to sustain this growing population until after the snow is gone. We need better options."

"I agree," he began again, "but it's not going to be easy. Then again, it makes sense, nothing's easy anymore. Okay, I'm in."

"We'll take a third truck then," I opined. "A third truck and a trailer. You seem to know what you're looking for, and Fred wears a cowboy hat so he's going to help your end of things. Any of this bedding, hay, feed, whatever you can find, get it and trailer it."

Cody and Fred both agreed and started talking among themselves while Jennifer eyed me.

"No, woman," I interjected before she could even begin. "You did great, but east of here is a big unknown and besides, you have a Hannah to help now."

"Oh!" Hannah nearly choked as she swallowed her water.

"He'll have someone to keep his ass in line anyway," Clara stated as she sidled her way up to the table. "I'm in."

"You're supposed to be taking it easy though," I reminded her. "Plus, with Frank out there, there's nobody to watch your kids in the evenings."

"There's plenty of people; they can stay with the Robinsons," she offered, and, forgetting who the Robinsons were, I neglected to argue. "Plus, cupcake, how long am I supposed to take it easy for? I need to get back into it."

"I'll see you before dawn at the motor pool, then," I relented. "Dress warm."

She nodded and smiled as she turned to head back to her seat.

We turned the conversation with the remaining members around my table to sustainability.

The world had ended, so far as any of us knew, and as had become apparent basically every single day, things we needed were in finite supply. Shelter, the number one thing needed, was handled. That was no biggie. Security? Eh, we were doing pretty well. In our immediate vicinity, the infected had largely became a non-issue. Scavenging runs allowed us to see that the world still wanted to eat or kill us, but mostly, especially for those who never had a reason to leave, it seemed lonelier here, more than anything else.

But everything else was a concern. There was the winter season coming up, and, sure, Henry's furnaces could help a lot but what about when it got really cold? How much could they help then?

Then there was food, medical supplies, even basic entertainment. We needed all three, in a sense, to keep morale as high as possible or there'd be even more issues. Bri was constantly commenting about how things were being reported missing from here or there. Shannon, Ashley, and Jennifer had a never-ending list of supplies they needed as well.

The armory, Rich's mad scientist lab, whatever it be called, as well as Tony. They both had their own constant grocery lists of what they needed.

None of it ever ended. And compounding the original threat of all the infected, we had every type of human you could think of at the end of the world. Some were just needy, alone, and needing a place to stay. Others were flat-out raiders on one level or another.

And the government. Or military. Militia? Whatever the hell they actually were, were a major concern now. The infected had shown us repeatedly that even their biggest and best couldn't pass our walls, and our moat. But those that craved flesh and bled from their tear ducts couldn't shoot at you.

The infected themselves. Aside from the obvious, their physical threat to our well-being, none of us still had any idea where they came from, what started it all, or how it spread, and so quickly at that.

All of this thinking was beginning to make my head spin, so I excused myself while the others carried on. Before I knew it, I was down in our apartment, then, out on the balcony with one of the few actual cigars I still had. A stale, dried-out Perdomo, but it was still my little heaven on Earth.

The commotion carried on from the rooftop above me, then eventually died down little by little as people left for bed, or their own evening vices. Eventually, it had not only died out, but all three of my own roommates, the girls, had come by to wish me a goodnight and go to bed themselves.

I should have gone, but my mind was just so littered with thoughts that all seemed pertinent, and coupled with my earlier nap, I just wasn't ready for sleep. Not just yet.

NINE

"Scott?" came the far away voice.

I mumbled, not even sure myself what my reply was.

"Hey, you okay?" a shake on my shoulder.

Damn it was cold. Where am I?

"You fall asleep out here?" It was Jennifer, so there's two mysteries solved.

I began a stretch, and nearly rolled out of the lawn chair I had apparently fallen asleep in, on our ninth floor balcony.

How long had I been out here? Out cold, in the cold, my lower face and beard tucked into my flannel jacket.

"What time is it?" I asked as Jennifer leaned in to give me a quick kiss.

"Time for you to go," she replied, smiling and handing me a thermos.

"What's this? You're kicking me out?" I jested. "I paid up until Tuesday, you can't do this!"

"Funny," she retorted, "I haven't seen your wallet in months, where did you get the money?"

"Right next to the toilet paper, it's worth the same these days," I chuckled, then held up the thermos. "Coffee or soup?"

"Couldn't coffee be a soup?" she asked coyly.

"Nah, more of a broth, I think," I suggested.

"Well either way you've got people waiting for you down below," she reminded. "Three trucks full of them, something about cows and feed?"

"Shit," I stated flatly.

"I've got a three-day bag packed for you," she informed. "Your rifle and favorite pistols are next to it on the table."

"Okay, love you," I said as I stood to give her a hug and a kiss goodbye.

"You better be damn careful," she started as she followed me back inside.

"I will, I promise," I told her as I wormed my way into the sling for my MK18.

"I know you will," she continued, "but I worry so much."

"Hey," I reassured, "we've been through the worst the apocalypse had to offer and we're still here, right?"

"Daddy bye bye?" Gwen asked from her seat at the table, a granola bar in one hand.

"Yeah, I'm leaving, kid," I answered as I picked up my Smith and Wesson 6906 from the table and clasped the drop-leg holster into place.

"You're going out there?" Hannah asked, the nerves showing in her face as she considered it.

"Wouldn't send my people out if I wouldn't hun," I explained, looking for the second pistol and finding it already secured into the chest rig leaning against my bag. I picked it up and inspected it. A Sig Sauer P226 Legion. It definitely was one of my favorites, and, whether she picked it by mistake or design, chambered in the same 9mm as my S&W. Less variety of ammo to carry made things nice. I only needed to worry about 9mm, and the .300Blackout for my rifle.

Gwen came over and wrapped her little arms around my leg and I placed a hand on her back, leaning down to kiss her on top of her head, momentarily enjoying the softness that was my little girl's bright blonde hair.

"Well, like Jennifer said," Hannah continued, "be careful. Now you've got three of us to worry about you."

"Keep talking like that," I joked, "and I'll adopt you. And we're weird."

"I can deal with weird," she corrected.

I began putting my chest rig on, realizing the mistake of slinging my rifle first, and removing that for the other. In a moment, I was suited up, opting to put my flannel on over the whole carrier and rig setup, then connecting the buttons only up high enough to secure my jacket from flapping, but leaving my pistol and spare magazines relatively accessible.

"You don't know Pfeiffer weird, kid." I smiled broadly and hugged her from beside where she sat. She tensed for just a moment before realizing and returning the gesture.

As Jennifer watched, I shouldered the heavy three-day assault pack, then slung my rifle back into place, allowing it to drop into place with the three-point sling. Finally, I secured my radio under my jacket and moved the earpiece into my left ear. Clicking it on, it immediately filled with chatter.

"On my way up to get him now, over," came an unfamiliar voice.

"No need, on my way down now. Over," I spoke into it, then, to the girls around the dining table, "Guess that's my cue! Love ya!"

Jennifer and little Gwen both returned the phrase, Hannah's mouth dropped open to speak, then closed just as quickly. I didn't think much of it as I closed the door behind me and turned into the hallway.

As usual, I drifted into thought, only to be minutely interrupted as Ryan stuck his head out of the command room door and called after me.

"Had no contacts all night," he informed, "and every road in our vicinity is mostly clear."

"Mostly?" I asked as I continued walking, mildly hurrying.

"Few infected popping up, nothing big or unusual," he advised.

As I had already passed and mostly cleared the hallway's length, I just replied with a thumbs-up over my shoulder, then closed it into a fist as I turned and burst through the doorway to the stairwell.

It had become so normal these days that I had to actually think to recognize how alien everything was.

I left a fairly typical family scene, for the most part. A family of three and a roommate, Dad getting ready to leave for work early. The rest of them gathered around the table for a simple breakfast. Normal, if you can ignore the patriarch strapping on a loaded plate carrier and three firearms, I guess.

Then I immediately leave my door and become 'Boss', being updated before I could even leave my own home building. Moments away from breaking shelter for a crisp, cool morning where we would go out into the world to take someone else's likely free-roaming cattle and possibly have to shoot at humans and monsters alike.

Who was it that first said, 'What a world we live in'? I'd like to shake the guy around a bit at this point, he had no idea what I wouldn't give to go back to how things were.

I cut the end of a stale cigar as I exited the stairwell to the first floor, pausing to light it in the doorway before leaving through the main doors.

"Ladies and gentlemen," Clara's voice chimed through my earpiece, "Elvis has left the building. Over."

"Can't be," came Fred's smooth country voice in reply, "Elvis was a handsome fella. What is *that*? Over."

"I'm armed," I warned, "and I haven't even cracked my thermos yet. Over."

"Shutting up. Over!" Clara chirped in reply.

I chuckled as I neared the ramp down into Henry's parking garage. The air was instantly heavy with humidity, as we had been getting a steady drizzle until late the previous day and the ventilation in the garage hadn't been turned on in months.

I nodded to a nearby group of mixed individuals, all equally as well-equipped as I, but with a bigger variety of weapons than any gun shop I had ever entered. And as I passed, they fell in behind me and began walking toward the short row of three large pickup trucks, two trailered, one empty.

I opened the door to the truck without a trailer and got in to find Clara, Fred, and Parker all waiting. Without a word nor ceremony, I got in and turned the key, waiting a moment for the diesel's glow plugs to cycle, then started the pickup.

I blasted the horn twice and began to pull up the ramp and back to ground-level as the other trucks fell in behind me, people rushing to mount up before we moved too far. I felt a few thuds and rocking on my own vehicle, checking my mirror to see four people pile into the bed of my own truck, the usual array of survivors that had flooded our originally miniscule population.

"You may very well have the largest standing army in the state," Clara joked, reading my thoughts.

"Doesn't matter if we don't know where we're going though," I replied, then pulled the truck past Rich's armory, and stopped just short of the inner gate at the end of the driveway.

"What's up boss?" buzzed the radio. "Problems with that Chevy already? Over."

"Just getting our heading, smartass," I called back lightly, "Over."

"Looks like we hit the outer gate east," Clara started, presenting a local map and tracing a line with her finger. "Then head due north to the avenue, follow it east, then we cross over here, and finally here. After this pretty much any east and west road that direction leads straight into the countryside."

"Find any good farms out there?" I asked her. "Anywhere to start a search?"

"Your guess is as good as mine," she said flatly. "I'm from the suburbs too. So, no, but don't farmers always have to fix fences?"

"What are you saying?" I asked, curious.

"Like, I don't know," She resigned. "You always hear about farmers mending fences and shit, so don't the animals break them sometimes?"

"You're saying," I suggested, "that even if we knew where a cow farm or whatever is, they could just be running around all willy-nilly like?"

"You fuckin' city idiots," Fred chimed in from the back.

"What the hell?" I said, turning in my seat to view his big toothy grin.

"Don't worry about it," he said, tilting his hat, "just drive. Y'all are half-right, they'll be there. But I do have to say, cows don't 'run around all willy-nilly'."

"Shut up Fred," I laughed. "Nobody likes backseat drivers."

"You'll like me," he said assuredly, "when it's a cattle drive."

"Fucker," I muttered and put the truck into gear as the inner gate took note and began opening.

As Clara said, I drove straight through the outer ring of our compound, and toward the eastern gate.

As I passed, I took note of just how much we had stripped so far. Much of the surrounding neighborhood was bare, with large squares of land where some houses used to be, already covered with hay and seemingly settled in for the winter; hopefully these lots would have crops growing in them after the cold weather.

The yards were nearly entirely empty, too. Almost all of the fencing around had been scavenged to bolster and thicken the outer wall. Henry had been convinced that even a tank would have a hard time penetrating them, especially with the dirt piled behind said walls from digging the tremendous dry-moat.

We approached the outer gate and slowed the truck, then stopped it as the gate on our side of the bridge over the moat opened. At this time, my driver's window got knocked on.

"Cody?" I interrogated as I rolled the window down. "You're supposed to be on another truck."

"I'm riding with you," he explained, "how else can I help look for places you need to check? You'd be past them before I could say anything if I was following you."

I rolled my eyes, shut the window, and waited just a moment before clicking the button to unlock the doors. Just long enough to make him think, maybe wonder.

The rear door swung open and the truck rocked a bit as the large man eased himself into the seat, squishing Parker between him and Fred. They looked at each other, and both cowboy hats nodded. This was going to be interesting.

As Cody eased into position, the gate finished opening and we pulled our truck through to wait for the inner gate to close and the outer to open. Once the outer had opened, we pulled across the gap and turned left, pulling up far enough to wait for the other two rigs.

The guys filling out the backseat spoke quietly amongst themselves as Clara retraced our route over and over again, her lips moving silently as she did so. She pushed her shoulder-length auburn hair behind her ears, the lighter color coming back in over time as it grew and she cut it, clearly having been dyed previously. She wasn't a bad looking woman, her angular features and deep-set eyes lending her an almost Eastern-European look if I had to guess. I still didn't know her age for sure, but I guessed late-thirties at most, despite the recent stress and conditions making us all appear older, wiser, and more worn than any of our years should have allowed.

"Boss?" Clara asked as I stared into the distance. "They're ready."

"Yeah, of course," I agreed blindly, and put my truck into drive and pulled away, the other two teams following me.

We hit the nearest main road above us on the map and took a right to head due East.

Most of the area around our compound had been cleaned and cleared, and every other day a crew went out that had no purpose other than freeing up the roadways, so it wasn't until maybe a half-mile from our little home that we ran into a few snags. Some spots were tight enough that while a truck could squeeze through, the slightly-wider trailers scraped. Every time we would cringe, wondering if the noise would attract runners, and therefore we kept the pace fairly brisk despite the dangers.

Occasionally, we would come across a totally blocked intersection, or, less frequently, an impassible roadway. It was always handled the same way.

The two trucks behind us would back up a ways just in case it was an ambush so our lead vehicle wouldn't be totally surrounded. While they did that, Clara would get out and attach the tow rope to the offending obstacle, and I would put the little Chevy Duramax diesel to work.

We'd found some clusters of infected, but they would be taken care of quietly and systematically. Several of the survivors manning the crews had small-caliber rifles and pistols that were fitted with oil filters using adapters for use as suppressors. Another of Rich and Ash's ideas, and, while not quite as effective as an actual suppressor, they did work quite well. For at least a limited amount of shots they seemed to quiet anything up to a 9mm down to not much more than a loud *clap*. Any advantage we could get, I was happy for.

The short line of trucks continued on mostly unhindered, all things considered. I had expected it to be a never ending stoppage of clearing traffic and debris. Thankfully, aside from the aforementioned, it had gone easier than expected.

As we traveled, the houses became further spaced apart. The trip eastward seemed to stretch the properties themselves, as if traveling across a black hole in space.

The weather even seemed to accent this, as we traversed more roadway, the morning transitioned from overcast, to mostly cloudy, and now even the clouds seemed to space themselves out more, almost as if echoing the property lines.

This isn't to say that we'd run out of the infected in these lower population areas. Everywhere you looked, you could catch sign or trail of them. Sometimes they could be seen openly wandering through overgrown lawns, or in stands of trees.

Other times, and much more unsettling, was the signs of a kill. Usually, not much more than a blood trail streaked up a driveway and into a home or other structure. Too fresh for the rain to have washed away, and a stark reminder that these things were still eating. Still thriving.

And something else. Something I wasn't quite sure if anyone had noticed, and I tried to make a mental note to bring it up in future meetings. The infected weren't just killing and eating in the open. Even out here, in the rural areas, they were carrying or even dragging their meals away. Were they merely hiding? Covering their tracks, even? Or could there be dens?

I dared not to let my mind dwell for too long on that last thought.

"I have to use the restroom," Parker spoke up from the back, which instantly sparked chuckles from the rest of us. The kid wasn't a child, though still in his teens or so. But he sure acted like one more often than not.

"Number one or number two?" I jousted.

"I have to pee," he nearly mumbled.

"I'm not stopping," I warned him.

"Use my spit jug," Cody offered him, offering the jug full of brown spit and tobacco to him. This set Fred and Clara into a fit of laughter as Parker visibly revulsed at the idea.

"Kid," I spoke, "we aren't stopping this truck until we get to grandma and grandpa's for Christmas dinner. We don't want to be late now, do we?"

"I really have to go," Parker said amongst even harder laughter from the others.

"Here," I said as I hit the switch to roll down his window. "Stick your body out and pee. Just, uh, point it behind us. Don't pee into the wind."

More of an uproar ripped through the truck as he sat irritated, lowering his head to look at the floor.

"Scott!" Clara shouted suddenly. "Brakes!"

I saw it just as she had and flattened my foot down on the pedal. I could feel it pulsing back against the arch of my foot as the ABS system took over.

Shouts of protest rang through the cabin as we stopped just short of the new blockage.

Before a single thought could gather, we were all rocked by a heavy *WHAM* as the truck behind us didn't stop nearly as quickly, making fast friends with our tailgate. Another, softer impact shook its way through the truck as the third vehicle hit the second truck's trailer, forcing them to give us a nearly motherly second tap on the rear.

"What the fuck?" I exclaimed, then grabbed my radio. "Everyone okay? Over."

The calls came back with nothing more than bumps and scratches, mostly from those riding in truck beds.

"Tail truck, back up twenty yards to the crest of the hill," I continued. "Then everybody dismounts. Over."

I waited a moment for the third truck to back up, pull forward to straighten its trailer, then take three more tries to back the distance before the driver finally got it right and was able to cross the distance to the top hill, then the truck behind us removed its front bumper from our tailgate and eased back one truck length.

As I reached for my door handle, the others did so as well, and we all left the truck, save for the guys in the bed who remained to provide cover from an elevated position.

"Log," I stated, rounding the front of the truck to look at the obstacle in our path.

"More like a whole fucking tree," Clara opined, eyeing it as well.

"This is a trap," I stated flatly, removing my eyes from the obstruction and scanning our surroundings.

We were right by the edge of what appeared to be a grass field. Maybe, at some point, it held crops of one sort or another, but by now it was thick vegetation every bit as tall as I was. To our left lay the field, with woodland preceding it; on the left was a solid patch of woodland the entire length of the hill.

"I don't like this," Clara said, the tension strong in her voice.

"Yeah," I agreed, "me either. And look at this."

I brought my rifle up to a low-ready position and motioned with my free hand. In several places, what looked nearly like deer trails had been cut into the overgrowth. Narrow footpaths here and there leading off of the roadway.

"First team," I said quietly to those around me, "get one end of this log and start pushing. Spin it and roll it off the road. I don't want to risk pushing it with the truck."

"You got it," Cody complied and motioned the others forward. They took a moment, and began pushing, moving the log only inches at a time. It had to be at least three feet thick, another fifteen in length. It had to have taken a team to move it into this position, and, looking at the cut ends, it sure didn't fall here on its own. This was definitely a trap.

"Second team," I spoke quietly into the radio, "to me. Now. Over."

They were around me in a mere moment, not really being far enough to use the radio to have called them, but it helped them all hear me at once.

"Team three, extra vigilant, boys, this is a trap we've wandered into. Over," I ordered into the radio.

"You're my lead," I spoke to the young black man I recognized as Harrison from a recent encounter with him.

"What's good, boss?" he said in return, his voice barely above a whisper.

"Nothing, that's what," I replied, then pointed out the paths through the vegetation. "This one. It looks fresher. Your whole team follows it. Quietly, and be ready to shoot. Whoever this is, they didn't do all this to invite us for dinner."

"Yes, sir." Harrison gulped audibly, then motioned to the rest and began a low crouch walk into the flora to our left. I joined my team in moving the log, all the while listening carefully for any sign of encounter from the second team.

Right about the time my team had grunted the log aside, and let it roll into the ditch with a slow, soft crash, my radio came to life. It was Harrison.

"Uh, sir? You need to see this," he suggested. "The path splits, go right at the fork for 20 paces. Over."

"Got it. Keep the channel clear," I instructed, then, "Third team, move your truck and team forward to meet the second truck and watch our asses from the roadway. Stay vigilant. We may have contacts. Over."

I listened to the affirmative reply and their truck started, a low rumble growing closer as I gathered my own people.

"Fred, is that all you brought?" I asked, motioning to his bolt-action hunting rifle.

"My backup won two World Wars," he patted the Colt 1911 on his hip. "I'll be just fine."

"Your backup," I growled, "is known worldwide for being pretty until it jams, and only carries eight rounds. Stay here."

I turned and approached the front door of our truck as the third team moved theirs into position and cut the ignition again.

Reaching into the floorspace of the front seat, I retrieved the rifle that lay there, grabbed the three spare magazines from the center console, and departed the vehicle again.

Approaching my friends again, I dropped out and checked the magazine for the rifle. Then, I rocked it back into position and chambered a round.

"An AK-47?" Fred nearly cringed. "Damn commie rifle if there ever was one."

"WASR-10," I corrected. "And while it's only semi-auto, it has more rounds in one magazine than both of your guns together, and you're going to use it. It works, and it works every time. Unlike those relics from the First World War that you carry."

Fred accepted the rifle hesitantly, and put the spare magazines wherever he could; one in his back pocket, the other two in his waistband at the small of his back.

I motioned to the other team to be ready and turned to speak to the rest in a hushed voice.

"Clara behind me, Parker, then Fred, then Cody," I instructed. "You other three, watch our backs."

I felt bad that I didn't even know the names of those with us, but I tried not to let it show as I hunched my back and crouched my knees to disappear into the underbrush along the path.

As we moved, carefully, quietly so as not to disturb much and make a scene, the vegetation thickened.

The path was narrow, and as we got farther in it seemed to reach from both sides to tickle faces and snag pant legs. Even this late in the season, into fall, it still held much of its green hue and more than enough leaf material. By the time we were ten whole yards into the mess, we couldn't even see the road we had left.

As we moved, my nose picked up another marker. The earthy scents of the outdoors carried a darker note with it. A note of copper. And rot. And what smelled like raw feces for a nice finish to every breath inhaled.

Another twenty-five paces, had we been walking normally, and we hit a splitting of the trail. As informed, I motioned and we took the trail leading to the right, which was much wider than that which we had just traversed.

The trail was much shorter, and as it began to open up even more, I took note of our other guys standing guard in a clearing.

I stood and sped up my approach, the rest of my group hot on my heels until we reached the clearing.

I don't recall what I was expecting, but I know what we found wasn't it.

The clearing was perhaps a dozen yards across and littered with several small tents around the outer ring, and a modest fire pit in the center. The fire had long gone, though there was still a barely noticeable wisp of smoke rising only a few inches from the center before disappearing into the atmosphere.

"Check the tents already?" I asked quietly.

"Yes sir," Harrison responded. "No good."

"No good?" I asked, approaching one tent and moving the hanging flap aside with the barrel of my MK18.

The smell that leapt out of the small space was that of rancid copper and soggy spoiled meat. I was assaulted so by the smell itself that I took a step back and nearly fired my rifle into the space. Yeah, it was *that* potent, the weatherproof tent material having not let any of it out in who knows how long.

"I warned you," Harrison said, and I could see the unease stapled across his features. "No bodies, just gross."

"No bodies?" I answered, speculating.

I stepped to the next tent in line, this time holding my nose pinched shut.

Sticking the barrel of my rifle in and moving the flap aside, much as before, revulsion struck me again. I didn't recoil, I didn't move, I stayed glued into one place.

A mass of gore that scarcely even resembled a human being lay to one side of the space, blackened and rotting flesh holding foundation to only a few rib bones and a pelvis, the rest of the mess either gone, or hidden deeper within the sleeping bag.

Alongside this, was the remains of a German Shepherd. The type of dog was easy, as the remains were little more than a head leading a length of spine, still in place with what little viscera remained, piled behind the teeth and lolling tongue like a bucket of muddy concrete had been dumped and painted red.

I caught sight of a gunstock visible right next to the tent entrance and reached in to pull it out. An old pump-action Mossberg produced from within the confines of the tent, attached by webbing to a medium hiking pack.

"Search this," I instructed, handing it to the early-twenties girl that had come in with Harrison. She took the pack and just kind of looked at me, unsure, so I repeated myself hastily, "Put the fucking bag, on the fucking ground, and search it."

She began frantically digging through the bag as we scanned the rest of the area.

"Did you check the other tents?" Clara asked Harrison, and he nodded.

"Some are a mess like the others, but no bodies or remains," he informed us, his hushed voice sounding twig-dry.

I began scanning the ground around the tents he motioned to and found a plethora of prints. This place had been heavily used, and the witness markings of foot traffic showed as much.

"Look here," I whispered, pointing to a trail along the ground, disappearing into the thick grasses and plants. Thick, crimson smears highlighted by deep drag marks. I pointed the drag marks out to Fred.

"Fingers," he said, deep in thought as he examined them. "Somebody was dragged from these tents. More than a single somebody, too."

He motioned to more nearby marks and streaks of blood, also all disappearing into the brush.

"This bothers me," Clara chimed in, already hoisting her AR-15 to the ready and scanning around. "It's been raining. These marks should have been erased if they were anything but recent."

As if to accent her statement, the brush on the far side of the clearing coughed.

Okay, the brush didn't cough, but something *in* the brush coughed, and all of our weapons pointed at that side of the campsite as a torrent of viscous red and black fluid shot forth from the strands of grass, covering the girl with the backpack as she crouched over it. Her scream may be something that will haunt me the rest of my life, and it continued on as she toppled over onto her back.

"CONTACT!" I bellowed as the entire edge of the clearing burst to life, the first visible runner shrieking that godawful tone as it hit Parker like a cop tackling a criminal before carrying on with the momentum and disappearing from sight carrying our friend. The beast moved so fast in the small open area we couldn't even get a shot on him.

Parker's screams carried deeper into the field as we lobbed shots into the parted grass he and his assailant disappeared into.

The backpack girl, covered in freak vomit, continued to lay on her back screaming as she writhed like a tipped turtle, her arms beginning to convulse as her hands twisted like those of an arthritic carpenter.

The cacophony of weapons fire and shouts drowned out all intelligible thought as I picked moving grasses and fired.

Another running infected burst through the barrier into visibility as she screeched her long war cry. Several of us must have already been focused in that area as she took several rifle rounds to the upper body and face, twisting her body to and fro as her run broke into a stumble. She hit the ground face-first, the earth nearly writhing under her with the puddle of projectile vomit that was meant for one of the men. She finished her dance when Cody pulled out his heavy S&W .500 revolver and launched a veritable cannon shell into the back of her head.

I screamed, "FALL BACK! *FALL THE FUCK BACK*!" but my words were lost among all the commotion. So many voices and screams at once, and the gunfire, it was like trying to pick a conversation out of a crowded club on Friday. I grabbed for my radio and tried again.

"EVERYBODY FALL BACK! ONE GROUP TOGETHER, MOVE AND SHOOT!" then continued, "Team three! Start the trucks, burn the left field, FUCKING MOVE! OVER!"

Cody lifted his FN FAL rifle from its drop on the three-point sling and started casting heavy 7.62 rounds into the brush, sweeping through a full magazine before stuffing the empty back into his chest rig and slamming a new one home.

"RUN!" I shouted into my radio again as I paused just long enough in my shooting to witness several growing clouds of smoke reaching lazily into the sky near the roadway, the scent of burning gasoline and diesel reaching my nostrils.

"RUN FASTER!" I reiterated, realizing the fire could also eliminate our escape route before we even reached as far. Might have been preemptive on my part, setting the field ablaze, but I couldn't exactly take it back at this point.

I stood by, the suppressed MK18 whispering its own .30 caliber variant into anything that moved and didn't have a gun. As most of both teams broke the entrance to the clearing, the grass came to life on a scale that made the previous onslaught look like an appetizer.

Clara turned to run and tripped over a fallen infected as soon as she'd twisted, cursing and already running again before she could even fully find her feet. As she ran, and Cody's large frame followed her, I ushered them past me, leaving only a few of our own in the clearing to fire into the unknown as more runners started to explode into the space.

Most ran straight across the clearing, hitting the field on the other side in a trajectory to intercept my own people. Just as the last of us started their sprint out of Hell, I recognized a runner. Parker. He no longer wore his glasses, but I recognized him regardless, his rail-thin frame just a flash as he bolted across the open spot alongside another freak. His eyes already dilated almost full black, a trail of blood streaming from each. He shrieked. Our Parker, shrieking like the dead.

I placed a single round into the head of the backpack girl as she started her own shriek while finding her feet and she fell into a heap, the force of her fall sending runners of the remaining vomit cascading on the ground. And I ran.

I ran like never before in my life, three of our own so far up my ass they may as well have been fake fox tails. We booked it out of the clearing, down the short path, and left onto the narrower passageway out of there, the smoke from the nearby fire already rolling in and lazily covering our surroundings.

As I stepped, nearly rolling my ankle twice, I caught a flash of movement to my left side just as the movement caught me.

Even as relatively large as I am, I went from a full-bore sprint to a cartoonish flight, my legs still kicking as my body was flung by the impact of a freak. It hit me mercilessly hard, but luckily high as we sailed into the briars and other thorns alongside the pathway.

We impacted hard, nothing but needle-sharp pricks to break my fall, but the impact sent the freak just a little further than myself. I had time to watch it sail past as it grasped the air and tried to latch onto whatever it could, and before I could find my feet and get my bearings, he had found his.

I began a frantic scramble to get away as the monstrosity found solid earth and bared its teeth at me and began a second full-charge.

Just as I thought I was about to die in some shitty field in Portage County, Ohio, the freak's head erupted like a rubber-banded watermelon. The concussion of the shot was a thing of beauty, as much physical as it was visual, thudding a single huge nail deep into my chest like a bass speaker. I looked up to see Cody reaching his hand for me, his full face and heavyset figure drenched in sweat, mud, and gore as he shouted something I could not hear.

I took the offered hand and began anew, heading toward the trucks as another runner took out one of the guys that had previously been following me. Before we even got close, it had gone for his throat. Nothing we could do at that point but shoot at him too, in case he decided to start trying to eat us.

The end of the footpath closest to the road was nearly completely engulfed in flames as we rushed through it, myself for one very happy that I had no hair to singe.

The trucks lay just ahead, up a slight embankment and not a half-dozen long strides ahead. Most of the others had already mounted up as my own door and Cody's lay open and ready. The metallic arms of a favorite thing at this very moment, waiting to embrace us both with safety.

I launched myself into the gap, into the truck interior, slamming the door behind me as I went and just in time to feel the truck rock as Cody did the same. Several more shakes and shudders rocked the vehicle as several infected tried, and failed, to make the same entrance we had just done. I turned back and saw a thing even scarier than what we had just encountered. Christ, I should have never looked.

The fuel-soaked grass was soaking the runners, and even a few shamblers that had started to breach the perimeter and find the roadway. These runners burst forth through the fire, soaked in the same fuel mixture, and flames covered most of them as they made beelines straight for the trucks.

Nightmare visages of lost humanity as they quite literally blazed paths right toward us, leaving black markings wherever they impacted the vehicles. Some couldn't quite reach that far as the heat contracted and charred muscles and connective tissues. These ones would nearly close into themselves, not in pain but with involuntary muscle spasms. I wasn't so sure they felt pain.

"Take it, SHOOT!" I ordered Clara as I shoved my rifle into her grasp, immediately more willing to hear the suppressed gunfire so close to me as opposed to the monster that was her .223 with a muzzle break.

The glass of the truck exploded outward as she opened fire, the rounds taking bits of window and the attached chain link protection with them as they stitched the chest and torso of several of the flaming beasts.

The vacancy of the window now added to the grisliness of the situation as the flaming dead could be *felt* as they neared the spot.

I slammed the truck into gear and squashed the accelerator like a cockroach as the vehicle twisted sideways, belching black exhaust and white tire smoke in unison. Several more thumps and thuds shook us as I took several of the infected freaks with the bumper-mounted bull bar in our escape. I watched the truck behind us fleeing in similar fashion, and could only assume, and hope, that the third was doing the same.

"Are you okay?" Clara asked, and I nodded so she started checking the others.

"Where's Parker?" Fred grumbled as he leaned back, almost as if trying to stretch a kink out of his back.

"Gone," I said, sure I was still shouting but not much able to tell after Cody's hand-cannon.

"Gone?" Fred and Cody echoed in unison.

"Yes, gone," I gasped, still trying to regain my breath as the truck rocketed down the center of the road. "He was one of the first, they fuckin' carried him…carried him away. No chance to help."

Both men in the back groaned as they sat themselves back, also trying hard to breathe. Clara extended a hand to my shoulder for comfort as Cody began to laugh.

"What the fuck is so funny?" she shot at him.

"Dude. This is bad enough," he started, almost delirious, "but wait until Smokey the Bear hears what we did."

"You're fired, Cody," I said flatly, slowing the truck now as we had outpaced our attackers.

"Fired from what?" he asked, amused.

"Talking," I stated. "Shut the fuck up."

They all got a little laugh out of that as the mood of the truck lessened just a hair and my radio began to crackle back to life.

"Team three," the radio informed, the female voice coming in tinny yet clear, "No KIA, one wounded from friendly fire. Over."

"Solid copy," Cody drawled into his own radio set so I could drive. "Team two, status check. Over."

"Team two at fifty percent," came Harrison's youthful voice. "We lost three, one wounded. Burnt. Over."

"Team one," Cody continued, "lost two, one wounded. Treat your remaining casualties the best you can, will figure the rest out later. Over."

Both of the other teams confirmed this, and we continued on, the truck swaying slightly as I dropped my speed to maneuver around small obstacles in the road here and there.

The infected still were not absent from our area.

There was a 'thin spot', in the area surrounding our adventure. That is, a much sparser population of freaks in the immediate area, as they'd all been drawn in and burnt to this point. Our escapades seemed to dog whistle every infected around beyond that, and it quickly reinforced the intelligence of the decision to flee instead of standing ground like we lived with the ghost of General Custer. The number of faces with gaping mauls and bloodshot eyes heading in the direction of our little field burning was a bit disconcerting.

Okay, it was more than disconcerting. It was downright terrifying. Hungry monsters that couldn't feel pain and wanted to eat us moved across the landscape in droves. Clearly the dinner bell had been rung.

So, wisely we made a hasty departure and in no time at all the situation had changed again.

We were officially, fully, and totally in the countryside. The land occupied by mostly field, forest, and farm was now overshadowing the amount occupied by house and grass. Occasionally, nice homes could be seen on either side of us, only to concede their territory to more field separated from another field by small strands of trees and underbrush.

So, the number of infected freaks we were seeing made no sense. At least, not at first. The country was supposed to be so much more sparsely populated than the dense city populations, right? Then Clara hit the nail on the head. They were spreading out. Leaving the cities. The numbers were not as compacted into a single area anymore, but they were still there, nonetheless. And there was no telling how many we weren't seeing as they hid among tall grasses and unkempt this or that.

Talk was kept to a minimum, and what was said wasn't deep or thought-provoking as Clara and I watched our path ahead, and the others watched all around.

We spoke lightly of Parker. He was a good kid, and a kid was exactly what he still was. Too young to have even qualified to rent a car in many states before the big collapse, now he was likely destined to roam the countryside looking for other humans to eat. No telling if there even was any Parker left, or if it was something darker wearing a Parker suit.

"Got one," Clara observed, pointing off to our ten o'clock. "Right there."

She was right. I pulled near to the left side of the road and tapped my brakes three times to brake light signal a stop, and then slowed until we were in fact parked.

At first, I only saw a single animal. A large black steer stood alone in a smallish field fairly close to our vantage point. The creature lazily chewed on patches of grass as if the whole world had never stopped spinning. Its eyes flicked in our direction, and then right back to the task at hand. Just a passerby of the apocalypse, not concerned with the greater scope of things besides 'chew grass, swallow cud, fart, repeat'.

The animal had been surviving healthily and unmolested due to the care of another. Where once a simple cattle fence had been, the supports were bolstered and made to hold lengths of chain-link fencing. The lengths of fence appeared to be held together with a mixture of ratchet-straps and industrial zip ties. Lengths of heavy, bare copper wire snaked its way through the weave of the fencing.

"Wouldn't touch that fence," Fred cautioned, as if he noticed this at the same time as me. "Looks spicy."

"I don't know if that's the right word," I chuckled, "but I agree. Hands off."

"What do you think?" Clara asked.

"We came all this way looking for farm animals," I explained, "that right there looks like a farm animal to me. Let's find out if he belongs to anyone."

"Hey Scott?" Fred asked.

"Yeah, Fred," I replied.

"I want you to notice that this fine specimen is, in fact, not running around all willy-nilly," Fred stated completely deadpan.

"Fuck you Fred," I stated just as flatly before speaking into my radio, "All teams, fifty-yard spacing, roll slow, we're gonna follow this fence and see if the owner is around. Over."

All returned in compliance and as I started rolling, letting the truck move on its own accord, they held back. Once I was about fifty yards ahead, the second truck began lumbering forward, its trailer creaking as it was once again put in motion. Eventually, the third truck followed suit.

We followed the length of fencing for a while, taking note of the blackened lumps lying around its perimeter. Every so often, what appeared to be an infected lay burnt to a crisp just our side of the barrier. In some places, a piece of ragged clothing hung here and there. Once, an entire hand, fingers still clenching an obstacle they would never pass.

We came upon a small road branching off from the main avenue and I turned the truck left to continue following the new direction the fence took. Before long, my truck was pulled alongside a gate near a barn and a driveway leading up to a colonial-style home at the end. Before I could even unbuckle my seatbelt, a trio of men in a John Deere Gator pulled near to the gate and parked.

One of the men dismounted the small vehicle and approached the fence. He was a bear of a guy, who looked as though he'd be just as at-home in a small country bar. Easily pictured slow-drinking a beer in a motorcycle vest with a trucker cap pulled low showing more of his black beard and neck-length black hair than it showed of his face.

The other two that were with him took position on the other side of the machine and kept low, their rifles positioned pointed skyward but able to drop to the ready at a moment's notice. I instructed my people to take similar stances, remain ready, and we'd see how this goes.

I disembarked my driver's seat and approached the same as he did, stopping maybe a half-dozen paces from my side of the gate. He did the same again.

"Nice day today!" I exclaimed, then immediately cringed internally. *That* was going to be my opening line. Really?

"We ain't much in the business of meeting neighbors," the man spoke. "State your business, or get the fuck on outta here."

"Sorry," I conceded, "let's start from the beginning. We need animals. We're willing to make generous trades if need be, but winter is coming and we're going to need to keep a bunch of people fed."

"And if I say no?" he responded, no humor in his voice. "What if I wanted to keep my cattle?"

"Well," I explained, "they're yours. That's kind of your say, I'd imagine. But we can help each other."

"You're no raiders," he observed. "The last two groups tried to strongarm them. They're buried in that field behind you."

"Let's try this from the beginning," I said, approaching the gate with my hand extended. "I'm Scott. Scott Pfeiffer. I'm the head of a large compound of survivors in the Falls. I enjoy a good scotch, classic cars, and being able to eat."

"Erik Kearns," the man replied, accepting my hand in his and shaking firmly. "This is my farm."

"Has it always been, Erik?" I asked him. "Pleased to meet you, by the way."

"Not always," he admitted. "The previous owner was attacked and killed by the monsters. A big one moved into his barn, too. We cleared it all out, put up a fence, started rescuing animals. It's mine now."

"Erik," I continued, flashing my best salesman smile, "my teams are awfully exposed out here. What say we open this gate and come in and talk. I think I have an offer you may appreciate, but I don't like having our backs exposed, especially since we were just very recently engaged."

"That you?" he asked, jerking his thumb at the smoke cloud rising with authority over the distant landscape.

"I believe that was," I explained. "Investigated a human ambush the infected had overrun, got ambushed by them instead. Lost six people."

"Alright," he stated and motioned to the two with him, "but, just inside the gate. Only two of you on the porch to talk, the rest have to stay with your trucks."

"Fair enough," I beamed, but a moment later, my confidence dipped slightly.

As he turned around and motioned again, the men from behind the Gator broke cover; one spoke into his own radio, and five more in total appeared from around various equipment and pieces of cover. I had thought we had him outnumbered. He was confident because, plainly, he had one man more than us in the immediate vicinity, no telling how many more waited around, then.

The gate swung open, and I watched Clara slide over to the driver's seat and put the truck in gear. At first, she pulled straight forward, then the reverse lights illuminated, and she backed the truck in and to her left, positioning it out of the way yet close to the exit and pointing in the right direction to depart the area quickly if need be. Good girl, I thought and smiled slightly.

A moment later the other two trucks approached and after lots of direction from others, each managed to back safely into the safe area inside Erik's farm.

I motioned for Clara and instructed the others to remain with the trucks. Clara came to meet me, and we followed Erik wordlessly to his front porch where he motioned for us to sit.

"What's going on?" a woman asked as she emerged from the house. "Who are these people?"

She was thin and appeared to be in her mid-to-late twenties. Her wavy dark hair was a mess and she had clear bags underlining her equally dark eyes. She wasn't ugly, but the recent turns of our world had definitely taken its toll on her. A little girl that looked much like her mother burst out of the door yelling for her daddy and was immediately wrangled by the mom and coerced back inside.

"My wife," Erik introduced. "Name's Angela. Angela, this is Scott, we're just having a talk. Business."

Angela rolled her eyes and kept a hushed conversation with Erik as she motioned repeatedly in our direction before spinning and storming back inside the house.

"We have kids here," Erik explained as he found a seat across from us, "she's just worried about their safety, new people here and all."

"I feel it," I assured him. "We have a couple-dozen or so at our own compound. It's a challenge keeping them separated from the world. That's one way we can help you."

"How so?" he questioned, eyeing me wearily.

"We hold twenty-five-ish square blocks of Cuyahoga Falls," I detailed, "surrounded by a ten-foot dry moat and backed by a ten-foot fence reinforced with earth. It's manned, guarded with armed sentries twenty-four seven, and only accessible by water or by a double-gated security fence."

Erik's eyebrows raised slightly as if to say 'Damn, bro' and he shifted his gaze to Clara. She silently nodded and rocked her head in my direction, and I continued my spiel.

"We have two-hundred survivors, approximately," I explained. "An armory, and an open trade route to another colony nearly on the same scale as our own. I offer safety, security, and longevity."

"But mister," he began, "we've been here since the beginning. We ain't doing great, but we're not doing badly, either."

"I never said you were, Erik," I corrected, "but your numbers are small. Your wife looks damn tired from just keeping up, and I noticed your guys operated that front gate like the wires running through it didn't matter."

"Wait, what are you getting at?" Clara asked me directly.

"Does your electric fence not work anymore?" I asked Erik.

"It does," he said, his gaze dropping, "but it runs on a generator. Without a steady fuel supply, we have battery-powered sensors up. One of them goes off, we run the fence for fifteen minutes."

"I see," I said flatly. "How many of you are here? And how many animals?"

"About fifteen of us," he described. "Six kids, five are mine. Dozen heifers, a steer, handful of pigs, goats, and sheep. About fifteen chickens, too."

"You've been caring for them all your own?" I asked. "How's food and supply here?"

He confirmed that they kept a team effort, not caring just for the animals themselves but the farm in general. Supplies were typically in short supply but they did the best they could with what they had, though the lack of a populated local area made scavenging for more a big risk, especially since they didn't have the physical presence to send out regular teams or stage any long-distance runs, such as what we were on.

"Come with us," I offered, and watched the surprise break his features. "We have everything you are lacking. We have a house ready to move into but there's no heat. We could definitely offer better accommodations in one of the main buildings if you prefer."

"I don't know man," Erik replied. "I don't want to agree and find ourselves in a bad situation."

"I get it," I comforted. "But look at it this way. You've already met the guy with the final say in everything there. Me. And, if we're wrong, I'm not exactly going to risk my people to hold you there. You'd be free to leave any time you wanted. All I ask, is that you do the same as the other two-hundred or so people there and do your part."

"Which would be…?" Erik asked for clarification.

"You've done well here, that steer on the way in was healthy," I offered. "I think you'd pretty much be doing the same thing as you are here. And if you like, you and your people would definitely be a help for us city folk at assisting Cody with regular agricultural duties too."

"Well," he spoke, "I still don't know. Let me lay it all out to my wife and our friends. You can stay the night if you want. But not in the house."

"All teams," I spoke into my radio, "set up camp for the night. We're having a sleepover. Over."

"I can trust you here?" Erik questioned.

"As much as we can trust you," I warned. "This isn't our first night in the new world, dude. We aren't looking for fights we don't need. You already said yourself you've had enough raider issues as well."

"Speaking of," Erik started, "what about you? Any big troubles?"

I explained to him what had happened in the past, the group from Old Northern High School, the small parties here and there who bit off more than they could chew, and I touched as lightly as possible on the new issues with Colonel Parker.

By the time the discussion was over, the sun was beginning to drop low toward the horizon. I turned to view the large barn closer to the entrance to the property and pointed.

"Unless it's strictly forbidden," I advised, "I'd like access to the top floor of that barn for no more than three of my men at a time."

"Just hay and feed up there," he said. "Long as they don't wreck it."

I spoke more instructions into my radio. Three hour shifts for each three-person team. One at one end of the barn, one at the other, and a third person to watch the other two.

I walked back to the makeshift encampment to find the tents set up on the trailers themselves and affixed by tow straps instead of tent stakes. They had been moved to encircle a small central area with a low-burning firepit. Several of our people sat around eating jerky and other snacks from their bags, several more already lay asleep.

I settled in around the fire and kept the conversation soft between us, but we talked of nothing important. We spoke of the past and things we had done or seen, the stories broken from time to time with soft laughter from one or more of us. The flames threw dancing light all around us as we reminisced.

Every so often as we spoke of our old jobs or school days, one of us would take a low shot at Fred and the fact that he was the oldest one around, in his 40s.

After a while or so longer, we heard raised voices from the household. I placed a hand on my rifle and twisted slightly to offer my ear to that direction. It was a woman's voice, and I assumed it to be Erik's wife, Angela. The voices quieted as quickly as they escalated, and I had assumed it was over.

A beat or two later however, Erik stepped out onto the porch just barely illuminated between the candlelight in the window, and the moon overhead. Another shadow, one of the other men, appeared next to him, leaning in with a bit of aggression to his body language. They hadn't broken a rough whisper as of yet, and even when they'd start to become louder, it was broken bits of conversation at best.

I was strongly getting the impression that Erik wanted to leave, or stay, and the others weren't in agreeance. The words 'my half' got thrown around a few times loud enough to hear, as if it were being used for bargaining purposes.

I sat only a few more moments listening to the scene as best I could before relenting. The world was going nowhere and whatever they were going to decide, I'd figure out in the morning. If it was really important, they could wake me for it.

"I'm going to sleep in the truck," I informed my friends and got up to head in that direction.

"Me too," Clara agreed and got up to come with.

"Excuse me?" I said, side-eyeing her, and she laughed.

"It's a crew cab, I'm lying in the back, you can have the front," she chuckled.

"I fart and snore," I cautioned.

"So do all men," she replied, pushing me forward.

I grunted a reply and climbed into the front of the truck, pausing for a moment to pick a scrap of, well, someone, from the fencing around the windows. I reached over and flipped up the center console to present a bench seat that would double well enough as a bed. I then stripped my shirt off and balled it into a pillow and laid down without saying a word as I felt Clara shifting until she found comfort as well.

Before I could even say goodnight, or at least think to do so, I was out cold.

TEN

Morning came, and the truck was miserable. Even after waking up at some point to crack the front windows a bit, the interior was an uncomfortable combination of chilly and stuffy.

I sat up to find Clara had stepped out at some point and I had the truck to myself. Rubbing the sleep from my eyes, I swung open the door and shuffled with my eyes nearly closed toward the front gate. Here I unbuttoned my pants and let out a stream of early morning urine, watching it sleepily as it steamed on contact with the cool ground. I pulled my noodle back in, stretched, yawned, and turned to see a scene I definitely did not expect.

Clara approached, offering a water bottle of MRE coffee and grinning.

"Does anything wake you up?" she giggled.

"Pee," I answered before taking a swig of the mixture. "But you guys should have woken me. What the fuck?"

While I slept, they worked. One more truck had joined our three, and only mine remained without a trailer. The others had been mostly loaded front to back with supplies, equipment, and what appeared to be half of the animals that Erik said he had.

"We'll have to make a trip back for more," Erik stated as he approached us. "Bedding for the cows and the rest of the feed and some equipment. Tractor and side by side too, if y'all want it."

"You're making a good choice," I told him, "I'll do my best to make sure you won't regret it."

"I sure hope so," he cautioned. "It wasn't the most popular suggestion we've had here, that's for sure."

"Everything okay?" I interrogated. "Heard yelling last night."

"That's just how she communicates," he laughed. "We're good, and ready to leave when you are."

"And the other guy? Outside?" I prodded.

"Yeah, Adam." He nodded. "Just Ange and our kids are leaving, we agreed to half, since we were here first. We keep half the supplies and animals and they keep the farm. When did you want to get on out of here?"

"Shit doesn't wait anymore, so let's go now," I instructed, walking back to the driver's side of the truck.

Erik and I both spoke the order to depart into our radios, and within ten minutes every person was rounded up and ready to go, every animal was double-checked and ready as well.

It was an interesting sight, seeing cattle strapped down to the flatbed trailers like large, furry lawnmowers. We were reassured a few times by Erik that this is how they got transported on open trailers. The smaller animals were merely left on shorter leashes and stood in place. Chickens? Yeah, they got the star treatment and rode within the truck cab of the pickup Erik supplied.

Every spot that didn't contain a human or an animal had been packed in tight as could be with whatever Erik was taking. Another flat trailer had been brought out and my own truck had been backed up to it. To this, several thick livestock blankets and numerous bundles of straw and hay were secured.

Equipment festooned the trucks and trailers from all angles. Belongings and generators, boxes and crates all strapped across roofs, bumpers, and trailer sides. Add the people, and there was barely room to fart, let alone add anything else.

I could not and may never be sure it was worth the trade-off, but I had hoped so. Every trip was a risk, and not just a risk of expendable materials but, as had been displayed the day before, life as well. Was a new family to feed and a bunch of animals worth trading the lives of six of our people? Can you even measure that?

Ready to leave, we pulled near the front gate and waited. And waited another minute.

"Right," Cody said, and got out of the truck to go open the gate.

I guess none of us considered that we weren't leaving anyone behind at a home base willing to do it for us this time.

Cody returned, rocking the truck once again as he entered and settled in, and we were off.

I cut a right onto the side road, then after a short distance, another right onto the main road.

The lengths of Erik's fence, or whoever's fence it was now, seemed to chase us as we left, a chain-link barking dog seeing its owner off, not knowing he may not be coming back.

We had made an offer to those Erik was leaving. We told them where we were, and what we were about. Gave them the same offer for trade and security between us all that we had with Hashman. We even told them about Hashman, too. It was a no-go. They explained that they felt safer behind their fence, and when the time came, they would find more members here and there.

Maybe they'd expand that way. Maybe they wouldn't. They made it clear though that they'd handle it on their own from there.

We traced the exact path we had come from. Mostly because we already knew the way, but also because we knew it was clear. If anything was out of place from the day before, we'd know to exercise care. And despite the urge to cruise openly under the assumption nothing had changed, I decided to err on the side of caution and maintain a steady thirty miles-per-hour, just in case it was fucked.

Within about fifteen minutes of travel, we came across the area we were ambushed at the day before. A number of infected littered the area, both dead and alive. Even with the windows up, the stench was immense.

A mixture permeated us that was worse than opening a fridge in the apocalypse. The wet odor of the infected mixed with the aroma of those burnt, heavily accented by the recent fire which still raged on here and there. The woods and field smoldered, and among the flames, they still roamed. The sick, the dead, the undead, whatever name you preferred, they still ambled about aimlessly. I knew not whether they searched for something lost, or just meandered, waiting for their next victim of opportunity. I didn't think it mattered, because they were there either way.

We'd adopted a heavy sweep and clear policy every time we'd scavenge, except in a couple of extreme cases. Extreme as in those kinds of cases where a single movement could bring three-thousand of these fuckers your way.

Either way, here was a good chance to cut down their numbers in one big heap, and we had open avenues to escape front and back. Take out more of them, there's less of them to trouble you in the future. Yeah, it's easy to joke about, or picture yourself as some kind of badass out here just mowing down hordes of them, but it isn't fun. It's grisly, it's terrible work, and if there were any other way, I'd take it. These aren't desk lamps, these infected, freak or not they were someone somebody loved.

But it still had to be done for the safety of those we still had with us.

I slowed the truck to a stop, the other rigs also presenting themselves in line.

"Get ready, lock and load. We're going to keep our M.O. and sweep and clear. Over," I instructed over the radio, then waited a few moments before issuing another order, "Fire."

Like a car crash early Sunday morning, the air erupted with noise. The cosmic typewriter clack of explosive small-arms fire ripped the air apart and left space for uncounted bullets to fly free as the vehicles vibrated from falling brass casings. Freaks started dropping on both sides of the convoy as bodies turned and contorted, tugged this way and that by the rounds we sent their way.

A few began running in our direction but barely made any progress before being removed from our plane of existence. One turned, and I recognized it from the day before. And from months before this point. It was Parker. He looked beyond ragged, and a good half of his face was burnt by fire and contorted into a permanent toothy sneer, but I'd have recognized him from a mile away.

Clara paused her firing form the window and turned to face me, having seen him herself.

"Yup," I said coldly, and she complied, turning back into position and digging her rifle deep as she unleashed a volley of fire that found a home right below the unkempt mass of hair that remained on the poor boy's head.

The ammunition expenditure lasted maybe another forty-five seconds before it really petered out.

"Cease fire, cease fire," I repeated into the microphone and all guns fell silent.

I turned and watched, all down the line of trucks and trailers, everyone had been firing. A wave of ammunition meant no freak was forgotten and none in near range was likely going to be any trouble for anyone now, save for the scavengers. If they still ate the infected, it seemed to depend on the animal.

Erik could be seen checking his rifle as he got back into his vehicle at the tail end of the line.

He had cleared his own swath through the monsters and did so without question or hesitation.

This worked great for both parties. I now knew that at least to some extent I could count on him. His wiry little wife even was going about the process of reloading a shotgun and putting it on safe, then doing the same for her pistol.

It also seemed to show a little of our own hand to Erik and his family. Yes sir, we were everything we said we were. Tried to be, at least.

I settled back in and put the truck back into drive and continued onward.

It was graciously uneventful the rest of the way back to our compound. The biggest event to be seen was watching a couple of the guys barely hanging onto the junk tied to the trailers as they policed loose brass to reload shells with if possible. They'd laugh as they went about the mundane duty, and each spent bullet casing they rounded up was treated like a mini celebration. Kids at any age, regardless of the firearms they carried.

We approached the road we departed the compound on, and our own wall came into view. I examined the face in the windshield of Erik's truck as best I could from my mirror. Unable to see much in detail I stuck up a single thumb and watched him return the motion with a broad grin that was finally visible even from my vantage. Yeah, Erik, you're home, buddy. You and your family can actually relax.

We took the final left before the wall and swung wide to park in front of the gate as usual, but this time was anything but usual.

One gate guard on the outside, and one in the makeshift guard shack with a radio was the norm.

This time, we were met with eight armed men. Not exactly children, not the younger end of the high school kids that typically filled in where needed, but men. One of them, Ashley's husband Zack, produced an electronic bullhorn. I hadn't seen hardly anything of the guy since the first day. He spent most of his time switching guard posts along the walls or helping with construction crews, rarely scavenging but he seemed to always make himself scarce. I'd not heard good nor bad of him, and therefore essentially forgot him most times. Surely, I'd never seen him lead a position of authority before, so I was taken aback a bit.

"DRIVER!" his voice boomed through the amplification. "STEP OUT OF THE VEHICLE SLOWLY AND APPROACH THE GATE!"

"Okay what the fuck?" I questioned to nobody in particular.

I complied, but not slowly. I pushed open my door and stepped out into the still-cool morning air. Walking around the door and pushing it closed behind me, I strode purposefully to the gate.

"What the fuck, Zack?" I demanded as I approached, watching all with him relax when they saw it was me.

"Attack last night boss," he explained. "You're going to have to vouch for these people or we're going to need to search everyone and everything."

"Open the gate and step aside, they're with me, of course I fucking vouch for them!" I instructed, then, "And put out a call for anyone with information to meet me on the ninth floor. Immediately."

I turned from the gate without seeing if Zack responded, and I didn't wait for a confirmation. I just shouted over my shoulder to open the gate now, not later, or I was coming through anyway.

I didn't even know if it was possible to bust the front door of our compound with a pickup truck, but luckily, I didn't need to find out. By the time I had slid into my seat, the outer gate was rolled clear and I pulled into position to wait for them to work the inner. I then pulled aside to wait for the rest to come through and pass, motioning for Harrison and the last truck to pull alongside me long enough to tell him I wanted the inner gate open and waiting for me.

"What the hell is going on, Scott?" Clara questioned me.

"All I know is we were attacked, according to them," I told, "and security has been bolstered. We're going straight in to command."

Harrison's truck pulled away and after a few seconds we were back in gear and following.

I drove through our partial neighborhood, and straight for the front gate, barely having to wait for the last trailer to clear as I pulled on in and flipped Noah off on my way by. The move was needless, but he was far from an 'alpha' of any sort, and the dickhead in me relished in the look of his face.

I parked my truck every bit as willy-nilly as cattle roamed and got out of the driver's side, barking orders as soon as my feet hit solid ground.

"Ash!" I shouted as he crossed the lot to head into the North Building, watching him turn and move in my direction instead. Good. I turned and started barking orders for anyone in earshot.

"I want these supplies staged out *NOW*!" my voice boomed. "Erik's stuff goes to an empty truck for them, start laying bedding in the first floor apartments' front rooms. Move the cattle and other animals into those rooms, they get the first floor now, just not the heat rooms with Henry's things."

People started moving double-time and cutting their stretching and conversations short to get moving on the new tasks.

"Fred, as the trucks and trailers get emptied, find someone to bring them to the garage," I spoke more quietly, as he was nearer to me. "Then you're in charge of the willy's and the nilly's. Find 'em all suitable homes, remove the front sliding doors for each apartment if you need to."

"Got it," Fred acquiesced and started barking his own orders.

"Ash, thank you for joining us," I said as he approached. "This is Erik. You got the most recent tour, take them around, show them the basics and go house shopping for them. This is our new farm family, the animals are theirs."

"Sure thing, buddy," Ash complied and took Erik by the shoulder as I motioned Clara and Cody to follow me. Within a minute we were walking into the command center.

It was already filled with more people than I expected, but what dismayed me the most was Tony sitting in my seat at the head of the table. That dickhead. Still my buddy, but what a dickhead.

"Get up, titties," I shot at him, "Daddy's home."

He moved amid the laughter in the room and I plopped down into the chair, motioning for a cigarette from Dave and lighting the stale stick of tobacco before beginning.

"Ryan! Rob!" I called over my shoulder into the brain of our facility, and they both stepped out, looking around at the sheer number of people in here.

I sat for a moment and surveyed the faces in the room as I watched the mood drop into silence.

"Start at the beginning," I said. "What happened while we were gone?"

The room erupted, everybody offering different bits of info at once. I put my hands up and waited for it to die down.

"Who was the first to see anything at all?" I reiterated, and Henry put his hand up. "Henry, what was it?"

"Bunch of guys with guns. I was on the South Building, Eighth Floor balcony on guard duty," he explained. "They came in with a little boat real smooth and quiet like. I ran back in; I was trying, brother. Tried getting to the bell to ring it."

The man looked so lost, almost like a puppy that had done something wrong but wasn't sure what yet.

"It's cool, man," I soothed my friend, "you saw something wrong, and went to alert the compound. That was your job."

"Thank you, my brother," Henry conceded. "They was gone by the time I hit the bell, but I rang it anyway. Somebody took a shot at me but that's all I know. I dropped down when they shot and tried to get to a lower floor."

"Who next?" I asked the group.

"Right here," Rich offered, and I could see the red blotch of blood on a bandage wrapping his left arm. "They shot me when I came out of my building. Must have thought they got me because I hit the ground, when they passed, I loaded them up with an M4 from behind. By then Dave started from a balcony with his AK, and all of a sudden, all of the balconies were firing."

"Does anyone know for sure if it was just a team, or if they were there from a larger group?" I questioned.

"Colonel Parker," Tony said.

"You know this though?" I asked him. "How are you sure?"

"Because we've got one tied up in the storage units below the South Building," Dave said coldly. "He was literally screaming Colonel Parker's name before the sun was even up. He may have bled out now though."

"Bled out?" I asked in response.

"Yeah," Tony confirmed, "He didn't start talking until I shot him in the balls."

"Well shit, that's convincing at least," I said, cringing a bit. "But no need to make anyone suffer. Rich, if he's not dead, go make him so."

"Aye aye," Rich said and got up to leave.

"Sounds like it was Tony and Dave, uh, interrogating the hostage?" I asked.

"Me too," Henry clarified. "Them fuckers shot at me. I got to help beat one up."

"That's fair," I offered, watching Henry relax again, the stout black man cocooning himself into the plush office chair. "So what useful info did you get?"

"They were here for you," Tony informed, "and me, Rich, Dave, pretty much all of us they could identify. Said if this failed, they were going to stage an assault in the near future, but we have reason to believe the guy didn't know exactly when, just that it was coming soon."

"We need to get ready then," I advised. "We'll send anyone that doesn't want to or need to be involved upriver to Hashman until this blows over or ends either way. Children first. No scouting or scavenging for the next few days to a week, and, no more overnight excursions. Nothing. We all guard the compound, or we leave."

"But if we all leave," Jennifer offered, "you included, won't they just give up and assume we've moved on?"

"Then they'll never stop looking for me. For us," I suggested. "If we face them here and crush them, they won't be looking for much of anything, and our neighbors and children will be safe. And if we don't face them here now, they'll just come back for us when we return. We're kind of stuck, in a way. Damned if you do type of thing."

"They have a tank…" she started again.

"APC," I corrected.

"It has a big gun and a lot of armor," she reminded me, "it's a fucking tank to me."

"They have a tank," I sighed as I rolled my eyes, "we have a Richard."

"This isn't the Avengers, you shit," she nearly growled.

"It's also not up for debate," I responded, then stood from my seat. "When Richard gets back, I want some of you to take more of you and go with him. Whatever way he has to limit the equipment they can use, I want it done. I don't care if we have to find a way to make this place fly, we do it."

"They have a gunship," Dave said. "Well, a small helicopter with guns, but they have one. We'll even have a fight if we fly."

"That's right! You guys," I motioned to Tony, remembering their detail I sent them on, "you're supposed to be scouting the Colonel, what happened to that?"

"Didn't take much," Tony shrugged. "Even in broad daylight the guy doesn't know dick about security. We pretty much snuck up between some houses and into another, saw everything he had from one place. They're currently set up in the parking lot of the old Market District."

"Well?" I urged him.

"About three-hundred people, all armed," He detailed. "They've got an AH-6, that Brad, a few supply or cargo trucks, and 5 Humvees."

"That's the bad news, what's in our favor?" I asked, eying my friend.

"I watched a fight break out over food, handful of people scrapping for scraps," he offered.

"And?" I urged.

"Tells me they're probably low on food," he continued. "I also saw very few people with any kind of drinking water, and about half his men are sleeping right outside with no cover."

"That puts me a bit more at ease," I confirmed. "We'll have to fight the military, and they outnumber us, but they aren't doing as well. Worst case, unless they can call for backup, it'll end up fairly even. And even stuck in here, the land is in our favor."

"What about using the infected to our advantage?" Rob suggested. "You know, like before?"

"The Colonel," I advised, "has the ability to break our walls in one way or another. I don't want the infected anywhere near us if that happens."

"It could help us though," Cody suggested. "Even if the infected got inside, it could interfere with the Colonel's ability to interfere with us."

"With the amount of effort and manpower it took to get them out before," I countered, "I'd rather not do all that again. They're going to get in one way or the other, but I'd rather not encourage a mass migration to move in."

At that moment, Rich returned to the command meeting room, hints of blood spatter on his face.

"Rich, you got red on you," I stated as the others laughed uneasily. "I want you to find any way you can to make the area around our base impassible. And I want it done today. Take all the people you need, y'all are the only ones outside of our gates until this is over anyway. Do what you can. Block roadways, topple buildings, whatever you need."

"Got it," Rich agreed and started ordering people to go with him.

"The rest of you, and those working with Rich," I issued, "get together with others. All children, and those not able to effectively hold and fire a rifle, will be on boats going up the river this evening. The rest of you are to remain armed, and on full standby until the threat is clear or a resolution is met. Rich, do you need anything else?"

"Henry's gotta finish the gun mount and install it," he explained, "other than that I'm ready to rock and roll."

"Henry, get working on that," I began, "take a young'un to help you. The rest of you have things to do, why are you still standing here. *LET'S MOVE PEOPLE!*"

The entire room emptied in record time and left just a few of us.

"Tony, you're head of security here," I scolded, "why the fuck are you still sitting there?"

"Oh, I didn't know you meant me," he said sheepishly and began to leave.

"Rob and Ryan, my two R's," I called into the room behind me, "twenty-four seven full monitoring. Grab some coffee or plan out shifts but neither of you leave that room. Where's Hannah?"

"She was listening from the doorway," Jennifer explained, "but she left when you mentioned the disabled and kids leaving."

I pinched my nose between my fingers and sighed.

"Okay. I'll get her rounded up," I stated as I rose to leave my seat.

"Hannah?" I called as I left the command area and entered the hallway.

I received no response. Where could she have gone?

"*Hannah*?" I called out again, more sharply this time as I walked into our apartment. Still nothing.

I checked through our kitchen, dining, and living areas. All empty.

"Scott?" came Jennifer's voice from the door. "I found her. You, uh, you need to come here."

I sighed heavily and followed my wife out of the apartment and down to the end of the hallway. Whatever this was, I didn't need it, and didn't have time for it. But when did I ever need, or have time for, any of this? I should be on my ass at work, cruising down the interstate eating cheap roller grill food and wondering where the union is going to stick their willy on us next.

Actually, I'd really rather be dealing with the unions. Useless, neutered, and giving out more concessions than an average little league game, but at least they weren't trying to eat us, shoot us, or do any of the other new bad experiences we'd been dealing with thus far.

Jennifer opened the doorway to the single staircase leading to the roof and motioned toward the back of the space, where I found Hannah behind a stack of cooking supplies.

The girl had sat on the floor, her knees drawn up tight to her chest and her arms encircling them. I couldn't quite tell, but she seemed to be crying. Great. I knelt down next to her, took a deep breath, and exhaled.

"I'm not leaving," she said defiantly.

"A lot of people are, Hannah, and it's not for good," I assuaged. "We'll be back. I promise. But it's going to be incredibly dangerous here and we don't want you getting hurt."

"This is home now." She tightened her arms around her legs and placed her chin on top of the whole mess.

"Yeah, mine too, which is why it's going to be pretty nasty here if we need to defend it," I explained. "Possibly, even more dangerous than the world outside the gates. We don't know what they could be capable of doing. Hannah, hun, they could level these very buildings. We just don't know."

"Your people saved me, and you made it comfortable for me," she reminded me. "You set it up so I would be safe and not have to be scared anymore."

Just then my radio crackled to inform me that all three of our boats had departed, and more were on their way down from the Hashman compound.

"I want you on one of those next boats, Hannah," I explained. "If I have to carry you myself. Think of it as a vacation. Hashman's compound is still safe. This one isn't for the time being."

"But what if you don't come back?" she cried out. "What if you get killed?"

"Kiddo," I began, "it's going to take a whole lot more than they've got to kill me. But, regardless, I want you safe, and you're going to be safe. I trust Hashman with my life. Actually, I have once or twice already. I'll send orders with you that you are his personal responsibility."

"I...I don't know..." she began.

"I do. Get up," I said firmly as I took her hand, feeling her momentarily recoil before relenting.

I brought the young girl into my arms and embraced her in a hug, kissing the top of her head as I did so.

"You know kid," I reminded, "you might just be worrying over nothing. Best case, the Colonel decides it isn't worth it and leaves us alone, and y'all are just buying us some space and time to bolster our defenses. You could actually just be going on a vacation."

"Vacations are for sightseers," she replied with no enthusiasm, "just be okay, okay?"

"Promise," I assured her as I led her hand to Jennifer's. "Next boat. I want both of you on it."

"I love you," Jennifer said as she took her own place in my arms, giving me a kiss and holding tight. I tried to break the hug and she still held fast for just another moment before ending the embrace. "Come say bye to Gwen?"

"Yeah," I agreed and followed the pair of them down the hallway and into the stairwell. About halfway down, we were forced to hug the wall as Henry and one of the older teenage boys passed by, carrying some big wrought-iron contraption and panting heavily, followed by two more teens carrying large cardboard boxes and breathing just as hard. Even in the cool air of the overcast day, they were sweating as they made their trek up the tight stairwell, and instead of his usual jovial banter, I was met with one a wide-eyed nod from our long-time friend and old neighbor.

"You have to promise me you'll be okay," Jennifer demanded after they had passed, and we renewed our descent.

"You know me, wife," I reminded her.

"Exactly," she semi-scolded. "Which is why I'm worried. You need to be damn careful. Promise me."

I was just about to let a quip fly when I glanced and saw the single tear streaming from her eye. I decided to rethink my response, and instead, merely took her hand in mine and squeezed.

"I promise, I will be careful," I assured her.

She replied no more, and we wordlessly made our way down the rest of the stairs, guiding Hannah the whole way and walking her over the uneven ground as we exited the building.

About halfway there, we met Carolyn with the last half-dozen children on their way to the boats to be ferried upriver.

Of course, little Gwen was on the edge of the pack, keeping a watchful eye on her surroundings. Hey bright blue eyes blazed with joy when they saw us approaching.

"Mommy! Daddy!" she squealed as she broke from the small group and made a beeline straight for us, toddler run in full stride and arms out. She met me first and I scooped her up, smiling despite the world at her happy giggles.

"We were waiting," Carolyn's heavy French-Canadian accent informed me. "She kept asking for her parents, we waited."

"I'm glad," I said as I squeezed my daughter tight and spoke only to her, "I love you baby."

"Love Daddy," she replied before stretching her arms to her mother, who accepted her readily.

"Take care of the kids just as you would here," I instructed Carolyn. "Hashman will make sure you have what you need."

I gave Hannah one last hug and led her hand to Carolyn's as she replied in the affirmative, then did the same for Jennifer and Gwen.

Jennifer's eyes welled with tears as she gave me one more solid hug, followed by three kisses. Our thing for many years. Three quick kisses, I, love, and you.

"Scott…" she began.

"Nope," I stopped her short, "I'll be coming back to get you guys soon enough. You go. Make sure everyone's okay. We'll, uh, well, we'll hold down the fort. Literally, I guess."

Radio chatter began as I looked past Jennifer's shoulders and saw three more boats pulling in, these ones offloading men and supplies before they were even thoroughly moored on the shore. The heavy loads they carried left them to anchor a little offshore on the river, forcing men to wade back and forth.

Dave and Tony guided small groups of men from place to place as Tony stood with his hands on his hips and Dave passed crates and boxes from the shore to different people.

"There's your ride," I motioned, cutting the emotional departure short, implementing the band-aid method as I was known to do.

Jennifer released her grasp and took Gwen's little hand as they both turned. She looked once over her shoulder, followed by Gwen, and I gave them a wave. Maybe a final wave.

Jennifer returned it, and Gwen stretched her free hand out at the realization that Dad's not coming. The tears breaking her eyes threatened to infect my own as Carolyn took the outstretched hand and garnered the girl's attention.

I watched as Rich appeared from his in-ground armory and stopped the group one final time to wish Carolyn goodbye. They hadn't seemed to be the closest couple, especially not since Rich had elected to move to the armory and Carolyn resided in the main building, but in the following moment, they appeared inseparable as they shared a goodbye embrace.

I hadn't even had time to process the tear dripping from Carolyn's nose as my radio began chattering.

"Go for Scott," I instructed.

"Look up," was the single command spoken by Henry, followed by a late and rushed, "Over!"

I craned my neck skyward to see the recognizable barrel of the M240 machine gun protruding from over the edge of the Eighth Floor balcony closest to our inner entryway to the main compound.

"We're all set up, my brother," Henry spoke into his radio as he beamed down from above, the corners of his mouth almost actually touching each ear, "Over!"

"Now we need somebody with machine gun experience to run it. Looks good. Over," I replied.

With not another word said, Ash's grinning round face appeared over the balcony and waved down to me.

"I've got it, mate!" he shouted.

I grinned and shook my head as they disappeared from view.

"Nice!" Rich said as he joined me, taking me by surprise. "Roads are all being blocked; we'll leave one way in and I'm decorating that with explosives."

He motioned to a nearby pickup truck. The bed of the vehicle was loaded with a few of the old large oil drums he'd used before, as well as a row of large water-cooler jugs filled with some kind of material or substance I couldn't quite make out at this distance.

"Blocked?" I asked, wondering what and how, and trying to get my mind to cycle up to speed again.

"Yup," he assured. "Dumpsters with the wheels cut off once they're in place, couple semi-trailers with the tires shot out. One road had houses real close to the curb so we're just going to push them with that old bulldozer and the excavator and fill the rest of the gap with abandoned cars."

"And you said you're leaving one area open but rigging it?" I asked.

"Yeah," he continued, "but, uh, you're going to want to wait a bit after everything is over before you try driving through."

"To disable whatever explosives?" I surmised.

"And rebuild the roadbed," he explained. "Their vehicles are pretty heavy; if we remove all the dirt under the concrete, put in a few two-by-four's for support, light vehicles should be okay but the second anything heavier goes over it…"

He splayed his palms vertically and then pushed them down to emulate the roadway collapsing,

"Think it'll be enough?" I asked.

"Should be," He said thoughtfully. "If it's done deep and long enough, it should be able to trap or disable a vehicle, I don't see why not."

"Those barrels," I motioned, "is that like before? When you helped with the school?"

"Kind of, but each one is a smaller bomb," he said, "and instead of a 'Wrinkle Free' setting, they're each wired to a sensor."

"A sensor?" I asked, wondering where he'd found something like that.

"They each have their own battery," he continued, "and each one is set to either a mouse trap or a couple of nails attached to a clothes pin. They can be set up so if anything drives over them or anyone steps on one, it completes the circuit long enough to set the explosive off."

"That's fucking genius," I exclaimed, clapping him on the shoulder.

"The mouse trap ones are easier," he kept on. "Once they're tripped the circuit doesn't shut down, so it'll power a heater coil inside the bomb until it heats and blows up, or the battery goes dead."

"Put one where you dig out the roadbed," I suggested, "so when it collapses, it triggers it and makes their situation even worse."

We kept talking, and as we did, the morbidity crept on me. We were sitting in what used to be a relatively okay neighborhood. It was once an amazing place to raise a family, then worse over time as the area changed, but it was still never anything less than decent. Until now, that is.

Now, most of its inhabitants were dead or gone, and we'd commandeered the entire corner of a neighborhood and were setting traps to kill other human beings. Six months prior, when and where we stood, someone was probably pulling into their apartment to enjoy the comforts of home. Now their home was a battle-ready fortress.

Rich broke our conversation to listen to his radio and issue a reply, after which we wordlessly said goodbye for now as he left to go handle the next stage of preparations.

Not one to ever seemingly be allowed to be left alone, Dave joined my walk into the main building.

"All the kids and people who can't fight are accounted for," he informed me. "All on their way to Hashman's."

Henry and his small crew were just leaving the front of the building and met us on our way in before we could continue.

"Henry! All good here?" I asked.

"Oh yes sir, we all the way good brother." He beamed again, proud of himself. "What's next?"

"What's next is the waterway." I motioned across the river to our north and west. "Whatever you can put between the water and the land, I want it figured out and done now. They came by water before. Let's make that more difficult."

"You got it, my friend." He nodded and began talking to his team to gather their materials before he even gained a full scope of the situation.

"Where's Tony?" I asked Dave as we made our way into the North Building.

"He 'went to help with the transplants' at Hashman's," he issued, putting air quotes around Tony's words.

"What the fuck?" I asked, shocked and more than a little angry. "They've got plenty of fucking people, why the fuck would he leave when we need him?"

Dave merely shrugged and broke into full-bore bitching about Tony and his work ethic, or lack thereof, and calling him every name he could think of. Okay, so it looks like I may be keeping them on separate duties, at least for a while. Sure seemed like Dave could use the break, and I fretted to hear what Tony would say in return. But right now? Yeah, not exactly what we needed at the moment.

I made it to my office on the ninth floor just in time to start cursing about my own issues that never seemed to cease, but my words were directed at the source.

"What the ever-loving fuck are you still doing here? The last boat is gone! Where's Hannah, where's Gwen?" I demanded.

"They're safe, they're on the boat and going with Carolyn to the other compound," Jennifer assured. "Look, I knew you were going to be mad-"

"You're fucking right I'm mad, dude what the hell are you doing?" I yelled at my wife, my voice reaching a crescendo. "Do you not understand what's about to happen here? Or that the girls need you?"

"You need me too and I'm not leaving your side," she shot back. "Who's going to make sure you keep your promise to be careful anyway? Dave?"

"I'm not in this!" Dave exclaimed, putting his hands up and departing hastily.

"What the fuck, woman?" I scolded her again, then, relented, "I'm not going to do this right now."

"Guys?" called Ryan's voice from the next room. "Scott? Hey this isn't good."

A radio message that seemed live was just beginning its repeat as we entered the room.

"-Colonel Parker with the United States Government. Scott Pfeiffer, we have your daughter. We have your friends. We are calling for your peaceful surrender. How copy? Over."

"I want confirmation on his claims," I snarled, feeling the heat creep up my neck. "Raise the last boat on their private channel. NOW!"

"That's the thing," Ryan stated flatly, "I can't"

"Give me the radio," I nearly growled as I snatched it from his grasp and immediately keyed it in reply, "Colonel. I want proof. Over."

"Oh, why hello, Scott!" he cooed cheerily. "Proof? She was on the last boat, correct? Little blonde haired toddler; my is she just simply adorable!"

"Proof, you cocksucker, or I bring a fight right to your doorstep, right fucking now."

"Scott?" Carolyn's accent sobbed through the radio. "Scott, is true, he took the last boat, I could not do a thing! I'm sorry."

A single grunt issued, cutting her off, as the Colonel's voice regained the line.

"Scott," he chirped, "I'll be honest, I'm done fucking around with you, son. Surrender yourself if you ever want to see them again."

"Come get me," I raged into the mic. "Walk over your dead men and arrest me. I will *not* be threatened."

I didn't wait for a reply before I flung the radio and watched it contact the wall and nearly disintegrate.

"Scott, he has Gwen!" Jennifer nearly wailed.

"I know," I replied from somewhere very far away, "and even if I surrender, do you think he'll just let her go free? Or any of them? We're fucked either way, so, we fight."

"Okay then," she replied. "How?"

"For now?" I asked, then, "We wait. Wait until our defenses are done. He won't come during the day anyway."

"How can you know this?" she asked.

"Because I wouldn't," I stated coldly. "He won't either. This isn't about arresting anyone or helping survivors, it's like Tony said. They're hungry. He doesn't care about us."

"Shit," Jennifer stated as the others in the room looked at the floor, dismayed.

"Scott? Scoooooott," the radio on the table cooed, taunting. Okay, apparently smashing the one did nothing when several around were all on the same channel. Oops.

It was him again. The Colonel. That bastard.

"Shootout at noon? Over," I returned, partially hopeful he'd say 'okay' and we could all end this thing before it got out of hand. He didn't.

"I'll be seeing you, Scott. Oh, and, no worries, I'll keep your little girl safe. Bye bye now. Over."

I stormed from the command center and right into the conference room where I snatched up a chair and began slamming it overhead into the surface of the sturdy table again and again until the wooden chair gave way, splintering and sending pieces of itself flying in all directions. By the time I was done, I slumped into my usual spot and placed my forehead onto the table. What, you thought I'd destroy my own seat? Mine was nice. I didn't like the one that now lay asunder all around me.

"Feel better?" came Jennifer's voice as I felt her hands on my shoulder. "It'll be okay, Scott. We'll handle this just like we always handle things."

"He has the kids, Carolyn, and whoever else was on that boat with them," I spoke into the table as she began rubbing her palms and fingers deeply into my shoulders.

"I know," she said. "One problem at a time. We take care of the Colonel, then we get our Gwen back. And Hannah."

The second name sent a new pang through me as I sighed and lifted my head, standing to leave the room as I keyed our compound-wide channel on my own radio.

"Everyone, they have Gwen, and they are apparently looking for a fight," I explained to everyone with a radio set. "Whatever duty you are on right now, finish it, and help whoever else is around you double time their duties, too. Meet around dinner time at the North Building main entrance."

"We need a plan," Jennifer suggested as we made our way down the stairs.

"We block their river access, Henry is on that right now," I recalled. "We block the roads, Rich is doing that one. Funnel them, take down their numbers the best we can, keep them tight, and hopefully funnel of death them to a sizeable number then mount a full defense at the central compound here once the guerilla defense falls down."

"Okay then," Jennifer resigned, forgetting that I always had a plan of some sort or other, even when I didn't actually have any idea what we were doing.

"We keep a few on lookout over the waterway, disable one entrance, and try to pin them at the other as another funnel," I continued on. "Then, by then, hopefully however many of them are left is less than what we've got left and we overwhelm them."

"What if it doesn't work?" she asked.

I did not answer. We had hit the second floor and I walked into, then through, Shannon's office as I was met by surprise reactions and questions that I ignored. I stepped through her sliding door, grabbed the lawn chair on the balcony, and tossed it over the balustrade to the ground only a dozen feet below. Upon hearing it impact and not hearing anyone yell up, I left the balcony. Then I turned and walked through the office again.

"Be ready to become combat medics," I instructed without pausing my steps. "Or stay put right here and treat wounded if they make it to you. Both sides. Patch up our enemy as well and maybe those under the Colonel will be sick enough of his shit to become friendlies."

Shannon and Ashley both exchanged glances and offered positive replies as I left and walked right back to the stairwell and down one flight to the ground level.

Upon exiting the building, I found the lawn chair, now slightly dented but still serviceable, and set it up, then rested my weight in it.

"It's about to be a long night, woman. Either get ready or find a public place where you can be seen and accounted for and take a nap." I instructed. "Either way, I want my kit sitting next to me when I wake up, please."

She just kind of stared at me for a moment before popping her eyebrows once and sighing 'okay'.

"Hey, you wanted to stay, you need to be ready too," I urged. "Both our kits by the dinnertime meeting."

"Okay," she repeated and turned to leave as I settled into position and closed my eyes. Stress and everything piled on me and didn't seem to matter. I was asleep before I could even think of any of it.

I did rest, though not well and definitely not thoroughly. I spent a few hours or so in that space between sleep and consciousness, sometimes aware of what was going on around me, sometimes genuinely asleep in spurts. Twice telling Rich to go away and work or rest, but leave me the hell alone nonetheless.

What finally brought me all the way back to the land of the mostly living was a sense of commotion building all around me.

Must be dinnertime, I thought.

Sitting forward and rubbing my eyes until my vision cleared and adjusted confirmed as much. People gathered here and there between the North Building and Rich's armory in loose groups.

I recognized many as our own, but there was a nearly equal number that I barely recognized, if at all. Hashman's men. I told him not to send people, just take ours. Apparently, he listened about as well as Tony usually does.

I sat on my plastic lawn chair long enough to get a feeling for the scene before me. Everyone was eating what was on hand, and that wasn't much, though mostly we didn't want for much. No big grilled meals cobbled together out of whatever, though, and MREs were finally beginning to be scarce, no longer rationed out but instead horded like gold and only eaten when necessary. Instead, the assorted men and women ate an equally diverse assortment of snacks.

Some passed around a bag of likely stale chips to a few friends, others feasted casually on power bars or bags of mixed nuts. A few here and there were eating canned food cold and straight out of the container.

I looked around for a moment longer and snagged one of the high school aged teens coming out of the building near me, her arms loaded with canned food.

"Pineapple," I said, watching her give a small startled jump before recognizing me and smiling as she handed me the one single can of pineapple rings.

I pulled the tab and opened the can, draining half the juice in one gulp before digging in and seizing a glorious golden ring of fruit with my fingers and pushing the whole thing into my mouth as if I hadn't eaten in a week. I felt the sweet juice run through the hair on my lengthening beard, touching the skin, and dribbling down to form a small puddle on my lap before being soaked up by my clothing.

I enjoyed it, not only because it was nourishment, not because I was so hungry, not even because I particularly enjoyed pineapple out of all the fruits.

I enjoyed it because, should this clash with the Colonel go on as I knew it would, it might be the last food I'd ever eat. And I damn sure didn't want that last meal to be the soggy fruit mix from an MRE.

"That's so attractive," came Jennifer's voice from my direct vicinity.

"How long's it been since you showered here, at the end of the world?" I asked her, opening just one eye to watch her think. "Days? A week? Longer? Don't talk to me about attractive, woman, we're all gross here."

She took it in jest and laughed while rolling her eyes.

"Everybody is almost here, I think," she observed.

"Looks that way," I replied. "I'd better get dressed then."

"Do you think this is really going to happen?" she asked, a tinge of nerves tainting her voice.

"I do," I stated. "I think it'll be soon, too. Go get everyone rounded up, I'll be there soon."

"Okay," she nearly whispered and left to do so.

I was getting the feeling that my wife had just realized her defiance wasn't a game to be played with this time. That she was now learning her choice to stay could leave our daughter parentless. Even as she left, I could see the look of far-off contemplation.

I rose from my seat and lifted my nearby gear onto the seat I had just occupied. A mismatched and cobbled together set of this or that, nothing on the Gucci level of Crye Precision, but serviceable nonetheless.

I stripped off my pants and donned a new pair of BDUs, one of my personal pair in a deep midnight blue and black camouflage pattern. Pulling off my Amon Amarth T-shirt was next and replacing it with a simple black long-sleeved affair with no design or pattern. I continued to add thin layers followed by my outer gear, also all in black and dark blue.

Checking my storage pouches and ensuring I had magazines for my weapons, I then proceeded to check the weapons themselves.

The MK18 MOD 0 rifle had quickly became my personal favorite. Not the best caliber there was, a .300 Blackout, but when firing subsonic rounds and paired with the suppressor it was startlingly quiet and carried fair accuracy between short and medium ranges. The only thing I didn't like was the damned tan-colored furniture on the weapon, but Cerakote wasn't exactly ripe for the picking since online services quit delivering after their driver's became part of the population of hungry infected.

I guess my real complaint was the ammunition itself. I could kick in the door on a quarter of the homes in the country and find 9mm or .223. But the .300Blk was a much scarcer caliber.

Slinging the rifle over my shoulder, I checked the first of two pistols. A basic Sig Sauer P226 in 9mm. Just my style. A common caliber loaded into a reliable firearm, no frills, nothing extra aside from the weapon mounted light. I slid it into place in my chest rig and checked the final piece.

Then the Smith and Wesson 6906 I had with me in the beginning, and on nearly every venture out into this hostile world since. Prior to the end, it had been my EDC. That's 'Every Day Carry', for those not aware. The small 9mm pistol had been in my waistband for years. It even held its place in concealment at my wedding. It fell naturally into the drop-leg holster I now wore for it and was secured into place.

By the time I had finished dressing and got a fresh pair of socks on with boots laced, it seemed as though the last few stragglers were rounded up and staged with the large group.

Thanks to Hashman, we had sent around half our population upriver, and received a similar number in return. Some looked a bit young to fight, but at this point, if they had no family left to claim and nowhere better to be, I'd take them as men and women for what was to come.

I meandered over near the group and took a step up the side of the bed of a nearby pickup truck and took a stand there.

"*LISTEN UP*!!!" I shouted through my cupped hands, my voice threatening to hoarsen over the effort. "Get as close to over here as you can, I'm not losing my voice for this."

I stood and watched as the crowd shifted and began to encircle the pickup truck. My mind slipped to fantasy as they worked among each other. I thought of the dilemma it would present me if they were all hungry freaks and left me thankful that I had never had to try fighting from an open position. Two-hundred odd men and women were imposing enough when gathered around you. It would have been terrifying if they were all blood-faced and hungry, spewing viscous infected vomit and clamoring to take a bite of you.

"Well," Dave spoke up from near the front, "we're waiting for you sweet cheeks!"

"Fuck you Dave," I grinned. "I will shoot you."

"It's alright," he quipped, "better you than me!"

"Okay everyone check it out!" I said, returning to the crowd as the chuckles died down. "Chances are pretty damned good that we're going to fight once again for our little place in the world."

Murmurs of conversation spread through the crowd, as well as several remarks about me stating the obvious and telling me that's what we're all here for. I waited another moment for it to start dying down and began anew.

"The waterways are blocked," I observed, noting the netting and fencing strewn across the river nearest to our location, "and the way to the water itself has been made difficult. The roadways are blocked, I'm assuming as well?"

"Yeah," Rich confirmed. "Exactly as planned, no difference, and we used your suggestion for rigging the trap pit to blow."

"We're boxed in," I explained to the crowd. "Fortified, but make no mistake. We are now backed into a corner and we must act like it!"

A dull rumble of concordance spread throughout the large group gathered around me, and again I waited. I didn't want to forcibly stifle the conversation, I wanted the crowd to do as crowds do and fuel each other. I didn't want fighters, I wanted warriors.

"A pair of you will break off and wade downriver, and another pair up," I instructed. "Check your radio gear and batteries, if they try the water, you'll be our advance warning system."

As I watched, a younger pair was pushed to the front of the crowd, then two more of similar age and stature. I knelt and spoke quietly to just the four of them, wishing them to be safe but advising they slept in shifts, one up, one down, and someone must always be vigilant. Trusting the alertness of our entire compound to a quartet of boys who didn't even look old enough to drive. At least, I thought, they'd hopefully be out of the line of fire if shooting started.

The pairs then departed, and I watched momentarily as one left behind my position, heading to cover the south of the river, and the other group skirted the crowd and disappeared around the near corner of the North Building, to cover that end of our territory. Godspeed, kids.

"Rich has all avenues to the compound by land blocked off," I continued, turning back to the crowd. "I want patrols of six each near the outer wall, and maintain line-of-sight with the next patrol down. I also want two teams of three on each main building rooftop, and roving guards throughout wherever possible."

"Roving guard?" asked a young red-haired teen near me.

"Ask anyone in camo, kid, they'll fill you in," I smiled at him, then regained my position. "We have maybe an hour of sun left. Get with Rich, Henry, or your section leader and start positioning supplies where needed. When we see anything that doesn't belong, kill it. Infected or not. Guys, we need to take care of ourselves first. Be safe out there."

"Your attention, please!" Rich's gravelly voice crooned from near his armory, where he, Henry, and Ash started handing out boxes of forearm-length tubes. "Black are smoke, white go boom! Plastic for ground level, metal goes up to the roofs and gets split between guard towers!"

I eased myself over the edge of the pickup truck, grabbing a pair of the pipe bombs from a box as one man ventured near me with it, and sticking them haphazardly into the cargo pocket of my trousers. I then patted the other one to ensure I had my old trauma kit in place, as they were made to fit such pockets.

I watched the trio at Rich's bunker hand out supplies, weapons, and personal med kits here and there to the thinning crowd as Dave and my wife came wordlessly to my side to take in the spectacle.

"Well, let's go," I murmured as I turned and went into the North Building and followed the corridor to the stairwell, then up, up, and up.

I passed by our apartment, then stopped and turned in to hand a box of water and snacks to Dave from near the kitchen area.

"The beef jerky and Sun Chips are mine," I cautioned, "don't even think about them. The rest is fair game."

I handed a few of our remaining MREs to Jennifer, and then we turned to leave the apartment and move up to the rooftop, where we'd watch from the east end of the building, looking out over our little walled-in neighborhood.

We settled in, each taking a barstool or similar and spacing out to look through the small gaps between plywood and solar panels as the sun took its last glance over the horizon behind us and dropped even lower, leaving a pink-streaked dusk to stretch across the sky.

The air felt different than usual, but, then again, maybe on this day I was simply more appreciative of it. The sky was beauty in itself and cast a wonderful soft-hued glow on my own favorite beauty, Jennifer. Gods, I wished she'd gotten on that boat. Part of me knew she'd likely be in the Colonel's hands now, but then she'd be there with little Gwen, and with Hannah. Then again, another part of me held the thought that she'd have been able to fend them off and get the boat to safety.

Then, Dave. As tall and as lanky as ever, he sat digging through a bag of honey roasted peanuts. He wore an all-black hooded sweatshirt to fend off the cooling air, and had his dreadlocks pulled into what he called 'his peacock'. The thick locks of matted hair brazenly displayed from the back of his head and tied to fall over the top of his crown. With the rest of us wearing the closest we could muster to our own military gear, he looked to be the most unusual of the bunch. Basketball shorts and hoodie, munching away with the ends of four pipe bombs protruding from the front hoodie pocket, and his now trademark AK47 cradled carelessly in his free arm. I was sure he'd have a pistol just shoved into one pocket, and various magazines and ammo shoved into others. And, of course, an old beat up cigarette pack with a precious joint or ten shoved inside.

I tore into my beef jerky as quietly as I could, but I was too late to hide it. Or maybe too careless. Or maybe women have a sixth sense or a dog's sinuses. I don't know. But there she was. Her head snapped in my direction and Jennifer's bright blue eyes focused in right on my hands.

"Hey!" she prodded. "What, uh, what do ya got over there?"

"Nothing," I said, and immediately locked into a stare down with her, her grin forming, pushing up her full cheeks as it went.

"Doesn't look like nothing." She pushed further, "Looks like something to me."

"Might be beef jerky," I admitted.

"Is it the kind that gets shared?" she questioned, her eyes gleaming and her face not showing any subtlety.

"Damn you, woman," I relented, pulling one of the two pieces out of the vacuum pack and passing it to her.

"Hey buddy!" Dave called over to join.

"Ask her, I'm tapped out," I shot as I pulled my piece from the pack and held the empty wrapper up.

They started going back and forth over it, ending with Jennifer tearing off a third of her piece and giving it to him.

I watched as the available light faded over our land.

In the limits of my line of sight, which shrunk as the light grew dimmer, I could make out the far wall. Guard towers were fuller than usual, and nearly everywhere you looked you could find a patch of darkly-dressed men and women following rigid paths through the neighborhood.

Where we'd dismantled entire homes and filled in foundations, less people patrolled as less people were needed, and groups could see one another more readily.

As I watched, something caught my eye off in the distance, nearly due south. Just a single point of light shown, then dimmed. I called it into my radio but our furthest team in that direction was still within the outer wall and much closer to the ground. Nobody saw anything.

"Want me to go check, Mr. Pfeiffer? Over," came the voice of one of the boys on river duty.

"Nah, stay put. If it's anything, they've got to come closer anyway. Keep your eyes on the water. Over."

"Uh, solid copy. Over," came the reply.

The late evening wore on into night as we sat at post making small talk among ourselves.

The only other noise around was the occasional radio chatter, and the low murmur of conversation similar to ours from the other end of the rooftop where Rich, Henry, and Cody sat and watched in much the same fashion as we did. I could also hear the occasional nerve-fed laughter from just below our position, where Ash and Harrison waited. Our gunner team on the 240 machine gun.

At one point, I'd noticed our newest family, Erik and his wife, enlisting help from a nearby patrol with carrying various sheets of plywood and road signs to the front of the building and surmised they must be blocking in and shielding the animals. Not having room on the boats, or time, the majority of what we'd brought from his pseudo-farm had been left here in the emptied first-floor apartments.

I glanced over and saw Dave ever-vigilant, his grey-green eyes doing their level best to pierce the nighttime and see any signs of anything, but as the moon faded in and out of the clouds, our view was very limited.

Jennifer, on the other hand, was slumped forward, nearly leaning against the nearby solar panel and half asleep. I didn't blame her. This duty was boring.

Was. Boy, I had no idea how much I was about to miss the 'boring'. Boring is nice. Boring is peaceful. Boring is, well, boring *was*.

"Command, front gate, over," came Frank's voice over the radio.

"Go for command," I issued.

"We're hearing incoming. Over," he informed.

"Say again?" I countered. "Hearing incoming? We're not getting anything here. Over."

"Sounds like vehicles, sir. Over," he said.

ELEVEN

"Sit tight," I advised before keying to all radios in range, "I'd like to remind you all now, there is no reason to fight stupid. The inner compound is our fallback. Retreat if needed until you are within the inner walls. We make our stand here."

I was starting to hear it, too. Though not quite what I expected. I was fully prepared for the rumble of trucks, or even outright gunfire. I was, however, only half-expecting it to be this first night, and even less prepared for the steady *whumpwhumpwhump* rotor blades in the distance.

I nudged my wife and watched her head spring up and start looking around wildly as if she were a startled rabbit before pausing to cant her head just slightly.

"What the hell?" she asked.

I didn't say a word but instead merely pressed my finger to my lips as Dave eyeballed me. I turned and looked over the rooftop to see all eyes focused in my direction, looking at me expectantly as if I had the answer they sought. Sorry guys. I'm just as lost as all of you, I just do a better job of hiding it.

The noise grew louder and louder and a shape began to emerge when the moon peeked from around a cloud. Just a glint, at first. Then the shadow of a small helicopter just over the treetops and moving swift and steadily in our direction emerged from the overcast night gloom.

As if it were uncloaked and sitting on our doorstep the entire time, the aircraft grew with the moonlight, an airborne lupine entity in any other world, I was sure.

"A helicopter?" I asked of nobody, astounded. "A fucking helicopter. Well. I don't know what to do about this one."

Before I could process any more thought, the mechanical avian was upon us. Pops of gunfire littered the compound as the chopper swept by overhead, pitching to climb just before the building I occupied.

"CEASE FIRE!" I bellowed into the radio. "Save your fucking ammo, he's moving too fast for you to hit anyway!"

No courtesy of an 'over' on that call, oops!

I didn't have time. The bird disappeared overhead as our tarpaulin roof blocked it from view, then the Earth broke.

At least, that's damn sure how it felt as the world-tearing vibration of automatic gunfire from above stitched its way through our makeshift rain barrier. It perforated neat little holes in a line as the helicopter opened up.

A few rounds found some of the supporting cable my wife had so painstakingly strung and the tarps overhead let loose with a series of *pings* and *pangs* followed by a heavy tearing sound as the wind caught it, once, twice, then lifted an entire triangular section away at once to expose us to our tormentor.

The shiny bubble of a Little Bird cockpit gleamed brightly in the waxing moonlight as a burst of light once again issued forth from next to the bubble. An M134 minigun spewed another volley of rounds into the opening as we all dove for concealment under the still-intact sections of rooftop.

"SHIT!" I screeched as rounds peppered the rooftop just behind our departure and the engine noise from the aircraft flexed in intensity and it repositioned itself for another volley.

The noise was otherworldly in intensity as another buzz saw of ammunition strafed the length of the rooftop and I watched Dave twist in response and dump an entire AK47 magazine skyward, serving a platter of return lead and copper back through the quickly fading blue and grey coverings.

I watched as the others at the opposite end also returned fire to the chopper and did their best to make a retreat into and down the stairwell.

The helicopter sent another heavy load of 7.62 caliber minigun fire in that direction. The rounds chewed a line through the concrete, the tables and chairs, everything in their way as they slammed into the return-sprung metal door upon finding their intended mark.

We remaining three on the rooftop started pumping rounds into the aircraft's belly as it started to juke and jerk, trying to throw off any bead we'd drawn before it nosed-up and scooted back through the air and just out of view.

A moment later, another burst issued forth from the mechanical dragon above as it sprayed the rooftop with death. Several rounds found the tank of an active propane heater near the stairwell, crumpling the canister and setting it ablaze to erupt into a minor explosion, further disabling all hope of reaching the stairs safely as the outer structure collapsed in on itself, leaving us with no escape.

As the orange and red infused plume of black smoke rose, the liquid black chopper lifted and spun again, moving into another direction. I stayed in place, perfectly motionless and watched as it hovered in this spot for another moment, then switched again. I could clearly see the pilot from my position, and it didn't take much watching him to realize he was searching for us.

I sat still, perfectly still and watched some more as the pulsing waves of rotor wash tugged and pulled at my clothing. I did not dare even scan the rooftop for my wife or my friend as the bird lifted and neatly spun once more, and paused a bit to scan that end before appearing to nearly slide sideways off the rooftop space as the pilot yanked the stick to the right and departed.

Then, the rotor wash disappeared, and the deafening roar of an angry AH-6 began to fade. At least, I'd hoped as much. I couldn't hear shit but my own heart pounding and the Liberty Bell itself ringing between my ears.

I looked around, getting a visual on Dave and Jennifer; both were huddled tightly into the corner of the roof maybe 5 yards from me, so I scrambled over to them.

"Are you okay?" I asked.

"What?" Jennifer shouted in response.

Their bells were ringing too, apparently, so I pointed directly at both of them, mouthed 'okay', and gave a thumbs up. Both of them nodded in the affirmative and began to move out of cover.

All three of us ducked and shrunk back into place as another ripsaw of helicopter gunfire split the night, and an explosion of small arms echoed in return. I rushed to the gap I had previously occupied and watched the trail of gun smoke fading behind the mechanical devil as it made a dead-straight passage right back out of our area of operations, presumably expending what ammo it had left on our people as it returned to whatever nest bore such a nightmare.

I caught sight of movement as I turned, and saw Jennifer bolting across the rooftop toward the largest of the several fires scattered around, grabbing any kind of fluid she could along the way. Dave followed and scooped up his own armload of water bottles and half-empty beer cans and they began hurriedly throwing liquid at the blaze, doing so little to quench it.

"LEAVE IT!" I shouted, my hearing returning and hoping theirs was as well.

It must have been, as they both stopped and backed away from the fire and turned to face me.

"We need OFF this rooftop, guys!" I shouted as I neared the place where the stairwell entrance had once stood proud, now a pile of collapsed rubble and destroyed door. The entire passage had collapsed and lay below, effectively barricading our way down. And...was that blood? Caked with dust and small fragments, it appeared as though there was bright red blood adorning the back wall below us.

"Status, who's hit? Over!" I barked into my radio.

"Two on the ground, ah, Thompkins and Vasquez! Over!" came Harrison's voice through the radio.

"Was that Thompkins? Or Thomas? We had a Thomas, he's MIA!" graced another voice. "Over!"

"Main building!" I nearly yelled. "Who's hit? Over."

"Henry took three rounds," Rich's voice grumbled into the radio, "I was grazed and might have took some shrapnel. Over."

"Is…Henry…alive…Over," I snarled in response, looking down at the new organic paint job in the shattered stairwell.

"He is. Shoulder and arm got hit but he should be okay. Over!" Rich breathed, it sounded like they were still running.

"We need to get off this roof." I turned to Jennifer and Dave, then looked around.

Before I could put together anything even resembling a plan, the nighttime air exploded once again, this time literally.

The *crack* of an earth-quaking blast split the night like a piece of firewood, and the source was no mystery as a flash of orange light enveloped our surroundings, though only briefly.

I half ran, half stumbled to the nearest gap in the rooftop façade in time to watch the orange of a blast in the distance fade into a fire, a few blocks past our outer gate.

"What just blew up? Over," I queried over the comms.

"The whole fuckin' road just exploded!" Frank shouted through my earpiece. "Looks like a tank caught up in the middle of it! Over."

"That'd be the AnFo," Rich informed, panting even heavier now, definitely running. "Oh, over."

Pops of gunfire began chattering in the distance, automatic and semi-auto mixed and growing in intensity.

"The AnFo?" I called back to Rich, then, "Frank! Is it the Bradley? Over!"

"A big tan refrigerator with a bunch of guns and antennae?" Frank questioned, his voice crackling as the comms tried to compensate and amplify it through the gunfire, "Over."

"That's probably it," I suggested. "Hit that fucker with the latex paint, come from the blind side and start shooting or smashing anything that looks like a sensor or antenna, and plug the exhaust up! Do fucking *NOT* let them run that machine! Blind and cripple! Blind and cripple, Frank! Over!"

"Solid copy! Over!" Frank crackled again as a corresponding burst of gunfire rang through both his radio and the distant air.

"Latex paint?" Dave said, nearly offhand.

"Yeah, blind them. No windows, no vision blocks, no sight," I informed.

I looked around the rooftop, now scattered with busted chairs and tables that were likely beyond repair. Various small fires leapt and crouched before springing forth again to emit light and acrid smoke as bits and pieces burned all around us. The concrete had been chewed all around as if somebody took a week's worth of methamphetamine and went to town with a sledgehammer. What an absolute mess.

"Guys, grab those cables!" I motioned to the steel line that once held the overhead tarps in place.

They both wordlessly complied as Dave took a knife from his belt and began cutting back the remaining scraps of tarpaulin free of the cable and pulled it away from its anchors with Jennifer's help.

As they worked, I planned and searched. I knew on this side of the building the command center was just below our feet. That was where we wanted to be, and that's where I was going to take us.

I grabbed the edge of the nearest solar panel and began pulling, trying my damndest to wrench it free from its mounts as the material creaked and dug deep into my palms, but gave no purchase.

"Here we go big guy!" Dave called as he took my lead and looped a length of cable around the top of the panel and doled out line to the rest of us.

We began a heavy grunting, cursing, straining match of tug-of-war as gunfire continued near the main outer gate, perforated by one, two, then three smaller explosions as excited chatter broke the radio waves.

A few more good pulls from the three of us in concert and the mounts busted free of the concrete, sending small flows of powdered building material to the roof surface as the panel gave way and fell with a clatter, nearly costing us our footing among the rest of the dust and debris around.

"Over the edge, let's go!" I ordered as we ran to the now-open gap.

We stopped there. Our jaws hanging agape as we surveyed the edges of our kingdom from this vantage.

Despite the night, despite the utter lack of all but the moonlight and some nearby burning barrels and tiki torches, we could see a fierce battle raging at the southern gate. Even several blocks away, various points of muzzle flash could be seen as pops and chatter reached us every time a bullet was given a job. Larger flashes of light could be seen here and there as improvised explosives were flung in answer to grenades, and Molotovs flew to start their own cheer section of screams.

Further back, behind the front row seating, I saw it. The Brad. As Frank described, a refrigerator on tracks, bristling with sensors and weapons. It appeared to be held fast by the trap trench that was dug out under the roadway, its tracks bound up and unable to achieve a climb angle even if they wanted to. I watched in awe as another salvo of bottled fire struck its surface and sprang forth into a petroleum-fueled bonfire of steel and rubber.

"Jesus," Jennifer uttered from next to my stand.

"So much for their tank," I said, feeling my neck grow warm as my palms began to sweat at the realization. Even at this range, I couldn't see a single hatch open. However many people that armored box contained, they hadn't left. The battery power reserve would only last the occupants so long, and it was doing no good for them at any rate as the flames engulfed the nightmare machine.

What once was known as an Infantry Fighting Vehicle was now an oven. I dared not imagine the horror as another round of glass bottles hit, their flaming cloth neckties fueling their contents. The inhabitants of that Bradley were being slow roasted. Cooked alive. I personally hoped they would wise up and use the topside hatch above the troop hold. That move may lead to them being shot on sight, but I think any end may be preferable to the option of being a living holiday ham.

I felt my stomach start to turn as I tore my eyes from that scene to peer over the edge. We were right above a ninth floor balcony, and this made my stomach twist in another direction now. I hated heights. Put a gun to my head instead, and I'd be so much more comfortable. A couple of steps up a ladder was usually my limit, even climbing into my own home at the beginning of all of this had been plenty for me.

"You first!" I instructed to my wife as she wordlessly straddled the riser and prepared herself.

I grabbed one arm, trying to help, and she pulled free.

"It's okay," she assured me, "I've got it."

I watched, helplessly, as she lowered herself to her belly, hanging precariously over the edge as another blast shook the night like thunder. Then, she dropped. My heart skipped a beat, two beats, even, as I watched the love of my life unceremoniously disappear over the edge of the rooftop.

I rushed over and looked down, and there she was. Casually looking up at me from a mere dozen feet below, dead center of the balcony. She looked up and gave me a thumbs up and toothy grin as she called something up to me that the wind took for itself.

More yelling came through my radio as gunfire began in a new direction, this time from the eastern outside gate, the smaller of the two. More pops and bangs started from downriver, near the shore where I'd sent the teens. They really were mounting a full assault. As if it hadn't hit me before, it did now. Like a fucking bulldozer. This was it. This was our fight. Suddenly, I'd rather be anywhere else but here, and that feeling intensified as Dave clapped me on the back with his hand.

"Over the edge or I'm pushing you." He beamed, knowing my holdup about this whole being up high thing. I hated heights.

"I'm going," I snarled, throwing a leg over the edge and immediately feeling every muscle in my body tense up. Dave chuckled and I turned to see him grinning, nearly leering at me as I gave him a one-finger salute and lowered to my belly.

Now or never, I thought, and I dropped. And I screamed.

I felt the wind rushing past my entire being, and I fell. I fell for what felt like way longer than I should have. In fact, I *knew* I was falling too far. Did I miss the balcony? Was this it? Was this the last act I'd make on this Earth? Flipping the bird to my dear friend, then just flinging myself off a rooftop?

Thud

Or, maybe, just maybe, I'm a pussy and I'm being over-dramatic.

I confirmed this to be the truth as I looked up and saw my laughing wife reaching her hand down to help me to my feet.

Dave landed easily next to me, dropping to his feet just as the painted-over sliding door next to us exploded outward with a blast from inside, then followed by another small shining fountain as more painted-over glass erupted forth from the door.

My first thought, as we scrambled away from the flying glass, was that somehow we broke the balcony and it was tearing free. I quickly realized my folly as several more chunks of the material disintegrated and became airborne shrapnel, followed by a familiar voice.

"YOU FUCKERS! FUCK YOU! THIS IS MY HOUSE!" Ryan fairly shrieked as he mag-dumped his weapon blindly through the glass.

"RYAN!" I shouted back, and was met by silence. "Ryan you fuck it's us! Friendlies!"

"Friendlies?" he stammered. "Prove it!"

I heard the sound of a fresh magazine being inserted into his weapon as he chambered a good round.

"What the fuck dude, we don't have a password!" Jennifer chastised him.

"Don't shoot!" I ordered as I maneuvered my head into view, through the many holes he'd made in his previous fusillade.

"Scott!" he gasped. "Oh thank fuck!"

I practically growled at his trigger-happy ass as I took my rifle loose of its sling and began to butt stroke the remaining glass out of the way. Then myself and my two comrades walked into the now open-air command center as I glared at Ryan and Rob, the pair standing now side-by-side.

"This live?" I asked, motioning to the computer screen bank nearest, the scenes of the battle below unfolding in full 1080p clarity.

"Yeah, it's live," Rob replied meekly. "We're losing people."

This statement was amplified as I watched a woman, one of our teachers, fall nearly front and center of one frame, then she received another salvo of rounds that perforated her limpening body as she lay and left streaks of high velocity spatter across the pavement and the house behind her.

I grabbed my radio as I watched the exchange in real time and pressed my earpiece nice and tight to begin issuing orders. The problem was none came. There was currently no order to give.

As oddly as it had seemed, everybody was more or less working and acting as they should have. This isn't to say that I had a couple hundred well-oiled machine-type warriors out there, but they didn't exactly scatter, run, and fumble like amateurs. Even as they lost ground to the enemy, it wasn't the fearful 'run and scream' I'd expected to see. Even though some tripped and fell and others still got shot, they kept face-forward, firing a couple of rounds then moving back further and then firing again as they covered a friend's retreat.

I could see it all from here, or, most of it at least.

Our teams had all appeared to fall back some. They no longer lined nice and tight around the entrances. They fell back, closer to the vehicles they had arrived in, many took positions in and around the remaining homes in the area, and while not visible to our attackers, I watched lots of smart movement.

One guy, it appeared to be Frank, would pop out from one house corner, fire a number of rounds, then disappear from sight only to pop up in a window, or another corner to fire again. We even had people firing through entire houses, lining up window to window and spraying lead at targets of opportunity.

It was encouraging to see them not just standing in the open and hosing areas down like this was a video game with infinite lives. That encouragement, however, was heavily dampened by the sight of better than a dozen scattered bodies on our side of the wall, lain casually in the street and sidewalks, a couple leaned against jersey barriers near the gate, one girl hung like a broken puppet from the upper window of a house.

Judging by the damage behind her, I'd say one way or another the entire room she was in had been exploded, leaving her limply dangling from the window frame by a single bracelet.

As I paused, glued to the monitors I watched multiple small explosives impact our security fencing at the gate. At first it was just a few here and there that shook the gating. Then one, two, and finally a third small blast rocked the gate again and our pride and joy drawbridge began a long squeak as it fell toward the Earth. When it hit home on the other side of the dry moat, it kicked up a shower of busted asphalt and dirt and ceased, likely the last movements it would ever make again.

I didn't have time to order or think on it any further as several of our cameras flashed white and lost all focus for a moment, only to return with only half the vision they had just held.

"What the hell?" Ryan questioned as he tried several commands to clear it up. I turned and went to the windowless sliding door and peered out across the landscape.

"Flood lights, adjusting," Rob replied calmly as he punched some commands in and brought the image halfway back to focus, but by then I had a good enough view from the balcony.

Several floodlights shone from the far side of the street from our fence, bathing the area in white and yellow luminescence. I presumed, or hoped, rather, that they were handheld but considering in several places there were two and four lights each, my stomach sank. This phase was planned.

I startled as Rob called over my shoulder to confirm what I'd already seen, but none of us could have predicted the next stage of the attack, as I'm certain it was planned to be a surprise.

A terrible rumble and a crash flooded the night sky like swamp water as another full set of lights exploded from the center of a residential block, clearly attached to another large vehicle as they gathered momentum, shredding both board and vinyl fences and even toppling a wooden swing set as it careened between houses.

"Ah fuck me," I fairly groaned as reality sank in, and I began yelling into the radio waves for all to hear, "FALL BACK! FALL THE FUCK BACK! *FUCKING RUN, PEOPLE! FALL BACK!*"

I pushed my way back to the monitors to get a look at the goings-on from the closer perspective of the CCTV monitors as I continued sounding the two-syllable order to everyone with a radio to fall back.

Our people began to scatter as the flat front end of an Oshkosh Mk. 23 truck burst forth through a hedgerow between two houses like a depraved sex offender, nearly tilting over and twisting as its jockey wrenched the wheel to one side.

The lumbering beast of a military cargo truck had circumvented the blocked roads by bulldogging its way right through the neighborhood, and now it careened into the front of another house as it cut a left and headed in our direction. One light visible clear as day, the other headlamp still obscured by a lawn chair as it barged its way down the street.

The beast corrected its path and let out a bellow from its air horn as it gathered momentum and speared the first of two closed outer gates, rending it like peeling the foil from a Thanksgiving turkey as it raced across the dropped bridge and contacted the second fence and did much the same. The fence barely gave a tug in defiance as it departed with the horrifying vehicle, sparks being thrown in contrast to its glaring headlight as the section of dragged fence picked a grown man up in passing and slammed him headfirst into a nearby Jersey barrier, a sound I could swear I heard even from here as his skull exploded on contact with the concrete, sending viscous matter in all directions.

The truck continued on as members from our side scattered in all directions, many finding nearby vehicles and playing catch-up as they lit the vehicle up from behind with small-arms as they also were pursued.

"We got infected!" Rob spat as he zoomed the view in to the scene behind the fighting. Streaks of infected ran left and right, nipping on the heels of our own pursuers as some of them matched our own retreat inward and began spraying rounds in both directions. Bullets now flew at us, and also at the new nightmare sequence behind.

Exactly the type of scenario I didn't want, but with all the noise we were making, what the hell did I expect?

"Not good," I muttered, and then recognized the steady *whumpwhumpwhump* of rotor blades increasing in intensity, adding to the chaos at hand. "Fuck, really not good. We gotta go!"

I began gathering what I could that I thought would be useful as the cyclic rate of Ash's M240 machine gun spun up and distant explosions rocked the night once again. I turned to the monitors to see why as Rob and Ryan followed the truck from their own electronic vantage points.

What was shown was a now-smoking rig still moving at a pretty good clip as Rich triggered IEDs alongside it, each blast peppering the rig with shotgun blasts of small supersonic shrapnel. It had nearly reached our gate as Ash's rounds found it and began ripping through the cabin of the truck like the backside of a shooting range. It was a mess before those inside the vehicle even realized they were dead, the heavy rounds from the 240 exploding the flesh as they ripped through, painting the inside of the vehicle with all the colors of the human body.

A final concussive explosion from Rich's devices rocked the front and wrenched the wheel, causing the truck to impact just off-center of our inner gate before the monstrous machine's journey found an end.

The hinged-side support took the mass of the impact, and that section of fencing fell inward with a loud metallic clang and bang, leaving a gap large enough to drive another equally-sized vehicle straight through, which worked to our benefit as several of our vehicles flew through, crushing the gating further and causing it to bend as they passed. They then promptly split and scattered in different directions. I turned back to the balcony just in time to see, hear, and *feel* our old Little Bird friend make another pass over the building.

"Rob, Ryan, get the fuck out," I demanded and watched as both men grabbed what they could and bolted out of the door for the command center, then I turned to my own friend and my wife, "Let's go, we need to get out of here!"

They both began gathering whatever might be useful as we started toward the door.

The sounds of the overhead helicopter rose and fell as it clearly searched both rooftops. Pops and claps matching pings and pangs as it took gunfire from below, occasionally spinning up its side-mounted minigun and returning a burst with a *whirr-brrrrrt*, signaling the likely demise of yet another one of our fighting men and women.

We reached the hallway and shot straight to the end, the only other person left here being Ash and his helper, manning the platform mounted machine gun from the balcony.

"Hit the stairwell!" I told my pair. "I'm going to grab Ash and whoever and meet you at the bottom; we're evacuating."

I watched as the dark clouds of realization spread over Jennifer's face first, then Dave's.

The Compound. The North and South towers, Rich's armory, Henry's garage, the graves of our friends and family, all of our work.

It was lost. We'd been overrun like some rookies by little more than a ragtag group that might not even still be current military. We'd been so confident. *I* had been so cock sure of us.

"You'll be right behind?" Jennifer asked, a tear forming at the corner of her eye.

"Right behind," I assured "Dave, take point, you have the heavier gun between you. I'll be right back, now *go!*"

Dave grabbed Jennifer by the wrist and got her started to the stairwell doorway as I pushed open the door to the space Ash occupied.

Jennifer gave one tearful look behind as she took her hand back from Dave and used it to balance her rifle, checking the chamber of her AR-15 and readying it at a run.

I pushed into the conference area and worked around the table to the glass door behind Ash, pulling it open and instantly regretting it as he unleashed a chest-thumping burst of hellfire at troops and shapes in the distance.

I grabbed the young teen helping him by the shoulder, nearly causing the kid to shit himself in surprise as I pointed to the doorways leading out behind me and mouthed a single word.

GO!

"Oi mate!" Ash cheered as he noticed me, then smacking the top cover of his gun, "Bugger's peppy! I like him! Help me make him a name!"

"We're evacuating, Ash! Let's go!" I called as the helicopter wooshed overhead, once again changing direction and angle as it harassed people far below it with quick belches of lead.

"I'm staying, mate. If I see my cousin again today then that's alright," he said, nearly emotionless. "I miss her, and I owe you one."

"Ash!" I challenged and was cut short as he flung several rounds at the tail of the hovering aircraft before pausing to check and clear a jam.

"No worry," he calmed, "this is my story, tell it well!"

"God fucking dammit, *let's go!*" I urged.

He shrugged free of my grip and picked a mangled casing from the gun's internals.

As he worked, the helicopter attempted to zero in on its new nuisance. The machine climbed straight up and raked forward as it evaded, then it made a slow turn and began searching, the pilot locking eyes with Ash and I on the balcony as my friend slammed the 240's top cover back down and worked the charging handle once before turning to me.

"Save yourself," he pleaded, then jerked a thumb over his shoulder, "Go now, me and this guy, we have some words."

"Fuck," I choked as I felt my feet carrying me backwards.

The helicopter got so close I could smell the fuel it burnt being carried by the rotor wash, then everything began to happen in sequence and so much slower than it should have, yet there was no stopping it.

Ash worked the charging handle once more, ensuring that he was on a live round and everything was ready to rock.

As he moved his right hand to the trigger, the AH-6 pilot found him, the bubble cockpit sweeping right to left from our perspective as the mounted minigun began that whine, as telltale to all around as the distant shrieks of the infected rushing to join the party.

I stumbled, twisted to run, and slammed full-force into a nearby office chair as the glass and wall furthest from us began to disintegrate under a barrage of 7.62 rounds.

The bullets ripped through glass, sending it inward like a shower of tiny razor blades. They chewed at brick and pierced the far wall, traveling straight through like it never existed.

As the helicopter began to feast on my command center, sending copper and lead clean through my own apartment as well, Ash brought his weapon into service.

The M240 and the bird's M134 arguing sprayed from balcony to sky and back and turned the world into one large cyclic vibration. As shrapnel of glass and building materials began to fly all around me, I briefly wondered if this was to be the last thing I'd ever hear, if the bird and the building strove to drive me both deaf and mad.

I began a fast crawl across the floor as I felt bits of building material slam into me from behind, and glass carve its way up my back as I went.

The minigun continued even as the rotor noise warbled, the helicopter coughed, and the gun continuing the barrage on our floor wavered.

I chanced a glance behind me to watch the wavelength pattern of fired rounds find Ash in his balcony, piercing the pressure board fastened to the balustrade and blazing through the man's lower half as he fell into his gun, the device kicking skyward to spray the rest of its rounds as the helicopter matched with a forward pitch. I had just cleared the corner and sprinted through debris once finding my feet and noting the cessation of rounds inbound.

A final destructive crash issued from the conference room and the entire building shook as I reached the stairwell doorway and nearly threw myself down the steps as I bounded downwards, feeling the pain in my shoulder on impact with the wall below.

I continued my rushed descent as the train wreck level commotion outside faded and changed, culminating in a series of loud smashes and crashes much lower.

I nearly ran into Shannon, Ashley, Dave, and Jennifer as I burst through the bottom door.

"Where's Ash?" Jennifer asked.

"Nope!" I uttered between hyperventilated breath, then turned to see past Shannon and see the lower door at the end of the hallway fly off its hinges with an explosive charge. The door skidded straight up until it lost momentum and fell flat, exposing men pouring in and already firing at us as I felt the hot rounds crack past my ears and find homes wherever they struck around us, and I repeated, "NOPE!"

Dave grabbed two of the girls by the backs and practically shoved them toward the main door, caddy-corner to our location and he and I followed.

Just as I felt freedom still looming in possibility, my world was rocked again.

I was wrapped in a scorching heat from behind as an explosive device of some sort chased me with its message, picking me off my feet like an angered Valkyrie and propelling Dave and I alike through the air, and through the open front doorway.

I hit the concrete and bounced, then slid a few more feet. Instant pain engulfed my entire being. I felt immediately as if two large men lit themselves on fire and held a sumo match on my body.

I winced, turning my head and caught Ash staring at me.

Well, it was Ash. Part of him. The man's upper half lay prostrate on the ground right near my own position among a pile of debris from the helicopter and the building alike. The smell of blood, bowels, and smoke washed over me as I peered momentarily into his remaining blue eye, held wide by the final throe of death and unmatched by the other as it liquefied on impact with the ground.

I pushed to gather whoever I could and get out of here and was held fast to the ground.

"I told you, cocksucker," came Colonel Parker's smooth, musing voice. "That pistol would be mine, and, no, I wasn't going to be paying for it."

I felt the tug back and forth as he fought to free it from the retention holster, then the pistol, my little S&W 6906, was pulled free of my body.

I opened my mouth to make whatever retort came to mind and push myself up again. Instead, all I could manage was an instant blinding pain across my upper neck and the back of my skull, and everything faded. The world went black, then came back, then lazily faded away again. The last I remembered of that event was turning to see my wife, Shannon, and Ashley all held at gunpoint nearby. Positioned on their knees as they were roughly searched and disarmed. Dave lay motionless nearby, lain on his back, eyes closed and face peaceful but thankfully not frozen in pain.

Then...

Blackness.

TWELVE

I awoke feeling heavy but feeling a sense of motion. All I could hear was the heavy sound of what seemed to be several fans. All around was a metal skeleton and above me every inch was covered by rounded metallic paneling. It felt like I'd been shoved into a giant airduct, but while I could hear the immensely penetrating fans, I couldn't feel the breeze they must be generating.

I tried to look around and observe my surroundings more completely but couldn't. It seemed as though my head had been immobilized, and my limbs as well.

As I lay, I heard a familiar voice call out for a nurse. Something about his arm, and some water.

I heard that same voice, a moment later, grunt an 'uh-huh', then fall quiet again.

Over the noise of the five-hundred box fans, I picked up various moans and complaints of one type or another intermixed with muffled conversations and sporadic beeps and buzzes of various equipment.

I listened and watched the ceiling, motionless, for just a minute longer before I felt a rough deep pinch in my right arm, and within moments, the world faded back to nothing, and the darkness welcomed itself back in my mind.

"And that's the extent of the events that led to you being with us. Here," Agent Jeff Grayson surmised, as if he thought out loud.

"That's what I can recall, at least," I assured him.

"Well, Mr. Pfeiffer," Grayson began, his eyes resting on me, calculating his words as he spoke them, "your story corroborates what we've learned from your others. I think we're done here. With this leg of life, at least."

"What are you saying?" I eyed him, my companion the headache still faintly straining in the recesses of my mind.

"You acted in perceived self-defense in every case," he informed me, as if I didn't already know that much. "And we can confirm, far enough at least, that Colonel Parker acted outside of his authority and without regard for guideline, public safety, or human decency. I'm moving to file the charges against him instead, as and where they'll fit."

"What was his reasons?" I asked, now damned curious as to why a Colonel in the United States military would continue to pursue and harass, well, little old us, until the bitter end of death if need be.

Before he could answer, one of the recruiting poster young men behind him exited the room.

"Must have needed the restroom," Grayson grumbled before turning to face me once again. "Colonel Parker fell out of communications and failed to report for some time. A common occurrence, these days. It was later found that he and his men had survived by taking advantage of the public, even going as far in several cases as to forcibly remove survivors from whatever strongholds they used for safety."

"That seems a bit excessive to me," I observed. "He hit us with a fucking helicopter *and* a Bradley IFV, dude. I'm not seeing where he would have needed all what he took."

"The Brad was cobbled together and didn't even have any rounds for the 25mm Bushmaster," Grayson informed me. "Nevertheless, Parker wasn't too apt to give up the luxuries he'd enjoyed in the world before it went to shit. His actions cost him dearly and he was trying what he could to survive. Had us convinced he'd brought in some big end of the world enterprise and it was going to put him back in favor with a government that doesn't exist anymore."

"Sorry, doesn't exist?" I asked, stopping and feeling the words in my mouth again before looking to Grayson for an answer.

"We're scattered, shattered, and smattered, Scott," he said pointedly. "We lost contact with SecDef months ago. He was our acting president. Now we're down to one, between you and I, absolute coward and show dog of a senator from Virginia."

"Where's the president? Dead?" I postulated.

"And several others meant to take the role if he died," Grayson surmised. "Air Force One went down. The events that caused this are, admittedly, still not clear to us. What we know is what we've got here and contact with a few shattered factions across the country but even with them, our communications are sporadic at best and nonexistent at typicality."

"No government, no president, sounds like a dream come true if you ask me," I chuckled, desperately trying to interject some humor into the conversation. No dice. Grayson looked as if he were a vet explaining a family pet's life-threatening illness.

"It's grim, Scott." As he explained, he became increasingly casual, less the government agent and more the man just trying to figure things out. "We concede a lot to those still out there fighting. The infected, the gangs, the raiders, Christ on a fucking mattress it's like a video game gone rogue out there. We condoned Parker's actions for the longest because, well, in part there was never a witness to testify against him."

"Then why would he risk bringing me here?" I questioned. "If I could be such liability to his run over what was left of civilization?"

"We demanded it, at threat of persecution," Grayson explained, "and death. 'Bring us one of these local warlords, or you're done, no more chances'. He probably assumed he could just steamroll you guys with his position in the government and walk away unscathed. I don't think he'd planned on interviews and interrogations."

"So now what?" I asked, and the question was tailed by a loud growling of my stomach.

"We go meet your wife and friends in the cafeteria for lunch," Grayson explained. "Munoz here will handle rounding up Parker, we still have due process and I want it followed. In the meantime, we'll explain what we can. Come on, I'll lead."

Munoz began packing his recording equipment and getting ready to go do whatever he does. I stood and immediately stretched, feeling the rubber bands that controlled my body all work at once and instantly felt better. Not completely, but still better than a moment before. Then my thigh cramped.

"Ah, fuck," I muttered. "Hey Grayson, I'm not a prisoner or whatever then?"

"No Scott." He smiled wanly. "You're just a survivor, like the rest of us, though I hope you make yourself as useful to us here as you did back in Ohio. Your choice, of course, but we can't exactly expend transport to see you back home."

"Where exactly is 'here', anyway?" I asked. "Can you tell me now?"

"Of course." Grayson forced a smile once again. "Mister Pfeiffer, welcome to Cheyenne Mountain."

I nearly groaned. Okay, I actually *did* groan, because it's all been just so typical. So much so in fact that if you were to make a book or television show out of this whole ordeal it would work, because it's all so...used? The government. The interrogation rooms. The...well, everything. Now, Cheyenne Mountain as well?

"I'm sorry," he offered, "it's not the Hilton. But we have Spam. Whole lot of Spam. It's, uh, well, let's go have some."

I cleared the corner of the table and approached the door to leave, following Grayson. Before I got all the way, I paused.

"Hey, Munoz?" I queried the tan-skinned man who had tormented me since my arrival.

"Hey no hard feelings," he advised, pausing to gingerly rub the bandaging he wore.

"I brought you a gift," I stated, watching his eyes narrow as I reached into my pocket, dug around, and produced a middle finger for his benefit. "You still a hoe, bro."

"Hey fuck you puto!" he challenged, though it was much less venomous than it had been previously.

I paced Grayson the rest of the way as he spoke softly to another man who met us past the doorway. I didn't pay attention; my mind and eyes were too busy taking in our surroundings.

The sterility of the hallways was no less imposing than it was my first time seeing it. The hallways still moved with all types of people, it nearly breathed with their movement. But something didn't seem quite right.

"Hey Grayson," I spoke, watching him acknowledge me from over his shoulder, "Cheyenne Mountain? From what I saw on TV and YouTube and such, it didn't look like this. They said it was like being inside of an aircraft carrier."

"Been in many of those?" he asked. "Thought you were a civilian?"

"Been in one, on vacation in Texas I think it was," I informed him. "This doesn't feel anything like that. It's… I don't know. It's like a hospital minus the clutter and windows."

"You don't think anything you can access via your TV is going to give you the whole grand tour, do you?" he inquired. "This is the VIP section. Used to be Top Secret, not like that matters much these days. It goes a lot further than the spring-bedded structures and five water reservoirs that they show you."

"Makes sense I guess." I shrugged, relenting, "Who's your friend?"

"Ah, yes, this is Doctor Silverman." He motioned his hand to the other man, who looked remarkably like Alan Alda minus the humor. The man nodded and awkwardly extended his hand and we exchanged greetings.

"Doctor Silverman will be taking a seat at our lunch table and answering what questions I'm sure you have," he finished, then added, "He's one of our top researchers for this…epidemic."

We continued down a few more short hallways and then our small parade turned and entered a cafeteria. The purpose of the room very clear to me, rows of tables and chairs, serving counters along most of two walls with a large window displaying a nearly entirely stainless steel kitchen.

Several tables were occupied nearer the doors, various types of military and professional sorts with men and women in white lab coats mixed throughout. At the very end of the room, I saw them. The mess of dirty blonde hair, the small child next to her, bouncing in her seat. The unruly red hair and tattoos sitting next to them.

"Jennifer!" I called, watching my wife's head snap in my direction as she rose instantly from her seat, "Gwen, Rich!"

We met nearly halfway across the room in a deep embrace. I pulled her in, feeling my tall wife pressed tight against me, burying my nose in her hair and her neck as a single tear fell from my eye.

I pulled back in time to see her wiping tears of her own but had no time to take it in as my legs were thoroughly assaulted by a much smaller embrace but matching in emotion and implied intensity. I bent down and scooped up my toddler, her nearly bleach-blonde hair falling to just above her shoulders. I gave her a big squeezy daddy hug and took in a sloppy little kiss before holding her out and checking everywhere I could on her little arms, legs, head and neck.

"I assure you," Grayson approached, smiling, "she's been in the best care we could provide."

"You can check my bunk for the Polaroid of Parker holding her. To taunt me and threaten my silence," I said coldly. "So, despite the recent turn in hospitality, Grayson, if my kid has so much as a scratch on her, I'm killing everyone in this facility."

"Please," he replied, "let's have a seat. I'll have lunch brought to you. And I'll grab that photo, if there's any way we can use it against him, I will."

I found a seat opposite Rich, Doctor Silverman, and eventually Grayson. My daughter happily sitting between my wife and I as she toddler babbled and poked my various cuts and bruises. So many rough patches from head to toe now that I nearly forgot about the relatively fresh gunshot wound near my ear. It all hurt, and ached, but I was here, with my family again and at least one friend.

We all spoke excitedly about the recent events, garnering more than a few watchful gazes as those nearby listened in. I figured it was their right to, there was no telling if some of these people had even seen the outside since the world went to shit.

And what a strange thought that was. Those famous blast doors probably slammed shut the moment it all began, which undoubtedly meant there were many here who had never experienced it. It was nothing more to them than a play on their monitors, or a story they'd heard from others.

At any rate, we were here now. Maybe, just maybe, we could find a way to be safe and happy as well. But I still had so many people left behind.

Rich informed me of the things I didn't know yet. Jennifer had been in the dark, as well, pretty much by my side until the end.

Many of our people had managed to use the final moments to escape. Several small groups took their chances overland, marching up the riverside toward the Hashman compound. Another larger group managed to flee in one of our remaining boats, cutting the netting across the river and heading out on the head of a hail of gunfire. Many others had died or been severely wounded. Unfortunately, Rich was unable to detail the who and how as of yet, we didn't even know how many of us were here.

Rich himself was ambushed in a way. He had made it down safely and was able to see Henry off by boat. He had returned to round up others and aid their escape, only to be caught in a blast. He said the wall next to him literally exploded and, when he woke up, he was in a large aircraft of sorts, head bandaged, and handcuffed in place. He didn't know much more than that and I wasn't going to push him.

The right side of his face had been patched over with gauze, and several strips still ringed his cranium. Despite this, the angry black-purple of bruising seeped from the edges of the bandages, contrasting the white of the material and the crimson spots of blood that still slowly wept through. The guy looked like he'd been held down and beaten by a Southpaw with a baseball bat.

"Well," Doctor Silverman interrupted, "I'm sure you have questions, and I have only a little while longer to remain before I return to my work. Shall we?"

"Yeah, Doc," I concurred. "So, you're researching what, exactly? The virus?"

"Not virus, for starters," he corrected, as we all fell silent and watched him, anticipating more info without asking. "What we know is it started airborne."

"But not a virus?" I asked, admittedly not the most well-studied in pathology.

"Not a virus," he confirmed. "An infection, of sorts. A parasitic bacterium, in layman's."

"What started it?" Rich inquired.

"No idea for sure," Silverman answered, splaying his hands to emphasize. "Our leading theory is the earthquakes. You'll recall the 'Big One' that happened in California several weeks prior to all this? Our forerunning theory is that it released a previously unknown organism into the air. It, essentially, it cracked the ground deeper than ever before if you will, and unleashed an airborne threat that humans have likely never before encountered."

"But that was weeks before people started attacking each other," Jennifer noted, "and it happened so quick. How could it take that long then just…poof?"

"You'll understand we are limited here, as for our research capabilities," Silverman explained further. "From what we've found, it was infectious without symptoms aside from those present with mild colds or sinus issues. The parasite rooted into the lungs of our, how you'd say, 'Patient Zero', and there it grew stronger and spread throughout the body while it waited. And with each subsequent infection, the DNA altered to be slightly better suited for the human genome, meaning each infection happened faster and hit harder."

"So a cough, a sneeze, anything could spread it?" I pushed him further.

"Yes. Exactly," he continued. "Given the theoretical six degrees of separation, quick period to infection, long incubation, it spread nearly silently across the world until something happened, of which we still aren't sure of. Some…biological trigger, perhaps? An unknown signal, or just bad luck and slow response from mankind as this started in Los Angeles, as opposed to China, India, or elsewhere."

"Jesus," I sighed, rubbing the stitching of my old head wound.

"Why does its starting point make it worse?" Jennifer asked.

"Point of origin," Silverman corrected, "the spread was likely quicker because of the population density of that region. Even more so as it's a major point for international and local travels, tourism, so many factors. And nobody was looking. With undeveloped and developing nations, the eye toward them is sharper. Nobody expected an epidemic of any proportion to come from America. Here? No, never heard of. Shanghai? Ahhh maybe, yes, but not L.A."

Before he continued further, a tray of fried spam, canned vegetables, and cartons of milk, juice, and water were placed before me. I was apparently the only one who hadn't been fed, as the others barely took notice of my feast. I began to dig in while I listened, barely tasting the food as I shoveled it into my mouth.

"What we do know is how it infects from a host, and how it controls the host," Silverman began anew. "It interferes with the autonomous nervous systems. Sympathetic, parasympathetic, it rides them like a work trolley and gains function control of the host like this."

"You lost me Doc," I said through a mouthful of mushy beans and corn. "Back to simpler terms."

"It, well," he started, sighing and pinching the bridge of his nose, "tt drives you from inside like a remote control car. It makes you perform the basic things it needs to survive. It sends signals and chemicals similar to adrenaline out to make you faster, stronger, and nearly immune to pain. But in bursts. It still needs sustenance. It still needs the body to rest. It needs a metabolism."

"That explains quite a bit," Jennifer noted. "The slow ones, Shannon called the shamblers. Why they always smelled like shit. And even why several times we had people reporting that they were almost kind of nesting together in shelter. But how did they infect others? And so quickly? And they seemed to, I don't know, like, choose?"

"Salivary glands, believe it or not," Silverman replied. "Once the virus had coded itself to humankind, and strengthened itself, it is able to inject itself very rapidly into new hosts through a bite. The same thing with their, er, vomitous attacks. This is the heaviest areas of infectious substance within an established host, and as it's already coded to 'go human', it has nearly instantaneous results on the next victim. Remarkable, really. We've never seen anything quite like it."

A sinking feeling began to spread through the pit of my gut as realization wormed its way through my conscious mind.

"Where and how are you learning all of this?" I questioned.

"Well," the Doctor confessed, "here. We keep a number of subjects on hand. Except for the big buggers, we can't seem to round one of them up without tremendous loss of life and breach of safety."

"A number?" I asked again. "What number, Doctor Silverman? How many?"

"That's quite confidential, Mr. Pfeiffer," he stated, narrowing his eyes at me. "Rest assured, it is safe."

"I doubt that," I told him, then to my wife and friend, "Find out how many of us are here from Ohio, and get everyone that wants to go gathered here in, say, 14 hours? I'm going home. Fuck this deathtrap."

"Agreed," said Rich quickly.

"I miss my clothes," Jennifer concurred, tugging at the ill-fitting nurses scrubs she currently wore, "And we forgot Gwen's favorite coloring books in Ohio anyway."

"Now, let's not be hasty," Doctor Silverman cautioned. "I assure you, they are locked deep away and safe."

"They're safe, but are we?" I started in return. "Look Doc, we had an outdoor compound that could probably have survived the end of the world just fine if Parker hadn't thrown a truck, helicopter, *and* an armored vehicle at it. Even then, even in the furthest reaches of our territory, we refused the idea of keeping these things caged up. Kill them. Or they'll do the same to you."

"Mr. Pfeiffer," Silverman began again, "it's not just merely for study, we are doing this in hopes of-"

"Fucking what, dude?" I retorted. "Saving them? Us? Kill them, don't get fucking bit. It's that simple. Have you even seen these out in the world? How they work together? How they set traps and *learn?* How they take care of the slower among them so they can all remain strong?"

"I've seen plenty of these infected, Scott." He glared over the table.

"That's not what the fuck I asked Doc and you know it." My voice began to rise. "You haven't been out there. You haven't lost-"

"Lost whom? Lost what?" his turn to cut me off as Jennifer placed her hand on my trembling fist. "Do you think we were allowed to go collect loved ones and possessions before the doors slammed shut? No. No I don't recall being given that option. My wife, my children, my grandchild, no. They sent a patrol that way. Want to know what they were able to find?"

"Continue," I grumbled.

"My neighbors. Scott," he nearly sobbed, "they brought my neighbors back here for me to run tests on. Infected. Thirty-seven year old Amy, eight year old William."

"And you couldn't even turn it down?" I interrogated. "Tell them, perhaps, no? That it's too dangerous? What are the safeguards?"

"Lock and key," he confirmed. "They're all kept confined, much as you were, except they don't get invited up for Spam and canned vegetables. And, no, I couldn't decline. Everybody down here has a purpose to one extent or another. If my purpose, my, usefulness, were to fall to the wayside, I wouldn't be down here anymore."

"What's the alternative?" Jennifer interjected.

"Topside," he stated firmly, motioning upwards with a finger. "We have a late-construction FEMA camp on the mountain. Mostly a cobbled-together shantytown, big tall chain link fence, guard posts, all draped with camouflage netting."

"How can we locate those that came in with us?" I asked, changing the topic. "Or, were brought in, rather."

"I'll put word out through Agent Grayson," Silverman assured. "We can have all of you meet here, in this cafeteria, post the dinner rush at around nineteen hundred hours?"

"Yeah that'll work," I agreed, seeing the hands of the clock positioned just after noon.

"Nineteen hundred hours?" Jennifer inquired.

"Seven PM," I informed her, to which she nodded and shrugged.

It turns out I should have argued for a reunion to happen a bit sooner. It got rather boring, and it did so rather quickly. For the time being at least, we were confined to our new room, the cafeteria, and the hallways between. Something that mostly went over my head about accommodations and varying permanency, clearance, blah blah blah.

Once we departed company with Silverman and left the cafeteria, we were led by a young man in military uniform to our new lodgings.

It was nothing fancy, though worlds better than my previous jail cell.

The same colorless tile, emotionless white and green two-tone walls, and glaring fluorescent lights from the hallways followed us into the room, doing nothing to complement it. Inside was spartan, bunk beds on both sides of a smallish room but instead of the glorified cardboard of a mattress, we were offered real cushion. At the end of each bed sat a single two-drawer dresser. The end of the room held another doorway, beyond which was an open shower stall, sink, and toilet. Not attached.

"Where are you going?" Jennifer asked as she plopped into a sitting position on the bottom bunk, setting Gwen on the floor to walk around.

"Shower," I muttered, stripping my clothes off even as our escort eased the outer door shut.

I left a trail of my coverings as I moved; I'd find out on my way back to pick them up if my clothing had stuck to the floor. I at the very least *felt* that filthy, and barely even let the water reach its maximum scalding…lukewarm temperature… before I found myself huddled under the meager cone of water emitting from the wall-mounted faucet. I had just unwrapped the bar of unscented soap I found nearby when the water shut off. I turned angrily, realizing after a moment that it was on a timer and twisted the single knob again.

After a while I was cleaned and searching for a towel, finding several folded and put on a shelf under the overhanging sink.

I left the shower area a new man, freshened up and smelling, well, neutral. I quickly ruined this effect by peeling up my dirty boxer shorts from the floor and donning them so as to save my daughter from the sight of naked dad.

"Your turn," I said to Jennifer as I approached her, three pecks on the lips, and sat on my own bunk. "Both of you, probably."

"What are you going to do?" she asked as she got up and took Gwen by the hand and led her toward the shower.

"Nap," I replied, the single syllable as comforting in that moment as the action itself. Naps are always good, and while some may not be able to sleep, that was no problem for me. I am an expert napper.

And true to fashion, I went under the covers and was asleep before their shower ended.

FOURTEEN

I'd love to say my rest was easy. I had been exhausted and clearly sleeping in the jail cell holding area hadn't quite recovered me, but every noise roused me.

Without fail, every time I awoke, my mind started drifting. Thinking about how many infected they possibly had here. Would we be allowed to even leave? Were we prisoners here now or would everything work out? Furthermore, what if our people decided they wanted to stay behind and I'd be forced to make yet another tough decision, leave them or stay as well?

Ohio was home. As much as I hated that shit state full of grumpy people, bad weather, and corn, it was home. And my friends were there. I could even confirm or deny my fears and swing through Missouri on the way back to see if my parents made it.

As my mind raced, yet faded between asleep and aware, I took notice of my wife. She had our daughter between herself and the wall, safe from rolling off onto the hard tile floor. In all her grace, she herself was splayed out, knocked out, and snoring like the jake brake on a Kenworth. Damn I love that woman.

Nonetheless, my final attempt at real sleep was cut short by a knock at the door.

I sighed, threw the blanket off, and sat up, promptly smacking my head off of the bunk above me which caused Jennifer to stir as well.

Making my way to the door, I opened it and found Rich standing there. His unruly red hair was freshly washed and lay about his head in a mess, but his blue eyes looked as if he'd only recently woken as well.

"1900," was all he stated, nearly yawning the word.

"Yeah, right," I replied, turning slightly to see Jennifer and Gwen emerging from their cocoons. "We'll be on our way in a minute."

Rich nodded and ran a hand through his hair before departing, presumably toward the cafeteria where we'd be reuniting with whomever was here from our group.

After a few minutes, we were making our way down the halls as well, looking every bit the 'slow shambly' infected. I'm surprised nobody called Silverman to come study us.

I led the way, and three turns later I was pushing open the cafeteria doors and ushering my wife and child in ahead of me.

Once I made my entrance as well, my heart sunk. Sunk. Shit, it fell through the floor.

Maybe a dozen people awaited. A dozen.

We had probably two-hundred people fighting on our side. Yet here sat a dozen people.

I eyed every person present. No big hugs, no showmanship or entry speech. Everybody looked ragged and worn, seemed every bit a post-battle crew having only had a shower and minimal rough sleep. I wondered how bad I looked as well. Bandages new and old, same old clothes I'd been apprehended in.

Henry was the first to speak.

"Yes, sir buddy," he offered. "We're all here, why the long faces?"

"Two-hundred people," I muttered. "I'm damn glad to see you guys, but is this all that survived?"

"Oh, heavens no!" Henry exclaimed. "We did lose quite a few, rest their souls brother but many of our family made it out before they could be rounded up."

"I've heard," I confirmed. "I was just hoping to be able to put some worry to rest. I see you, Rich, hello to Dave, Shannon, Ashley, Cody, Clara, Erik. But we have my kid and one of the others, some of the high school students but what about the boat Gwen was in? With Rich's wife? And the dozen other children she had with her? Did everyone make it safe? Who's left?"

"I opened fire when they took the boat, just in view of our compound," Cody informed me. "I couldn't quite see, but the boat did shove off in the confusion, maybe they got away after all."

"You opened fire with my kid and others present?" I eyed him furiously.

"Relax," he assured. "Suppressing fire, just to work them up and break their focus. If Carolyn got away with the boat, then it worked."

"Fine," I conceded. "And, thanks."

"Kinda funny," Erik spoke up, the large man offering a half-grin, "but it probably worked in your favor; they brought your kid here and we know she's safe."

"Yours are too, I'm sure," I comforted him. "Angie, right? Her and your kids were on one of the first boats to leave."

"Still no confirmation that anybody made it at all," he advised. "We were out of radio range to your buddy upriver, so we don't even know if the boats got there."

The thought caused a sour turn in my gut as I mulled it over. He was right. We had nothing but blind faith that the entire plan worked in the first quarter even, and it damn sure didn't hold up through the entire game.

"I mean, anything is possible," reminded Shannon as Ashley quietly eyed everybody present. She looked so lost here, like she was looking for something so simple as what to say in the faces of others.

"I think they made it," I offered, "or they'd be sitting right here, right?"

"This looks like maybe a third or less of the people he took," Jennifer noted. "So if that's true, where is everybody else?"

"Shit, they could be back home already," Dave suggested. "They might have just hidden and never got captured. If Parker didn't leave any men there to watch the base, I'd be fixing things right this minute."

"That's possible," Shannon agreed. Nobody else seemed to pick up on the out-of-character optimism from Dave, but I did. Maybe he and Bri really were closer than I assumed.

"Well," Clara interjected, "I'm going home. I'm worried about Frank and my own kids. I'm not going to stay in Colorado."

"Yeah nah," I agreed. "Did they tell you guys they're keeping an undisclosed number of the infected here?"

I assumed not, as this news sent a murmur of worry and protest throughout our small grouping as others in the room observed cautiously. We proceeded to bring everybody as up-to-date as we were and considered the job done when every question had to be answered with a clueless shrug.

Nonetheless, three people, the high schoolers chose to stay behind.

"We have nothing left in Ohio," spoke a girl whose name I believed to be Anna. "Our families are gone, and we just think it'd be safer here. Surely they wouldn't bring those…those *monsters* here to keep unless they could do it safely."

"All that's happened," Cody spoke up in her direction, "and you still trust the fucking government to do anything right? They couldn't even get shit right *before* the end! I definitely am not staying here. No way."

"Do you think it's any easier out there?" started another teen, a boy with dark hair whose name I couldn't place. "How far do you think you can travel without being overrun? I've heard the stories from teams that come back, I listen!"

"Well then stay the fuck here!" shot Erik. "We don't need lightweights taking up our food supply anyway! Sit here and piss yourself, you fucking girl!"

"Fuck you dude!" the boy nearly spat. "It's quiet around our compound but you go in any direction and they're still everywhere! You're insane!"

"Guys!" I broke in, not wanting an argument to persist. "Yeah, it's insane, but I've got to know, and I've got to be back home. Why the fuck are y'all arguing for anyway? Nobody is making anyone stay or go to begin with, what's arguing about to solve? Shut up!"

"He's right, everyone, why we gotta bicker?" Henry helped.

"Yeah, chill. Shit's about to get crazy anyway, if you don't want it, then stay here," Rich opined.

"Well, we don't have much with us, we can talk to Grayson," I suggested. "See if any of our gear was saved and if we can get any going away packs."

I didn't have time to continue when all the lights blinked once, twice, then went out.

In their place came a glow from the many emergency lights around, followed immediately by oscillating red strobes and a mechanical *BUZZZZ BUZZZZ BUZZZZ.*

"Oh great," I murmured, looking at all the scared faces around us. "Ah shit."

I backpedaled among my shocked friends and half-ran to stick my head out of the cafeteria door. At just the right moment, I caught sight of a white button-up shirt and salt and pepper hair as it passed at a jog.

"*GRAYSON!*" I shouted over the alarm buzzer, and the man turned. It wasn't him, but upon seeing me, the guy put up one hand, mounted by a single index finger.

"One sec!" he mouthed, then disappeared around a corner as he put a radio up to his mouth, holding it sideways like all cool guys do.

I felt a presence next to me and turned to see Rich on one side, Clara and Jennifer on the other.

"Guys, get everyone gathered up and get back into the kitchen," I ordered. "Block all the doors but this front one until we figure out what's going on."

We started ushering personnel toward the kitchen; most went willingly but I did watch Cody grab one man up by the shoulder and nearly give him a kick start in the right direction. Once the cafeteria was devoid of people, I'd turned to go in with them, into the stainless steel safety of the kitchen area.

Just as I'd reached the door, the entrance to the kitchen burst open.

"Pfeiffer!" Grayson shouted, and I whirled around.

"What the fuck is going on here, Agent?" I countered.

"Parker!" he shouted and motioned that I come with, to which I turned back to the kitchen, pointed at my fighters, Rich and Clara.

"You two come!" I ordered, then to Jennifer and the rest of the Ohio all-stars team, "You guys, keep everybody hidden until I come back, we don't have weapons so find anything you can use! Stay low, stay quiet!"

Before even Jennifer could jump to stop me, I was gone again, hot on the heels of Agent Grayson who was moving too fast to speak about where or why.

Now, I thought we were moving at a pretty good clip, but apparently not as we got nearly shoved aside by a large group of men in gas masks toting rifles as they blazed past us on the way to whatever was going on.

My big ass was nowhere near as quick, but I kept on Grayson's heels as he barked multiple times into his radio handset and led us through several left and right turns.

We finally reached a set of double doors that bore a sign overhead-
NO UNAUTHORIZED PERSONNEL BEYOND THIS POINT

Here, Grayson stopped and grabbed the lead of the next group of soldiers to make it to our location. He issued orders into the man's ear that I couldn't quite make out, then called me in closer.

Even tight in with him the sound of the alarm buzzer made it difficult to discern his statement, but I got it, nonetheless.

"You're with me!" he ordered. "Parker is making a play."

"Fuck do you mean 'making a play'?" I shouted back to him.

"He's removed the safeties," Grayson admitted, "he had men all over this base and he's trying to take it over. Killed three of our guys when they went to arrest him and got away. He's in the C3."

"C3?" I questioned, having never heard that term before.

"Command center," Grayson stated then grabbed me and ushered me to the stairwell and motioned for my friends to follow.

"Why do you need me?" I asked as I started down the steps behind him.

"He got here using you!" Grayson shouted over his shoulder, the alarm drowning out parts of every word. "I don't exactly have a plan. But let's go!"

We ripped through three full sets of stairs, each split and doubled-back like the stairwell in our apartment building, but much wider.

Finally, Grayson pushed through a set of doors at the bottom of one flight and into a hallway packed with personnel.

At the far end, perhaps a hundred feet away, there was a 'T' intersection backed by large plates of glass as the main hallway broke and went around a central room, terminating not far down either end of the rough 'U' in sets of double doors.

The relative distance, dim accent lighting and red flashes made it hard enough to see, I was helped slightly by the monitors, displays and banks of devices within the room. If this was the command center for everything, it fit. There were perhaps three rows of computers with state-of-the-art displays, then the back wall was a huge multi-pane unit set into the wall and framed with steel doors on each side. What most stood out to me in this room was the figures standing in the middle.

It was Parker. Colonel fucking Parker. He had another man held at the end of his pistol and was currently leaning forward shouting at him.

Filling the rest of the room with him was what appeared to be several civilians, an entire family, huddled together as kept in place by several men in military uniforms.

Between the emergency lights and the banks of monitors, the Colonel's face was cast in such a light as to show the monster he really was.

As we approached, Grayson began barking orders and demanding updates.

"Sir!" a young man in uniform reported at Grayson's demand for an update, "We're getting overrun at all lower levels, tactical retreat has been initiated and we are sealing all doors as our men get pushed back!"

"How the fuck did he get the president in there?" Grayson growled loudly, jabbing a finger in the direction of the control center. I realized it as he spoke it; the man Parker currently had a gunpoint was none other than the Governor and acting president of the United States himself. This just took an immediate turn for the worse, I thought.

"They were the ones watching him this shift sir," the man continued, motioning to some bodies near Parker. "I-I'm sorry, we didn't know!"

"Don't apologize you jackass, if any of us had known this wouldn't be happening!" Grayson snapped, showing a side I hadn't yet seen nor expected from the older man. "Can we get these fucking buzzers cut?"

The man nodded quickly and began speaking into a radio piece held in place near his shoulder. A few more beats, and the pulsating lighting remained the same, but the buzzer immediately silenced itself. All that I'd been missing auditorily came back in a rush, and suddenly the space held too much sound once again.

Men and women moved around in every direction. They coordinated plans and issued orders. Many just stood by, watching, seemingly helpless in the flashing red darkness. Off in the distance, multiple distinct pops that I recognized as gunfire echoed from somewhere far away as some nearby gasped at the sounds and began moving away, back up the stairwell.

"Why the fuck don't we have charges on those doors yet?" Grayson began shouting, grabbing one man by the shoulder and pushing him forward, directing him around the corner as he left.

I approached with Rich and Clara, only to wince back a step as Grayson grabbed a rifle from one nearby uniformed woman and fired three shots into the glass.

Parker merely paused, and looked in our direction, first at Grayson, then at me, then the rest of the people in the hallway. He motioned to one of his men to hold the President, then approached the glass partition with an eerie grin and clicked an audio button.

"You could have just knocked, Agent," his voice drawled sweet and slow through the comm box. "You knew those rounds wouldn't penetrate."

"Open the doors, John!" Grayson ordered. "Let's talk through this, we can work together!"

"Tried that," he nearly groaned as he continued grinning. "You showed your interests to still be…small. I'm here to begin healing an entire nation."

"What's your angle?" Grayson challenged. "You have to have an end game."

"You're about to find out, Jeffy," Parker taunted Grayson.

"Jeffy?" I questioned, to which Grayson put a hand up without even looking my way.

"Christ John, come on, there's got to be another way we can both meet goals," Grayson nearly pleaded as the doors on each side of the display behind Parker began shaking with impacts from forces trying to gain entry.

"My dear brother," Parker replied, "this is the only way it could have panned out. You've known it's the path New America needs, you just lacked the fucking gumption to get things done. Your due process and panel decisions. You could never measure up!"

"Brother?" I interjected. "What the fuck, Grayson? What the fuck dude? Brother? Jeffy?"

"Doesn't make us on the same side," Grayson assuaged, his cool eyes lined with fire and meeting mine for a moment before he turned away. "He's fucking lost it."

"The only thing I've lost, Jeffy," Parker mused in torment at his brother before turning behind him, "is my patience. Jacoby, bring the boy forward."

The man I assumed to be Jacoby pulled a young boy of maybe six years old to his feet by the back of his neck and used it as a control to force him to Parker.

Parker, without so much as a mere hesitation nor flinch, raised the pistol he held to the boy's stomach and squeezed the trigger once. The shot rang loudly through the comm box on our side of the wall as people in the room screamed and the boy began a long, low, haunting wail of pain, doubling over to fall face first into the floor and gripping his belly as he writhed in agony.

Clara gasped from behind me and pressed her face into the back of my shoulder as she let out a sob. Rich tried to snatch a rifle from the man next to him, only to be pointed at by the barrels of three more.

I stood in utter shock. The sweat that had been slaking my entire body dipped in temperature as if I'd just walked into a meat freezer. There was tremendous commotion all around me, yet I couldn't do any more than focus on the new developments right in front of me.

My surroundings slowed into focus as every man and woman that was on the back side of the control room came flooding back in from each end of the "U", shouting about being overrun and to seal the doors.

Bright flashes issued as the steel safety doors were thermite-welded into place and those nearest the front of each group took positions with rifles, and a single man wielding an M249 Squad Automatic Weapon. They all focused their attention down the hallways and at the doors they had just passed through and sealed off as the doors began to thud. Once, twice, then a full-on barrage of bangs and thuds, each one causing the thickened steel to dance in its frame.

Atop the thudding, came a tidal wave of ear-piercing shrieks that could only have been made by those damned infected. How many did he say? If reports were correct, they'd doubled in number thanks to the local population feeding their ranks, turning pure terror and panic into hunger with a single bite. But a double from *what*, exactly? Because they were winning, and the doors were only barely doing their job to hold back a flood.

Parker casually stepped over the boy, motioning for his man to release the child's father to fall over his boy, hysterical. He stopped right next to his comm box again, positioning himself to speak into both the box and the room.

"Mister acting president," he stated, as if he was issuing a bad test score, his croon sending shivers further up my spine, "your son has been gut shot. If he doesn't receive medical attention immediately, he will die. The nukes. That's all I ask."

I felt all color wash away from my skin and come rushing in again with that singular word.

Nukes.

"John, for fuck's sake!" Grayson called through the comms, desperate. "Let's talk about this!"

"Talk is over, baby brother. Just watch instead, we're about to get to my favorite part!" the Colonel drawled soft and slow again as he raised his pistol and put three rounds into the comm box, then turned back to the president.

We could no longer hear anything as the man fairly wailed from his knees, clutching his son close to his chest as the boy's blood began to pool. Red-faced, anguished, the man just continued shaking his head as he bleated words we could no longer hear.

"Go to Jennifer!" I ordered Rich. "*Find* weapons, anything at all, keep them there, in place, and safe. I'll be coming soon!"

"Got it!" Rich agreed and hauled ass back to the steps and out of sight so quickly it was like he was on fast forward. Or, maybe, I was still on slow.

I turned back around to see the Colonel send another bullet, this time to the president's daughter in nearly the same location before grabbing up the man's wife and pressing the pistol to her temple, sending him into hysterics and a series of clear pleas.

Within moments, Parker had dropped the body of the woman after receiving no compliance. The shot was silent with no comm box, but the red and hair splatters against our window spoke all they needed to. He yoked the president up like a puppy and pushed him to a console where the man set to work, wincing at every noise and shout issued by Parker.

As the president began issuing the needed codes, the doors on the right hallway burst forth and fell flat as the entire area burst into shrieks of the monsters and a barrage of gunfire.

I grabbed Grayson by the collar, and Clara by the arm and nearly yoked both of them off their feet to set them in motion.

If there was a way to stop Parker now, that way was clearly lost.

The hallway flooded so quickly with so many well-fed runners that they reached the first line of riflemen as if they weren't even being shot to pieces.

We hit the stairwell in front of the group of others, moved to one side and turned to watch as infected began pouncing on people like lions in a freshly-stocked savannah.

Clearly, they were set to full-turn, with no intentions but to swell their ranks as every person they tackled began those horror shop convulsions and spasms before the monstrous sires even took their full weight off of them.

Go on, Silverman, explain how it happens that fast, I thought.

"We have no choice," Grayson resigned as he pressed in the large red button next to us and reached his free hand up to pull an emergency lever. Thickened steel doors dropped from the ceiling to seal the hallway from the stairwell.

As it fell, it caught the last woman through right on top of her head, propelling her forward and fairly scalping her in the process.

I felt Grayson pulling my arm as we three followed the stampede up the stairs, one floor, two, then a standstill at the top, our way out.

"The emergency doors are sealed!" someone shouted from up ahead as all stopped and began looking wildly at each other.

We were trapped. Steel ahead, steel behind, and a whole two floors to live our remaining minutes upon. Right. Bullshit. I'm getting out of here.

I tapped Grayson and Clara and motioned as we went back down one flight to what I assumed to be the second floor, provided we had started our day on the first.

As we moved into the second floor hallway, a handful of people here and there were scrambling for the stairs still, some others tending to injured that had been in fights with Parker's men, or during the stampede to leave. I could only assume it was the people who'd already fled that took the same mentality as we and slammed the doors shut behind them as they went, so I couldn't really be too upset with them.

"Wait!" Grayson hushed as he pulled us into a small side room and pressed his finger to his lips.

A moment later, a half-dozen soldiers I actually recognized from Parker's crew passed by, shooting into the bodies of those that still lay in the hallways or within visibility from the surrounding rooms. As they reached the end of the hallway, they slammed the security doors shut behind them.

Okay, it was roving death squads that probably sealed everything from everything else, not panicked people from elsewhere in the facility.

This put a tight knot deep in the pit of my stomach. If these guys were sealing the doors, and the first floor, which held my wife, kid, and friends was sealed already...

I didn't have time to think about it further as Clara opened the door cautiously and then stepped out, crouched low and moving as close to silently as she could.

"Grayson, there's got to be a way up," I nearly pleaded. "I have to get to my family, and we need to get the fuck out of here."

"Clearly," Grayson started flatly but was withheld from further comment as the formerly red flashing lights turned to a blue pulsing glow. Fade in, fade out, then back again in a smooth pattern.

"What the hell is that?" I asked.

"He's..." Grayson began, then pinched the bridge of his nose with his fingers as I watched a tear fall down his cheek, "He just launched nukes."

"What the fuck?" I gasped, as I watched the little color pale Clara had recede. "How many? Where? Now?"

"I don't know, but, yes, those blue lights are to warn of a launch," Grayson admitted, exasperated.

"Are there any maintenance vents?" I asked, still urged to get out, maybe now more than before.

"That I know of?" he questioned from somewhere far away. "No. To my knowledge they're barred and have fans every fifteen feet in case we need to back feed the system and exhaust the entire complex of contaminants."

"Fuck," I muttered, then saw Grayson's expression change for a moment.

"Come on," he ordered and took the lead from Clara. We moved low and quick through the empty hallway, passing many rooms in various states of disarray. One in particular caught my eye as we passed it.

The door hung wide open and lying nearly centered to the room was a body, face-down, and arm outstretched. Whether the previous owner of the item was reaching for it, or had dropped it, there was exactly what I needed to feel better. A handgun.

"Hold up!" I called as I skidded to a halt and ducked into the room, checking left and right and finding myself, my two friends, and the guy on the floor to be the only obvious occupants of the space.

I approached the body, passed it by, and snatched the firearm off the floor. A little Ruger LCP380. Nothing fancy, yet better than nothing. The tiny silver and black pistol was so small it could be concealed entirely by my hand. The small .380 cartridge was on par with a .38 revolver, or 9mm, so while it wasn't a massive machine gun, its power would be on par with the sidearms I'd had all along.

I pressed the release and dropped the magazine to witness six rounds within. Pulling the slide back just enough to check the chamber shown one more. Full capacity for this firearm, not one shot had been expended.

I grabbed the business jacket on the body of the man nearby to begin checking for spare magazines, not knowing if this guy had even originally possessed such a small piece.

One pocket, empty, the next containing a set of keys. I went for a pants pocket, and the man grabbed out at my arm, which I dodged back from.

I saw his bleeding eyes at the same moment Clara issued a warning. He opened his mouth to show a gaping tunnel of death that he clearly wanted to drag me into just as that tunnel filled with a crimson and black sludge and expelled it at me. I jerked to one side and only just caught a splash on my pant leg as the rest of the fountain torrent flew past me. Before I could even react, Grayson brought an office chair down on the monster's head.

The first was a glancing blow as the freak started a shriek from Hell itself and began scrambling for purchase to stage a lunge for me. Grayson swung again and connected solid, the skull giving way with a sickening crunch as his head met the hard tile floor and began leaking everything he knew at our feet.

The shriek wasn't alone, however, as clear half a dozen more echoed from further down the hallway. Grayson lunged for the door and slammed it shut just as the first mutated monstrosity reached our position and bashed herself headlong into the heavy wooden door.

"Desk!" Grayson gasped and motioned as he fought to keep the door shut and latched, then realized it had a lock and spun it into place, deadbolting it as the door leapt in its frame with more and more impacts.

We slammed a large metal office desk into the door, the agent just moving out of the way in time to avoid being steamrolled by the heavy furniture. He then braced himself against it as we searched around.

"Drywall walls, right?" I asked Grayson and he nodded. "Just drywall? No core?"

He nodded more emphatically, and I promptly kicked the shit out of the wall furthest from the door, feeling the sheetrock cave under the force of my Doc Marten.

As I kicked, Clara reached into the gaps I was creating and began breaking away lose material and throwing it aside as the door behind Grayson began to crack and split, bowing more inward with every strike.

The freaks were trying to get through the door nearly as fast as we were getting through the wall, but we were beating them.

The far side didn't have as much give, but we forced a hole the best we could, only to be met with a smooth metal surface. Great.

"He said no core!" I growled.

"Filing cabinet!" Clara corrected. "It's okay, help me push!"

We reached in shoulder to shoulder and gave our best as the heavy metal cabinet on the other side toppled forward with a tremendous crash.

Nearly immediately the grinning face of a fresh infected missing half of one cheek appeared, it started that godforsaken screech and before it could even reach full pitch, I pulled the tiny pistol from my pocket and jammed it in her mouth, squeezing the trigger once and blowing the base of her skull out as she crumpled in a backward heap before us, exposing a break room of sorts behind her.

I pushed the pistol through the hole first, flagging the room for threats, then followed it and made sure all was clear.

I motioned, and in a moment, Clara had pushed her way through into the room behind me, turning to call behind her.

"Agent!" she shouted. "RUN!"

Grayson twisted and grabbed the chair he'd used once already and braced the front edge of the desk with it as he scrambled forward and made a break for it, nearly crashing through the narrow hole between the studs as we slammed the filing cabinet back behind him.

Clara fell back against the wall, drenched with sweat and panting much the same as myself and the older man. Here, we caught our breath in silence, save for a few muttered curses from each.

I was the first to move, and I reached out and placed the little pistol right to the side of Grayson's head. Just enough to brush it along his temple and watch his entire body tense as he froze, only bringing his hands up slightly to placate and show he didn't intend to be a threat.

"Scott, what are you doing?" Clara interjected.

"Stay." I motioned her with my free hand. "Your brother, Grayson? Your fucking *brother*?"

"Half-brother," Grayson breathed. "Biological to my mom, different dad."

"I don't give a fuck if y'all are family to the pope," I snarled, pressing the little gun into his head before relenting to make sure it stayed in battery. "That monster is family to you. How much extra allowances and freedoms did that purchase him, Jeff?"

"More than I should have given him," Grayson admitted, turning his eyes toward me. "No amount of sorry can cover that, but I assure you, we aren't on the same side of things. I don't share anything with him but blood now, and even before it wasn't that inclusive."

"I'm going to tell you right now, and only once," I cautioned as I withdrew the weapon, taking his chin in my hand and forcing close eye contact, "you better find religion, because you're coming to Ohio. You'll be treated as a less-trusted member, but one of my crew nonetheless."

"I don't have anything in Ohio," he stated flatly. "Then again, I don't have anything at all."

"When we get back to my home," I continued, tightening my grip, "every single soul we've lost at the hands of your negligence over blood will cost you. One square inch of skin for each person. Starting at your scrotum."

I released his face as his head fell in shame.

"This isn't the time for this," Clara admonished. "Agent Grayson, where were we going to go? Let's get to safety then worry about everything else."

"We're in office storage right now," he thought. "The room across the hall should be maintenance. Every other floor should have access to the electrical shafts for maintenance reasons. If we can take out the wall in the back of this office, it should give us access to the shaft and ladder up."

"You're sure?" I checked.

"Positive," he confirmed. "Each office is set in the same location relative to the shaft. Just because this floor doesn't have the access panel doesn't mean we can't get there from here."

"Well then, we go now," I directed. "I'm going to find my family. Straight across the hall?"

"Straight across, door-to-door," he confirmed.

I moved to the end of the room, it had windows, but the blinds were drawn and the glass itself had been frosted. No shadows appeared to move on the other side, however, and I tried the door to find it locked.

Working the little twist knob, I spun it counter-clockwise and tried the handle again. It leveraged low with a barely audible *snick* just in time for the world to be filled with screeches and footsteps again and I froze. Stuck there with the door but an inch open, watching the dim-light and blue pulsing hallway beyond as a woman screamed on her way past the door.

She hadn't made it but a dozen feet past the door I held in my hands, looking over her shoulder, when a runner from ahead plowed into her. A sickening thud echoed the hallway as he impacted, leveling the woman like a dump truck as the other runner caught up and slammed into the first, having nowhere else now to displace his momentum.

This sent both freaks flying as neither could cope with the new force, and they got up looking like martial arts wrestlers locked shoulder to shoulder as they fought each other right above the woman they were both meant to prey on.

In a bare moment, they both remembered why they were there. She tried to scramble away on all fours and the larger of the two monstrosities, the one to hit her first, grabbed her by the legs.

His disgusting mottled-grey flesh rippled with muscle as he swung her by her ankles, contacting her head with the wall and issuing a watermelon-smash thud as the woman went limp and both monsters dug in deep.

I was pinned in place not so much by fear, this was nothing new in our world now, but I knew if I moved, I'd be noticed. I had no other move but to watch as both once-men pulled shreds of flesh from her back. Her head lolled to one side and I recognized her as the orderly that glimpsed me naked just recently as Munoz collected me from my cell.

This sent an involuntary wave of guilt as I watched her get eaten, unable to have done anything without risking my own exposure.

I barely noticed as Clara reached just above my head, an object pinched between her middle finger and thumb. I recognized it as the spent casing from the .380 just as she sent it flying with a flick.

The little golden casing arced angrily over the freaks' heads as it flew straight down the hallway. It contacted the ground with a metallic tinkling and, luckily, bounced the wall before disappearing around a corner to finish its journey.

Both infected snapped their heads in that direction and launched from their current corpse to go possibly make another one as they scrabbled with each other and tore through the hallway.

Clara eased the door open and nudged me ahead softly, Grayson glued to our backs as we tried the door across the hall and found it graciously unlocked.

This door opened easily, and we disappeared inside just as the meaty footfalls of the freaks were making their way back to our vicinity.

I eased the door closed, and engaged both the handle locks, and the deadbolt as quietly as possible while Grayson checked through drawers until he pulled out a small folding blue work knife.

The sounds outside the door grew in intensity as both monsters regained position on the woman and the sounds of their feasting returned. The sounds never failed to sicken me and turn my stomach, and it was somehow made worse by my brief contact with their victim when times were 'good'.

Within a few minutes time, Grayson had knifed a large square into the wall and begun very slowly, very quietly prying away bits of building material.

The work was slow and fraught with obvious danger, but before long he was through one layer, had the insulation cut and pulled away, and had begun work on the second layer.

The sounds outside of the door calmed, and while I didn't dare look, I had hoped this meant the beasts had moved on, satisfied with a belly each full of fresh meat.

"Got it," Grayson whispered. "Let's go."

I watched him disappear into the gap in the wall and continued watching as his feet left our view before Clara pushed her way through and joined him.

Once she was through, it was my turn, and I stepped into the vertical shaft and placed my weight on the ladder, looking at the walls and below, I could make out dozens of large wires and network cables disappearing into the darkness, the space only dimly lit by LED lights on small boxes here and there that I had assumed to be some kind of junctions. Looking up, I caught a view I hadn't prepared for.

"Hey Clara?" I asked, quietly.

"Yes, Scott?" she replied, a note of confusion in her voice.

"You been doing squats, or is it just the lighting?" I asked trying to lighten the situation any way I could.

"Keep looking and I will kick you!" she half snarled, half laughed.

We moved in our tight vertical train several feet further up before it stopped, and I nearly ran into Clara's feet on the rungs.

"Found the hatch," Grayson murmured, "but not how to open it. Anyone got a light?"

"I do," I offered as I fished a BIC lighter out of my pocket and passed it up the ladder to Clara, who then passed it Grayson.

"Thanks," he stated. "Can't see a damn thing up here."

"You're telling me," I added. "All I can see is Clara's butt."

"*SCOTT*!" she snarled, and I dodged a foot that was clearly meant for my forehead as we all chuckled.

"Got it!" Grayson called as low lighting flooded us from overhead.

Before I knew it, we were all free of the shaft and standing in a maintenance office nearly identical to the one we'd just left.

"Well," Grayson commented, "off to meet up with the others?"

"You first, Jeffy," I prodded.

"Don't," came his single-word response, and I let it drop for now.

I wasn't sure if I was comfortable, nor would I ever be, with having the brother of the guy that just fucked everybody in our midst. One thing was for sure, I wasn't about to hide his identity from those with us and I wasn't planning on hiding it from those back home. It may be wrong to ask one to atone for the sins of their kin, but I'd let the group make that call. Maybe put it to a vote.

While I was on another planet considering all of this, the other two had already reached the door to the hallway and were turned around wondering what the hell I was doing. They didn't have to say it, I could tell by the looks I was receiving.

"Right, sorry," I muttered and joined up behind them as Grayson eased the door open.

The hallway was empty. The same tiles, hideous paint, and pulsing blue warning lights as everywhere else, but not a creature moved here.

Regardless, we all waited. For several minutes, I don't think a full breath was taken by the three of us put together, let alone individually.

After a few beats longer, Grayson stepped out into the hallway. He ran one hand along the wall to keep his balance as he kept to a low crouch, followed by Clara, then myself.

One by one we snuck down the hallway. Every doorway, we'd freeze, Grayson would peek in, watch, listen, and so far, we'd simply keep moving.

As I was about to comment how eerie it was that we had seen nobody and nothing thus far, it happened.

Footsteps.

Clara slipped across the hallway and fairly pulled the agent and I inside, easing the door mostly closed as she went. I pushed Grayson and her back and drew the tiny pistol from my pocket. Just as I eased into a comfortable kneel, two voices could be heard from the end of the hallway the door wouldn't allow me to view.

"Nukes though," Voice One said casually. "Jesus dude."

"Those cities needed it," Voice Two stated. "Cities were pretty much all filled to the brim with those…things."

"Filled with survivors, too," Voice One replied.

"Negligible," Voice Two offered, as they both drew nearer, slowly. "Any survivors left were outnumbered. We did them a favor. Urbanites suck anyway, now the nation can grow up the right way. Without 'em."

"How many did he launch?" Voice One inquired.

"Dozen. Maybe two dozen," Two replied. "Don't remember. He says guard, I guard. I don't ask questions and he keeps me on the easy jobs."

As he finished the statement, the two men strolled lazily past our position.

One had a rifle, kept low and hanging, the other one had a pistol in a holster, but I couldn't see much else for either man. Both wore some semblance of military uniform, but no further than what I'd seen from Parker's men previously.

I took the opportunity and stepped out from behind the door, even among the whispered protests of my companions.

The man with the rifle was, thankfully, a good half step or more further behind than the other, and that's who I went with.

Coming out of the doorway, I watched his legs as he passed. His right one began to swing forward for another step, and that's when I placed my knee against the back of that leg.

Before he could even react, I had one arm constricted tight around his neck, his balance in my hands, and that little .380 pistol very visibly to the side of his head.

"Don't even reach for it," I cautioned, not wholly convinced myself at whom I was talking to, but it worked. They both froze.

The one with just a pistol took a step back, barely getting a syllable out before Clara approached out to one side, and Grayson the other.

"You won't take out all three of us," Grayson warned the other man. "Give it up."

The man merely dropped to his knees, put his hands behind his head, and looked down at the floor. His resignation was apparent as Clara removed his pistol and gave him one solid stroke across the back of the skull, dropping him in a heap right there in the hallway.

I moved to snatch up the rifle from the man I held as I shoved him flat down to the ground. Grayson reached for the rifle and I pulled back, handing him the little Ruger instead. He took it and inspected it wordlessly before returning his gaze back to me.

"Is it always going to be like this?" Grayson asked me.

"Don't know," I replied, looking over the M4A1 I'd just acquired.

Checking the magazine and chamber showed it ready to go, and I switched the selector to full auto and covered the man that held it before me as I turned him over and grabbed the two spare magazines he held, watching Clara do much the same for the man that held her pistol before her.

"Fair enough, I guess," surmised Grayson.

Before long we were on the move again, and after two hallways of much the same nothingness, we reached familiarity, and with that, the cafeteria.

I moved much more quickly in here, pushing a few chairs aside and making as straight a line as possible back to the kitchen area, which I reached in almost no time at all.

The problem was what I was looking for was not there. Where my loving wife and trouble-causing child should have been was a pair of bodies, though definitely not theirs.

It was a pair of infected women, neither of them familiar to me. They had each been decently ventilated with bullets, and the resulting fountain of blood splattered across the stainless appliances. One appeared to have been brought down, then shot, as the splattering around her head on the floor was immense, and there wasn't much left of a head on this one.

What I didn't see among the gore was my family nor my friends.

"Guys?" I called out, drawing a matching glare from each of the people I was with. "Don't care. Hide if you don't like it, but if either of them is gone, then shit ain't worth it anyway to me."

At that, the walk-in freezer at the end of the space slowly began to open, drawing the muzzle of each of our guns.

I lowered mine the instant I recognized my wife, our toddler holding onto her leg, both of them grinning at the realization of who stood before them.

"Oh, thank God!" nearly fell out of Jennifer's mouth as I rushed to shush the "Daddy!" that spilled forth from little Gwen.

"You waited...here?" I questioned her.

"No way was I leaving you," Jennifer replied.

"And these? You have guns now?" I motioned to the two bodies.

"They were hunting us, and we hid in the freezer," she explained. "Somebody shot them, but I'm not sure who. It wasn't us."

She couldn't quite get much more out before the blue lights around us cut off mid-pulse, and the faster, harsher flashing red lights returned.

"Launches are over," Grayson sighed, resigned that there would be no hero work today, it was lost at the hands of his own blood.

"That was an awfully long fucking time for missile launches," I advised.

"I can only assume that's because there was more than a few of them, Scott," Grayson explained.

"What fucking missiles?" Jennifer fired at us.

"Wait, what?" Dave challenged.

"Nukes," I stated flatly as I watched realization wash over every face present, save for little Gwen, who had not the slightest clue what was going on.

"Grayson's brother fucked probably every major city in the U.S., at the very least," Clara added, which added to the group's confusion.

"Grayson's brother?" Cody asked. "Who the fuck is his brother and why does he suck so much?"

I thought, among the questions being fired back and forth, I'd heard something very familiar. Familiar, and very unsettling.

"Wait, guys," I started, trying to listen above the growing noise from my companions. "GUYS! Shut the fuck up for a minute!"

"Bad word, daddy no say it!" Gwen chimed in just as everyone else got silent. Jennifer covered the girl's mouth as several present tried to withhold laughter and we listened for a moment.

Somewhere, deep behind us and into the facility, came a screech. And, the more we listened, the closer and louder the shrieks became. They were coming.

"How?" Shannon asked, nearly wailing like a child with a stomachache. "The facility is sealed, how?"

Nobody knew the answer, but we did agree it was time to start moving. I began pushing everyone forward, at a walking pace at first, then slightly more hurriedly as the sounds grew.

Before long, we were all moving at a brisk jog. Clara took point, Grayson and I brought up the rear, as the three of us were the only ones armed with anything more than kitchen knives and chair legs.

We had nearly reached another bend in the hallway when a flurry of movement caught my eye behind us. About fifty yards back, an uninfected child of around ten came barreling down the hallway, with another hot on his heels. I nearly stopped to help as the one following jumped on the boy's back and dragged him to the tile floor, biting deeply into a leg then nearly dragging the boy's body to shove it behind him as he sprung forth after us.

The shriek that ensued was drowned out by the M4A1 as I squeezed a burst out and missed, chewing up the wall at the end of the hallway. I then corrected and launched two more bursts of automatic gunfire, the second one shredding an irregular grouping high into the freak's chest, disabling the spine and making it useless as it fell at a running pace. Upon impact with the ground, it slid, then stopped, never to be of any more use than to lay there motionless, bleating out one long shriek after another as his final victim vaulted over his sire and took several rounds himself, high into the chest and lower skull, killing it in a hail of 9mm weapons fire from Clara.

Then, another humanoid shape appeared, now one-hundred yards away as we caught another bend in the hallway and picked up view of the entrance to this great facility as the halls tightened. I didn't stop to fire, and neither did Clara.

Eventually, we were backed up against the infamous vault door to Cheyenne Mountain.

Grayson went fast to work on a terminal near the door as the majority of the group huddled nearby.

I slipped the .380 from his pocket and passed it off to Erik, as he was the closest to me. In that human grizzly bear's palm, it looked like a toy.

"You got, like, six shots dude," I informed him before the three of us with firearms stood off with the far end of the hallway.

Effectively creating a barrier between the unarmed survivors and ourselves, we stood. And we waited. The sounds of the infected, possibly following the scents of such a large meal on the move as we were, drew nearer.

And still, we waited.

Grayson slammed the 'Enter' button home one final time and the nearby red lights were replaced with a flashing yellow as the door slowly unbuckled itself from position and began to work free.

The first infected appeared at the end of the hallway, two-hundred yards straight down the alley.

"Hold," I ordered, not wanting to expend ammo unless we had to.

Behind us, Grayson took over ushering survivors out the door and into a pair of trucks nearby in the large, open exit tunnel.

A veritable highway carved right through the mountain, this had to be the way out, the entrance and exit that fed this vast facility in times of peace.

As they filtered out, I urged my two companions in arms backwards step by step with a tap and tug each as more room was made between us and the door.

One-hundred yards.

Grayson followed Jennifer, the last of the unarmed and moved through himself.

Seventy-five yards.

I pushed further and watched as Erik, then Clara slid through the door.

Now twenty-five yards.

"GRAYSON!" I bellowed. "DOOR!"

"The control panel!" he called back to me, and I turned to locate it.

Not outside, with us, but inside. I raised my rifle, certain I could hit the panel. It was the size of a pizza box and only a dozen feet away. Of course, I could hit it!

Zero.

I unleashed a volley of deafening rifle rounds from the carbine. And right into the chest of the first infected.

The high velocity little copper-jacketed insects passed straight through the freak and buried themselves into the panel for the door, setting off further alarms and buzzers inside.

A shower and fog of Halon fire chemicals and much more, I was sure, began pouring in all directions inside the outer room from various nozzles around the door as one more freak tried to take a lunge through the chemical.

The swinging door knocked it askew and caught it mid-sternum as the multi-ton weight slammed back into place in its frame. The locking systems spun and slammed themselves into place as what was left of an infected middle-aged woman did little more than flop and shriek nearby on the ground as Clara casually placed a pair of bullets into her.

"Let's go!" I urged as the others fell back to the vehicles. Cody was already in the driver's seat of the nearby 7-ton troop transport as our people occupied the back section meant for them and whatever cargo.

Grayson was in the lead vehicle, a M1035 HUMMVEE marked for medical purposes by the military. I could see Jennifer and Gwen in the back seat of the vehicle, and I vaulted the tailgate and waved inward to them from the covered cargo area.

Turning and looking, I could see I was essentially cushioned by wooden crates and plastic totes of different types. If we were taking this vehicle, I only hoped it contained enough good stuff to benefit us.

"You have keys for these trucks?" I called up to Grayson.

"They're military vehicles!" he called back, irritated. "They don't have keys, only switches!"

As if to punctuate his statement, both trucks fired up nearly in unison and Cody began charging the air system in the Oshkosh as we prepared to set off. I guess I should have interviewed the guy better, as I had no clue he could operate such a machine.

A moment later, we were in motion, the truck tugging me backwards a fair bit as Grayson accelerated, the troop truck behind us, doing its best to keep up but falling well short on acceleration. Regardless, we were moving now. The banks of lights flashing by overhead just as if we were traveling down any mountain tunnel in the United States.

Apparently, the way had long been cleared. Grayson made mention of it, and that the vehicles were staged as they had been sending out regular sweep-and-clear crews and scouting teams, much the same as we had done back in Ohio but clearly, on a larger scale.

I started drifting in thought as we broke from the tunnel and into the crisp Colorado air, the sun already down low enough in the horizon to play peekaboo as we started our journey.

It would be a long way back to Ohio, and I settled in. Much as a kid on a family vacation, I had little to do but watch the scenery as we passed, leaving Cheyenne Mountain and its hundreds, if not, thousand or more survivors behind, and Colonel Parker as well.

Good. I hoped they never got to him. No civilian rescued him, and no freak made it in to feast on him. It would give me a slight, crooked smile for life to learn that he had felt nothing but the pain of starvation as he lay trapped in that control room with the stench of death and body odor to keep him company.

We traveled for what seemed like a hundred miles or more, Grayson using Clara as navigator and pointing us east, but away from any major population centers. Partially, we were kept humble and scared by the higher number of infected in those places, but we also just weren't ready to see if *all* had been nuked, and unfortunately nobody in our car knew much about exclusion zones and what would be safe or not safe to inhabit after a bombing.

Jennifer, Erik, Dave and Rich all sat quietly as I turned and began detailing the story of Grayson, Parker, and the nukes. Several looks were given toward Grayson, and he nearly became exhausted explaining how little he had to do with Parker's end plan. Swearing up and down that he knew not one single word of it. I wasn't fully convinced, but I didn't feel alone in that regard. As I recounted everything we knew, I watched several times as one person, then the other, would shoot Grayson a penetrating glare.

Eventually, we pulled alongside a desolate stretch of road as Cody had started flashing his headlamps.

He was low on fuel, the gauge in his truck having dropped into the red.

Clara spent time with her nose in the map, and finally found a nearby motel that would suffice.

We rolled several more miles to reach it and found it relatively empty. No healthy, living people nearby, and oddly enough, not an infected in sight. At least, none we could see.

Taking this as an omen for the positive, we set up a guard schedule and agreed who would share which weapons with each other.

Several of us took to blocking the stairwells on each end with spare beds, dressers, and a vending machine. A few rooms were opened, convincing their locks by force to let us enter; the doors were propped open as we inhabited the interior spaces, huddled under blankets from other rooms to add to those in our own to find comfort.

Having opted for second guard shift, I lay back on an amazingly soft pillow and stared at the pair of blonde heads on my chest. One of my wife, the other my daughter's.

They were already fast asleep as I gently placed a kiss on top of each of their heads, then lay there myself, staring at the ceiling.

The wind outside blew gently. Just enough to cause the occasional commotion outside as a nearby guard would rush to the window or the railing to investigate.

Aside from that, and the steady footsteps of a guard here and there, I had only my thoughts as I drifted slowly into a deep, deep sleep.

END

AUTHOR'S NOTES

Okay, cool, is the editor gone now? I can speak freely? Ah, good! Not that I have anything against editors, you have a tough job, but this is *my* little spot. So, go pour a drink, have a stretch, you've earned it!

Now, on to the rest-

Thank you. Yeah, you. My reader. My friend. My family. My fan. Whatever name you go by, you...fucking...ROCK.

I'll probably never be rich, nor will I likely ever be famous. So, all of this? Over a year on each story so far? Yeah, this is for you. And whether you hated it or loved it, I want to take a moment to thank you from the bottom of my heart for taking the time to check out the Scott Pfeiffer Stories. It truly means more to me than I think I'll ever be able to express. Thank you.

A special shoutout, of course, to my mother and father. My wife, beloved offspring, my friends who have been there and inspired a truly amazing cast of characters, those that have heard me drone on and on about 'maybe this, maybe that' as I build this story, the gods themselves, I could keep going but at the end of the day, if you're reading this, thank you for the part you've played in my life.

I'd love to stay and grovel even further, but I can't. I have more writing to do! So, on that final note of gratitude, I'm off. Off to begin the next book in this series, and maybe start formulating the backbone for a much, much larger project I've got in store for the future!

CHECK OUT OTHER GREAT ZOMBIE NOVELS

Z BURBIA
by Jake Bible

Whispering Pines is a classic, quiet, private American subdivision on the edge of Asheville, NC, set in the pristine Blue Ridge Mountains. Which is good since the zombie apocalypse has come to Western North Carolina and really put suburban living to the test!

Surrounded by a sea of the undead, the residents of Whispering Pines have adapted their bucolic life of block parties to scavenging parties, common area groundskeeping to immediate area warfare, neighborhood beautification to neighborhood fortification.

But, even in the best of times, suburban living has its ups and downs what with nosy neighbors, a strict Home Owners' Association, and a property management company that believes the words "strict interpretation" are holy words when applied to the HOA covenants. Now with the zombie apocalypse upon them even those innocuous, daily irritations quickly become dramatic struggles for personal identity, family security, and straight up survival.

ZOMBIE RULES
by David Achord

Zach Gunderson's life sucked and then the zombie apocalypse began.

Rick, an aging Vietnam veteran, alcoholic, and prepper, convinces Zach that the apocalypse is on the horizon. The two of them take refuge at a remote farm. As the zombie plague rages, they face a terrifying fight for survival.

They soon learn however that the walking dead are not the only monsters.

CHECK OUT OTHER GREAT ZOMBIE NOVELS

VACCINATION
by **Phillip Tomasso**

What if the H7N9 vaccination wasn't just a preventative measure against swine flu?

It seemed like the flu came out of nowhere and yet, in no time at all the government manufactured a vaccination. Were lab workers diligent, or could the virus itself have been man-made? Chase McKinney works as a dispatcher at 9-1-1. Taking emergency calls, it becomes immediately obvious that the entire city is infected with the walking dead. His first goal is to reach and save his two children.

Could the walls built by the U.S.A. to keep out illegal aliens, and the fact the Mexican government could not afford to vaccinate their citizens against the flu, make the southern border the only plausible destination for safety?

ZOMBIE, INC
by **Chris Dougherty**

"WELCOME! To Zombie, Inc. The United Five State Republic's leading manufacturer of zombie defense systems! In business since 2027, Zombie, Inc. puts YOU first. YOUR safety is our MAIN GOAL! Our many home defense options - from Ze Fence® to Ze Popper® to Ze Shed® - fit every need and every budget. Use Scan Code "TELL ME MORE!" for your FREE, in-home*, no obligation consultation! *Schedule your appointment with the confidence that you will NEVER HAVE TO LEAVE YOUR HOME! It isn't safe out there and we know it better than most! Our sales staff is FULLY TRAINED to handle any and all adversarial encounters with the living and the undead". Twenty-five years after the deadly plague, the United Five State Republic's most successful company, Zombie, Inc., is in trouble. Will a simple case of dwindling supply and lessening demand be the end of them or will Zombie, Inc. find a way, however unpalatable, to survive?

CHECK OUT OTHER GREAT ZOMBIE NOVELS

900 MILES
by S. Johnathan Davis

John is a killer, but that wasn't his day job before the Apocalypse.

In a harrowing 900 mile race against time to get to his wife just as the dead begin to rise, John, a business man trapped in New York, soon learns that the zombies are the least of his worries, as he sees first-hand the horror of what man is capable of with no rules, no consequences and death at every turn.

Teaming up with an ex-army pilot named Kyle, they escape New York only to stumble across a man who says that he has the key to a rumored underground stronghold called Avalon..... Will they find safety? Will they make it to Johns wife before it's too late?

Get ready to follow John and Kyle in this fast paced thriller that mixes zombie horror with gladiator style arena action!

WHITE FLAG OF THE DEAD
by Joseph Talluto

Millions died when the Enillo Virus swept the earth. Millions more were lost when the victims of the plague refused to stay dead, instead rising to slaughter and feed on those left alive. For survivors like John Talon and his son Jake, they are faced with a choice: Do they submit to the dead, raising the white flag of surrender? Or do they find the will to fight, to try and hang on to the last shreds or humanity?